TO BUILD A NORTHERN NATION

● ● ●

A Novel of Canada and post-Civil War America

Al McGregor

Library and Archives Canada Cataloguing in Publication

McGregor, Al, author
To build a northern nation: a novel of Canada and post-Civil War America / Al
McGregor.

Issued in print and electronic formats.
ISBN 978-0-9689207-2-5 (pbk.).–ISBN 978-0-9689207-3-2 (kindle).–
ISBN 978-0-9689207-0-1 (kobo)
ISBN 0968920721

1. Canada–History–1841-1867–Fiction. 2. United States–History–1865-1898–Fiction.
I. Title.

PS8625.G735T6 2014 C813'.6 C2014-903346-X
C2014-903347-8
Cover Design: Quantum Communications

Maps and Map Art: courtesy of Chris Partridge

Published by: Al McGregor Communications

www.almcgregor.com

For all who encouraged me along the way...

Introduction

For a few days in 1865, the Union celebrated. The cruel Civil War was over. But a single gunshot ended the celebration and produced a new round of uncertainty and tension. President Lincoln was dead. Across the northern border, the leaders of the British provinces not only felt the shock and pain, but within days they were forced to deal with fears that the assassination plot had been conceived in Canada.

To Build a Northern Nation begins in the aftermath of the assassination and continues to the birth of the new Dominion of Canada in 1867.

My first book on this era, *A Porous Border*, dealt with the immediate impact of the war on the British colonies: the thousands of men who crossed the border to join the conflict; the Confederate raids from neutral territory that threatened to spread war across the continent; and the effect of the war on the drive for Canadian Confederation.

Now, *To Build a Northern Nation*, illustrates the aftermath of the war. Vanquished rebels flee to the British colonies in search of sanctuary; former Union soldiers join an invasion in support of Irish independence; and the Canadian people and politicians must contend again with events beyond their control.

Many characters are based on historical fact, while others are fictitious. All must struggle with an unpredictable future.

History tells us the outcome. The people on the following pages face a future that is uncertain, at best. Only a few will actually meet, but each expands the story of the new northern nation.

I

Quebec City, Canada East
April 10, 1865

Journal of Paul Forsey,
Government Clerk

The telegraph has just delivered momentous news. General Robert E. Lee has surrendered his Confederate army at a tiny railway depot in Virginia. The military authorities believe it signals the end of the American war, but it has not ended the uncertainty.

The rebel raids across the border raised the tension between our colonies and the United States, so there is a nagging fear that the American war will be replaced by a war here in the North. With a million-man army, the Yankees could quickly overpower our small British force.

Government and military leaders are on edge and wonder what to expect next from the fractious neighbors to our south.

Quebec City
April 15, 1865

"Come on! Move!"

Paul Forsey again slapped the flank of his reluctant mount. His attempt to find a carriage had failed, and there was no time to waste. The large, lumbering draft horse was all that was available. He jerked on the reins to force the animal up the driveway to Spencer Wood, the official British government residence. After what seemed an eternity, he slipped awkwardly to the ground and ran to pound on the door.

"I need to see the governor general," he panted to the chubby servant girl who answered the door.

"And don't the whole world." The Irish accent suggested a recent immigrant. "His lordship don't come out for any John, Dick, or Harry."

"I have urgent government business," Forsey said, trying to push forward.

"And his lordship will have me job if I bring in any oaf who calls before breakfast."

"Then get me Godley. Get his secretary. This is a matter of life and death."

"It'll be my death if I wake them and it's not important." The woman was standing firm.

"Take me to him. I'll wake him!"

"A fat chance of that! You could be a burglar!"

"I am Paul Forsey, a clerk with the ministry. I need to see Captain Godley."

The maid only scowled.

He yelled at the top of his lungs, "Captain Godley!"

A second shout brought Godley's reply from the top of a staircase.

"What the bloody hell is going on down there?"

"President Lincoln has been shot. He's dead!" Forsey shouted.

"Oh, me God!"

The maid made the sign of the cross.

Godley was stunned but began to take control. "Wait there. No. Brigid, take him to the library. I'll bring the governor general."

Unwashed, unshaven, and clad in dressing gowns, Viscount Monck and his principal secretary shuddered at the clerk's report.

"It came in over the telegraph. It happened last night. Lincoln was at the theater, and someone shot him. The line from Washington went down for a while and when it came back, it said he was dying."

"Oh, me God!" The maid had remained in the doorway. "Yesterday was Good Friday. Like our dear savior, Mr. Lincoln left the world on a holy day. Perhaps it's a sign."

"That will be all, Brigid." The governor general gently guided her to the hallway and closed the door.

"There's more," Forsey began as Monck crossed the room to his desk. "William Seward, the secretary of state, was also attacked and may be dead too. And just as I left, there was another telegram. It said the assassins—and I checked: it was plural—the assassins might be headed for Canada and that the Americans should close the border."

"Bloody hell," Godley kept repeating.

"All right, Dennis! We agree!" Governor General Monck snapped.

"The border. They could march right across," Godley warned. "I'll call out the garrisons, but we'll need the militia too."

Monck opted for caution.

"We don't know enough. Send an order for extra surveillance. The border guards are to report anything they see. But let's not set anything off. The Americans will be on edge. Just a watching post until we know more."

"I'll draft the order," Godley said, hurrying off. "And I'll draft one for the militia in case the extra men are needed later."

"You're a government clerk," Monck said, trying hard to place the face.

"Yes, sir. I'm Paul Forsey."

"I'll need to speak to the cabinet. Could you call them together?"

"I can't, sir. Most are off to London, remember? Georges Cartier, Alexander Galt, George Brown, and John A. Macdonald left several days ago."

"Yes, yes, of course. The meetings are to discuss the Confederation plan and imperial defense. They'll be on the ocean. Well then, no cabinet meeting. I'll handle it."

"Yes, sir," was the best that Forsey could muster.

"I'll return to the city shortly," Monck continued. "I need you to collect every scrap of information. You'll be my unofficial eyes and ears."

The governor general leaned on the desk for support.

"We worried about the American war spilling across the border, but somehow I had the feeling that Lincoln wouldn't approve an invasion. The Union would have been face-to-face with the British. The Americans must be beside themselves. They will be doubly suspicious and almost certainly dangerous."

The room was silent before the governor general turned to the clerk. "You can go! Pull the information together."

Forsey didn't move.

"Is there something else?" Monck asked.

"If it's all the same, sir, I'll wait and ride down in the carriage with Godley. The horse I rode is about done in."

• • •

Montreal, Canada East
April 15, 1865

"You've seen the afternoon newspapers, Mr. Hogan?" the desk clerk asked as the hotel manager approached.

"Yes! Horrible news, and if the newspapers are right, the man responsible is a former guest here at Saint Lawrence Hall."

"Do you believe it?" The clerk went on. "Can you imagine John Wilkes Booth involved in something like that?"

"I try never to judge my clients, and neither should you."

The clerk felt the sting in the manager's tone and pretended to find other duties.

"But we must also keep your eyes open," Hogan added softly as he checked the register.

"What of our Confederate guests? Mr. Thompson, the leader of the group, has checked out?"

"Yes. Left rather suddenly but paid his bill. I think he was heading for the coast and a boat to Europe. If he waited only few days, there would be a ship leaving Montreal but he was in a hurry."

"And Mr. Lee, the new Confederate commissioner who is replacing Thompson, is he still here?" Hogan ran his finger down the list of names.

"Yes. He was down for breakfast."

"And George Sanders? Another commissioner and one who always claimed to know what was happening."

"I haven't seen him today. But he picked up his mail last night."

"Well, that's fine then. I was just curious."

"Mr. Hogan? Do you have a minute?"

The hotel manager turned to face a teller from the nearby bank.

"Of course, Mr. Campbell. What can I do for you?"

"Perhaps we could speak in your office?" The teller followed close on Hogan's heels as he led the way across the lobby.

Hogan offered a chair when the door was closed. "What can I do for you?"

"I won't keep you long but I had to talk to someone." Campbell was flushed, the perspiration shining on his forehead.

"The Booth business. Are you going to the authorities?" he asked.

"What on earth for? Mr. Booth was here. He paid his bill. He did no damage. What more is there to tell?"

The clerk hesitated. "I wondered if he concocted this business at the Saint Lawrence Hall...er, in Montreal...I mean. I checked the bank records. He was here in October and took out a bank draft."

"Mr. Campbell, I try to respect the privacy of my guests."

"Perhaps it's different with a hotel. A banker has to be more careful. I'll excuse myself."

"Uh, Mr. Campbell, wait. Since we're having this *very* private conversation, another of our Southern gentlemen, Jacob Thompson, checked out in a hurry. Did he do business with you too?"

"Yes, as a matter of fact, he does—well, he did. This must be confidential. He closed out his account and took all the funds in cash."

"Really, Mr. Campbell." Hogan began to rock in his chair. "I don't think we have to worry about going to the authorities. They will be coming to us."

• • •

Quebec City, Canada East
April 16, 1865
"The first ship."

The relief was evident in the governor general's voice as he watched the vessel break through the last pieces of ice and glide toward the wharf. The first ship had become a welcome sight for Charles Stanley Monck since his term as chief British representative in the united province of Canada had begun four years earlier, but the sight was never more welcome than in 1865. The winter isolation was broken, and with the Saint Lawrence River open for shipping, British troops or fresh instructions could come quickly from England. Domestic politics had dominated Monck's term. He had become comfortable dealing with the feuding factions in the province, but the threat of armed conflict was a different matter.

"London will be unaware of the president's death and what we may face as a result," he muttered absently to his chief secretary. "When the transatlantic cable is restored, we will have instructions instantly."

He turned away from the window to face the scowling assistant.

"Now what's the problem?"

"I must ask that you allow me to do my job." Dennis Godley was at his most officious when he was angry.

"The British forces are quite capable of collecting intelligence. That clerk is gathering nothing but rubbish."

Monck rubbed his fingers through his beard. The government town, always awash in rumors, had been flooded since the Lincoln assassination. Everyone had a theory.

"My men say the Yankees are nervous," Godley continued. "The Americans are supposed to check everyone that crosses the border and they have pictures of the suspects but don't have authority to share them with us. Still, they are staying on their side of the border crossings, and we have no reports of unusual troop movements. Their Vice President Johnson has been sworn into office. He's asked the Lincoln cabinet to stay on. My guess would be they will bury the former president before they consider what to do next."

"At least, we know what we are dealing with in the cabinet," Monck settled into the chair behind his desk. "But Johnson is a question mark. He's from Tennessee and spent the last few months as a military governor. One must assume he'll have a grasp on the domestic affairs, but he'll know nothing about international relations. The British legation in Washington will have to educate him."

Monck tried to recall what he had read of Johnson. His selection as Lincoln's vice president had come as a surprise, but the American political system was often filled with surprises and unexpected change.

"Is there any more on the assassins?"

"That's a problem for us," Godley explained. "The latest telegrams suggest a Southern conspiracy engineered by the Confederate commissioners here in Canada. The man in charge is Edwin G. Lee. He's a distant relative of the Southern general, but of course, he's just arrived so he can't have been involved. We know Booth spent time in Montreal. The manager of Saint Lawrence Hall confirms he was there. And here's a strange one: Booth's theatrical luggage, his costumes, have been salvaged from a ship that sank last fall. The ship was owned by Patrick Martin, one of the Confederate hangers-on and a blockade-runner. But we won't learn much from him. He went down with the ship."

"Keep on it," Monck ordered. "In the next day or so, we should have a message from Washington. Our embassy will know more than we do."

"And the clerk." Godley was insistent. "Can we send him back to the ministry?"

"What's he turned up?" Monck asked.

"Rubbish," Godley pronounced. "The kind of material fit for a cheap novel; worthless public drivel gleaned from the provincial papers."

"Such as?"

Godley began to sort through the file the clerk had submitted.

"He notes that the Western District was supposed to be full of Confederate sympathizers, but the mayor of Windsor ordered all shops closed on the day of the funeral. He heard that the Confederates at the Queens Hotel in Toronto cheered and celebrated on hearing of Lincoln's death, and that's not a surprise. I suspect there were cheers in the barrooms at the Saint Lawrence Hall and other places Southerners gather. And do we really need to know that men at a barn raising near Amherstburg were so upset they couldn't continue their work? Or that a Southern sympathizer fired a few rounds at the Union Jack in Lucan in Canada West? He didn't agree when the flag was lowered to half-staff.

The rest of it is simply newspaper reports and editorials, mostly kind words for Mr. Lincoln, churches planning memorials, and so on."

Monck gathered his thoughts before he spoke. "It is not military value, but I'll let Forsey down easy. I'll let him keep the notes. It will be a record of his service at an historic moment."

"We certainly won't need the tripe he collected for the official records. Look, someone has written a memorial called 'Maple Leaves from Canada for the Presidents Grave.' Maybe next he'll find someone who created a wreath of oak. It's a waste of paper and government time."

"Come now, Dennis." Monck smiled. "Let the clerk have his day. As for us, there's little we can do but watch as events unfold."

• • •

Detroit, Michigan
April 17, 1865
Across the river, Tom Hines could see the lanterns glowing in the windows of the Heron House; and just down the slope from hotel, the ferry unloading at the Canadian dock. The boat would tie up for the night after the return trip to Michigan. The American soldiers who had carefully inspected the passengers as the ferry left Detroit were leaving for the day. He had watched as an officer nailed a poster to a wall. Even from a distance, he knew it was the image of John Wilkes Booth.

Hines ran his hands through his hair and felt the residue of grease. He had washed the latest disguise away, dunking his head in a horse trough to remove the gray hair-coloring. The false beard was safely stowed in his carpetbag and a blue forage cap and jacket had been tossed on the railway track between Cincinnati and Detroit. A rumpled suit matched his mood. Deep sleep had been impossible with surprise inspections by conductors and armed guards, and with each inspection, he silently blessed the forgers who had made his papers.

Word of Robert E. Lee's surrender had been followed with shocking speed by the Lincoln assassination, and when he heard the name "Booth," he knew he had to escape. Anyone associated with the rebel operations in Canada was at risk. His own attempt to bring revolution to Chicago and the American Northwest had failed, but the Yankees had long memories. Some people said he looked like the actor, and so the sooner he reached British sanctuary, the better.

Across the river, the ferry captain appeared to be in no hurry. The Windsor-bound passengers were still leaving the boat. Only a few had appeared for the return trip to Detroit.

The smell of fried onions and roasting meat drew him to a waterfront saloon. The room was dim—lit only by grimy lamps—the oily smoke from which mixed with the scent of tobacco. Hines chose a seat at a table near the door, leaned against the wall, and through the dirty streaks on the window watched as the last passengers left the ferry. It would be at least a half hour before the craft returned to the American shore.

A bowl of stew and a piece of bread was served quickly. From habit, he scrutinized the other customers. Factory workers, he decided, or based on the grease on their overalls, perhaps railway men. One was leafing through the pages of a newspaper and began to laugh.

"Here," he said, pointing to a page. "A pastor delivers a sermon and says Lincoln's death was divine retribution. Old Abe should have known better than to go to the theater on a holy day. No mindless entertainment on Good Friday. God was not amused."

"Keep your voice down," a companion hissed. "People don't want to hear anything said against Mr. Lincoln. They're in a foul mood."

Hines wiped the bread around the bowl. The meal was like a quick bivouac during a mounted raid with Confederate General

John Hunt Morgan. He had learned to eat fast whenever food was available. The next meal could be hours away.

The tavern cook approached. "You want more? Only another twenty-five cents."

"Yes." Hines politely laid out the cash.

The cook scooped the coins before he returned to the kitchen but stared at Hines through the open door as he ladled a refill. "You from around here?" he asked as he returned to set the bowl on the table.

"No."

"Didn't think so." The cook moved off but continued to study the customer and in only minutes was back.

Hines pushed the empty bowl toward him, but the cook had no interest in his china. Instead, he lunged at the customer and attempted to seize him in a bear hug.

"Help me with this son of a bitch!" he yelled. "It's Booth. Come on, boys! Help me hold him! There's reward money here!"

Other customers rose and gawked as Hines writhed to escape.

"By God, you're right," a diner spit food from his mouth. "It's John Wilkes Booth."

Hines kicked to upend the table and block the rush of other customers. He drove his right elbow deep into the cook's gut and was greeted with a welcoming groan as the arms released.

He dashed through the door and across the hundred yards to the ferry dock. A glance over his shoulder showed a tavern posse gathering for pursuit.

The final passenger had stepped onto the wharf when Hines careened by and onto the boat. A moment later, the man who held the mooring line felt the snout of a gun.

"Let her go," Hines ordered and watched the rope drop instantly into the Detroit river. The current caught the ferry and began to carry it downstream.

"Stay here," he ordered and bolted up the ladder to the wheelhouse.

The captain swore and fought to bring the craft back to the Michigan shore.

"Other side!" Hines pointed to the lights on the Windsor shore and shoved the gun in the captain's face. "Canada. It's one last run for a single passenger."

II

S he was reassured by the hand that gently guided her forward.
For the first time in weeks, Sarah Slater felt strong and vibrant. Her days as a Confederate courier could be relegated to
the past. Her rebel colonel, now dressed in civilian garb, was at
her side.

"We'll go right on up to Pennsylvania Avenue," Dan Mcgruder
whispered. "Detectives will be checking the hotels. We're safer in
the crowds until we catch the evening train."

Washington was wreathed in black. Crepe hung from government buildings, offices, and private homes. Men and women
quietly lined the empty street, kept in place by the soldiers who
policed the capital's main thoroughfare.

Sarah wore a long, black gown and a matching hat and
veil, and so blended easily with the other women in mourning
attire. She decided that Mcgruder appeared elegant, his muscular build straining against a simple black suit. There was no
evidence of the money belt strapped around his waist, and the
rustle of Sarah's clothing covered any sound from the paper cur-
rency sewn into the lining of her dress. The money would pave
the way for a new life.

Mcgruder had played his role to the hilt on their trek from the temporary sanctuary in Virginia. He told Union patrols that he was taking his sister to family in Vermont. A recent sickness had sapped her strength, and she must avoid the heat of a Southern summer. "One doctor thinks it's cholera," he had whispered at one checkpoint and was quickly allowed to proceed. Only after news of the assassination did the troops begin to pay closer attention.

"I met him," she whispered after rigorous questioning at one river crossing. "Booth came to the Washington boarding house while I was there. He was meeting with John Surratt and some other men. I didn't know he was a famous actor until John spouted off about his friend the next day."

"I never met him," Mcgruder confided, "but I heard all about the plan to abduct Lincoln. And I suspect his name was in the war department file I salvaged. I'm glad now that the file was lost in the confusion when we left Richmond. Best to let sleeping dogs lie."

"Will they help him?" she asked. "He was true to their cause. Maybe Southern associates will help him escape?"

"I don't know," Mcgruder growled. "And I don't want to know. All I care about is getting you to Montreal, and first we have to get through Washington."

Pennsylvania Avenue was lined five and six people deep, and more men and women filled the open windows that looked down on the street. White faces registered the shock of the recent days. The black faces showed abject despair.

A single bell began to toll, and on cue, it was joined by the bells from other churches. Minute guns from the forts ringing the capital erupted in final salutes, the reports a sharp contrast to the silence that fell across the crowd. The funeral cortege of President Abraham Lincoln was moving from the White House to the Capital.

Mcgruder tugged Sarah gently and moved to a doorstep. She joined him and was able to see above those on the sidewalk.

"We shouldn't be here," she whispered.

"Too late now," he told her.

A soldier in a crisp, new, blue uniform stepped up beside them. "Mind if I join you for the better view?"

"Not at all, sir," Sarah said, instantly regretting speaking. The accent could give her away.

"From the South?" He studied the couple.

"Southern West Virginia." Mcgruder spoke before she could. "We were too damn close to the rebels."

"I understand," the officer replied. "I spent time there before I was transferred to the War Department. Did my part to put down the secesh from behind a desk but I got the job done."

"Make way! Make way!" A sweating officer called to the crowd blocking the entrance to Sixth Street. "I've got a regiment coming up."

Seconds later, an army band marched into the intersection and halted. Behind it were rows of blue-clad troops.

"They're darkies," Sarah said in shock.

"Yes, ma'am." The officer smiled, mistaking her tone for approval. "The Twenty-Second United States Colored Troops, just back from Richmond."

The band members marked time before breaking into the "death march" and swung unto the avenue. The regiment of black soldiers followed in perfect order. The officer drew in a sharp breath.

"It's messed up," he told them. "The colored regiment was supposed to bring up the rear but it's leading the way. I'm glad I won't have to explain this."

"A symbol of the new America," Sarah told him sweetly. "What is it they say? Bottom on top?"

She felt Mcgruder's elbow in her ribs. His eyes flashed a warning.

She counted slowly to ten and began to sniff. Again, she felt the elbow but ignored him.

By the time the casket passed, she was ready with heart-wrenching sobs.

"Why do they have to take him so far away? There must be someplace other than Springfield, Illinois. They should bury him with the former slaves at General Lee's estate in Arlington. He loved those people. There's already a burial ground. He should be laid to rest with them."

Mcgruder's eyes flashed a violent danger signal.

"Take me away." She flung herself against him. "I can't watch anymore!"

"I'm afraid my sister is overwrought," Mcgruder apologized. "We'll move so as not to disturb the solemnities."

He gently guided the sobbing woman to a quiet side street.

"You fool," he snorted. "You could have had us both arrested."

The street emptied as they moved farther from the cortege.

"I am truly sad," she admitted. "But it's not just for Lincoln. It's for everything that's gone. But then, I'm happy too." She squeezed his arm. "We'll be starting over together."

• • •

Washington, DC
April 20, 1865

"Hah! What a delicious mistake!" It was the first time that Secretary of War Edwin Stanton had laughed since the assassination.

"The Negroes were at the very head of the procession?" Stanton could barely contain himself. "And of course, weren't our anti-abolitionists and the Democrats put out at that. Hah! It looks good on them, but Captain," he turned to the aide, "how did it happen?"

"The men were nervous. Many of them hadn't slept on the ship coming up from Richmond. They were hurried to the parade route, so when the music started, they marched."

"Wonderful," Stanton chortled. The military miscue helped to ease the tension of the search for the assassin.

Lincoln's funeral train had left the capital. The engine was draped in black, and several cars filled with politicians, old friends, and army officers rode with the remains of the president and his late son, Willie. Mary Lincoln demanded that the child be reburied with his father in Illinois but she was too emotionally drained to make the trip. The train would reverse the route that brought Lincoln to the capital in 1861, and there would be ceremonies in all the major Northern cities.

"To business, Captain," Stanton barked. "I want orders sent to every commander along the route. If they suspect anyone of causing the smallest problem, arrest him and lock him away. The loyal people demand a solemn send-off for the late president."

"Already done, sir," the aide responded.

"The hunt for Booth," Stanton asked, "what's the latest?"

"Those same black troops that led the parade have been sent to Maryland to comb the swamps and the back country. Black people are more likely to tell them if they've seen anything—or at least more likely than they would be to tell white folk. We already have detectives on the ground, but the area has a strong rebel tradition."

"Booth?" Stanton demanded.

"We've tracked where he was in the capital. He kept a woman, an apparent prostitute over in Hooker's Division, and she may have tried to kill herself."

"Guilt-ridden?" Stanton seized on the possibility.

"No sir, it was an overdose of laudanum. The girl is very pretty but not too bright. It could have been an accident."

"Booth was seen with Senator Hale's daughter," the secretary remembered.

"We think she's innocent," the aide replied. "Booth took advantage of her."

Stanton raised his eyebrows.

"No, No!" the aide explained. "Well, at least not that we know of, although he did have a way with women. In the Hale case, he used her to get to the father and to get special passes and the like."

"Pretty innocent stuff?" Stanton asked.

"Yes, we think so."

Stanton was silent as he considered his options. "We may need the senator's vote. Let the topic wither away. The senator will deal with his daughter. Perhaps she is a candidate for a convent. We have bigger issues. What about this connection to the War Department?"

The aide shifted nervously. "We're working on that. Booth had accomplices beyond those at the theater and the pair at Seward's house. They planned to kill President Johnson and completely disrupt the government. Booth was seen many times at the boarding house of Mary Surratt. We picked up a man there, along with the owner, but a fellow from our department lives there too."

"A spy?" Stanton snapped.

"We're not sure. He had access to the prison camp records. He may have given information to the rebels but he is the nervous sort—Louis Weichmann is his name—and we don't think he would have the guts to do much."

"But he will talk? Stanton asked.

"Oh, almost certainly. He is being questioned at the old capital prison, but I must warn you, the jail is filling up with potential suspects and known rebels."

"Little crowding won't hurt them," Stanton barked. "Let them rot!"

"Gladly, sir!"

"Why don't we have Booth?" Stanton was losing patience with the manhunt.

"He may be using the old rebel underground route to Richmond."

"You're sure he's gone south?" Stanton demanded, slapping the stack of papers on his desk. "There's a sighting from Detroit. A fight in a bar, and the man escaped to Canada. Then there's a sighting at London in Canada West. And what about this Canadian ship supposedly waiting for passengers on the Chesapeake?"

"We'll check all the reports, sir!"

"What about Jacob Thompson?" Stanton asked. "Lincoln would have allowed him to get away to Europe, but I reversed the order. He was headed for a ship from Maine or Vermont."

"We haven't found him. He may have slipped back into Canada."

"That whole Canadian Confederate operation must be arrested, and Thompson was the leader. I want a list of names by the end of the day, Captain. We'll offer a reward to smoke them out and when we have them, we'll have the link to Jeff Davis and the rebel hierarchy."

"You'll have it, sir!" The aide faced a long day, but Stanton wasn't finished.

"I don't trust the Canadians or their British handlers. They stood by, allowed the rebels to mount raids against us, and then hid behind neutrality laws. All kinds of people slipped back and forth across that border. It leaks like a sieve."

Stanton lifted another paper from his desk.

"Like this one. George St. Leger Grenfell arrested in the Chicago conspiracy. He spent time in the provinces after he left the rebel army. The old bugger was in this office last summer claiming he wanted to hunt in Canada and then go home to England. Instead, he was working with the rebels to incite a rebellion and free the southern prisoners at Camp Douglas. The lying bastard thought he had put one over on me. Well, Judge Holt and his court took care of him. The man will hang, British or not. And here's another one: Bennett Young. He's supposed to be in jail in Toronto, but the Canadians allowed him bail. He led the Saint Albans raid. I want him back on American soil."

The aide nodded in agreement.

"And leave no stone unturned, Captain. There were too many British running about in the Confederate camps and dashing back to British territory. The British know a thing or two about gathering intelligence. They've been playing with royal intrigues for centuries. Ask about in our government offices, Captain, at the War Department and the State Department. See if we can find any sign of an orchestrated British effort to undermine the Union."

"Yes, sir," the aide responded.

"Nothing is too farfetched at this point, Captain; nothing. Not even our own people. There were war profiteers and underhanded deals on cotton. Congressman Ashmun was one of Lincoln's old friends. He was the last one to see him to talk business, and what did he want to talk about? I'll tell you: permits to trade cotton with the rebels. Ashmun is a good Republican, and I know he wasn't involved in the assassination. But there might be others. And, there are other issues. General Sherman has been far too generous in the surrender terms for Joe Johnston's rebel army. That will not stand. We have the rebels down and we'll keep them down."

• • •

Toronto, Canada West
April 23, 1865
George Denison studied the young man who fidgeted in the parlor. Denison hoped someday to tell the Southerners in his extended family how he saved the partisan raider from the gallows. Denison, while a Canadian militia officer, was an active Southern sympathizer. The few lessons for Bennett Young might be part of a final act to support the Confederacy.

Young was barely twenty, but if his extradition to the United States were approved by a Canadian court, he would be unlikely to reach twenty-one. As a leader of the Confederate raid on Saint Albans, Vermont, he was a special target for American justice. Another raider John Yates Beall had fallen into American hands and been hanged. Beall's failed attempt to free rebel officers from a prison camp on Johnson's Island in Lake Erie produced charges that he was more pirate than soldier. Robert Kennedy, yet another Confederate raider, had been hanged for his role in an incendiary attack on New York City. Young could easily become the next victim.

"Your lawyer is doing an admirable job but we'd have more influence if a man like Cameron is actually by your side in the courtroom." Denison began to explain the nuances of the Canadian court.

"John Hillyard Cameron is a close friend of John A. Macdonald, the attorney general. With him in the court, the magistrate will pay more attention. They never know when a senior position might open on the bench, and the magistrate won't want to upset anyone with influence. And you won't need both French and English lawyers, as you had at the trial in Montreal."

Young rubbed his eyes. He found it hard to remember all the names. From the well-connected lawyer J. C. Abbott to the young law clerk, Louis Riel, a bewildering stream of lawyers, notaries, and assistants had navigated a legal maze.

The charges filed when he returned from Saint Albans moved slowly through the courts of Montreal only to be dropped, but then mere hours later, he was arrested again and whisked off for a new court appearance in Toronto. This time, he was charged with violating Canadian neutrality. He spent a week in jail before a judge agreed to bail, and George Denison stepped forward with the four thousand dollars to buy his freedom temporarily. Denison's Toronto mansion was a convenient place to prepare for the next court appearance.

"Godfrey Hyams's testimony may hurt us, even if we convince the court he is a turncoat, a liar, and a sell-out," Denison said, thumbing through his notes. "This business of planning the Saint Albans raid last summer while in Canada. You must convince the court that everything was hatched when you were in Chicago."

Young began to speak but the older man raised his hand.

"And, I don't want to hear anything but what you testified to in Montreal. The last thing we need is a perjury charge."

Denison, Young decided, needed only the clerical robe to drive his sermon home. He would have been a stronger lecturer than the meek professor in theology classes at Toronto's Trinity College just a year ago. Those classes, a way to put in time, had actually prepared him for future encounters. Without them, he would have been lost discussing the Gospel with that fetching young girl as he scouted Saint Albans before the raid. He felt a tinge of remorse when he remembered her face as the rebels began to herd their captives to the village green. He hoped she would see that the raid was not robbery but a legitimate act in time of war.

"We'll prove that Hyams is in the pay of the Americans," Denison was saying. "He's apparently told the American counsel that he's willing to tell all if well paid. He's a Judas willing to sell you out for a few pieces of gold. How well did you know him?"

"Hyams...not well," Young replied. "Well...he was always around. But we didn't say much in front of him, didn't like him—didn't trust him."

Perhaps, he thought, it was because Hyams always claimed to know more than he should.

"He used to tell us he did important service for the Confederacy but then he'd laugh and say he'd have to kill us if he told us any more."

"What do you know about a so-called bomb factory?" Denison pushed on.

"Bomb factory? What bomb factory?" Young asked. "A fellow in Windsor mixed the Greek fire, but the chemical concoction never seemed to work no matter who mixed it."

"No." Denison shook his head. "I mean the explosives stored in Toronto."

Young appeared stumped, but then the smile returned. "There was a house on Queen East. Yeah, six Queen East. Hyams claimed he had a stockpile of ammunition and hand explosives, grenades. But I thought he was spouting off."

"He's still spouting off," Denison reminded him. "The men sent to clear the house missed a box, and the police constables found it. A New York newspaper has the story. If they run it—and they almost certainly will—it will look bad. By the way, did you have any explosives in Saint Albans?"

"No, just the bottles of Greek fire, and they didn't work or there would be no Saint Albans."

"Careful with that kind of talk," Denison warned. "The judge doesn't need to hear that."

He leaned forward with another question.

"And the Greek fire was made somewhere in the States?"

"No, it was made…" Young began to understand. "Yes, that's right. It was carried in by one of men…uh, from somewhere in New York State. I don't recall exactly where."

"Good. Stay with that."

"Couldn't we just arrange for Hyams to disappear?" Young asked. "I can think of several men to do the job."

Denison shuddered.

"He's already made a statement to the American counsel and the police. If we can get him on the witness stand, we can catch him in his lies."

"Maybe some of the other fellows can challenge his story," Young suggested. "Tom Hines is back in Canada. He had no love for Hyams."

"No!" Denison was emphatic. "Keep the others out of it. With the assassination, the Americans are looking for any excuse to collar Confederates. And the Canadian authorities may yet take a dim view of sheltering fugitives. Hines has to lie low, just as you will."

"What's the big problem?" Young wanted to know. "Is it Booth? I only saw him once in Montreal, and he didn't tell me anything."

"Don't admit you saw Booth," Denison thundered. "The less you know the better. I'm giving the same message to all of you. Hines, Surratt—it doesn't matter—all of you."

"Surratt." Young thought for a moment. "Tall fellow, about my age, dresses like a dandy?"

Denison nodded.

"I met him on the Richmond line when I went down last year. Big talker! What's he got to do with this?"

"In the last few months of the war, Surratt was running messages from Richmond to Montreal. He was also sent to New York State to scout the prison camp at Elmira, and find a way to free those men, but since the assassination, he's been hiding in Montreal. His poor mother has been arrested for conspiring with Booth. So be very careful. Too much talk and anyone here could be drawn in, and it wouldn't be for violation of the neutrality act but for the murder of their president."

"But I only saw Booth the once," Young told him. "He was talking with Patrick Martin about shipping some stuff through the blockade."

"Every time you speak, you dig yourself deeper," Denison warned. "Take my advice. Forget you saw Booth and forget you saw Surratt!"

• • •

Washington, DC
April 27, 1865

"They are sure it's Booth?"

Edwin Stanton's fiery gaze was aimed at his young aide. The boy stood at attention just a few feet from the secretary's desk. Hanging from his arm was a saddlebag.

"Er...yes..." the young soldier stammered. "The body is being brought back from Virginia. And Herold, the conspirator that was with him, is in chains. He'll be returned here too. And —"

"We'll deal with Herold quick enough," Stanton interrupted, "but we must be sure we have the right man. I want any intimates of Booth rounded up. They can identify the body. Was it burned or mutilated? I need a positive identification."

"No, sir." The aide thought of the messages from the search party. "Booth was shot, but was pulled out of a burning tobacco barn, and he died a few hours later."

"Did he say anything?" Stanton demanded.

"Something about his mother," the aide answered.

"I don't care about his mother! If he was alive for hours, he might have said something more. I want to see the detectives the minute they return. I want to interrogate every one of them. See to that, soldier! There's a reward at stake. Every one of them will want their share, but I'll determine who gets what."

The aide could do little more than nod.

"And that Maryland doctor who treated Booth's leg, where is he?" Stanton rummaged through the papers on his desk before seizing a dispatch. "Mudd...Dr. Mudd...what a fitting name for a traitor. Where is he?"

"The old capital prison," the soldier answered, silently praising himself for having checked.

"He won't be there long," Stanton hissed. "As soon as he talks, he'll hang. That will finish the story. Now, the body of Booth. I will decide who sees it. And then the body will be destroyed. There will no gravesites or relics for Southern traitors to visit. Burn it or weigh it down with rocks and sink it in the Potomac. I don't care how, but Booth will disappear forever."

"Understood, sir."

"But not yet!" Stanton barked. "Be sure it's him. Those rebels are devious. He might have slipped away. He may have gone deep into rebel territory or be hiding with his Canadian friends. Perhaps we have someone who only looks like Booth."

The aide suddenly remembered the saddlebag and removed it from his shoulder.

"The officer in charge in Virginia sent a special dispatch by rapid courier. It was to be given to you alone."

"And when were you going to give it to me?" Stanton snarled and stepped quickly from behind the desk. In seconds, the saddlebag was open and a small book removed. The secretary was silent as he thumbed through the pages.

"A diary..." he murmured and returned to the desk. "Leave me."

The soldier saluted and began to turn away.

"And no paperwork on this, nothing for the department files. Leave it with me."

• • •

Buffalo, New York
April 27, 1865

"Buffalo Depot," the train conductor called, "The army has ordered a delay on all trains. It will be a few hours before we move again."

Charles Hemmings glanced through the window to the crowded platform and hoped again his contact was in place. He carried no luggage but slipped a small brown derby onto his head. Tucked in the hatband was a single yellow dandelion.

"Move to the rear of the platform," a Union army officer ordered as the passengers stepped from the train. "You'll be able to see more when these cars are moved."

Hemmings pushed his way toward the passenger waiting room but stopped suddenly as a hand came to rest on his shoulder.

"That's a dainty little flower." A man pointed to Hemmings's hat and added quietly, "You are in the right place—follow me. I have a carriage waiting. Stay close. It's a busy night in Buffalo."

The carriage was one of a long line parked beside the track. Most drivers and passengers were staring silently across the train yard.

"We're not going anywhere for a while," the man began to explain when they reached their vehicle. "But the army is running things by the clock. So, we may not have to wait that long."

"What's happening?" Hemming asked. "I only got word a few days ago to come tonight. I've been hiding out on a farm near Dunkirk and I'm out of touch. I was on a raid and got separated."

"You knew Lincoln was shot?" his guide asked.

"Yeah, I heard that a couple of days ago, just before I was told to make my way here."

"Thank your Confederate friends for finding you. In the grand scheme of things, you are a small fry, but the rebels are taking care of their people."

A train whistle shrieked in the gathering darkness, and a single locomotive inched off to the west. Armed Union soldiers leaned from the cab and clustered on top of the wood tender.

"That will be the pilot engine," the guide announced. "It's running ten minutes in front of the funeral train. Yankees are making sure nothing more happens to their dead president."

"The body is here?" Hemming began to grasp the reason for the crowds.

"Yup and there was a public viewing all day. Thousands of people went for a look. They say he's in good shape. He should be. A pair of embalmers freshen him up each day. He'll be looking pretty for a showing in Cleveland tomorrow."

"And that's why all the people were clustered along the track when my train came in? Some of them had bonfires going…like they were waiting for something."

"They won't see much. But we may have lucked out. The border patrols will relax tonight. The newspapers say Booth is dead. Yankees caught up to him in Virginia, and with the assassin dead, they're going to care less about people like you."

"Did Booth shoot it out?"

"Don't matter." The guide shrugged. "He's as dead as the Confederacy."

"So have the armies all surrendered?"

"No, there are diehards down South, but I don't see what they can accomplish—"

The words were cut short as the whistle sounded on a second steam engine. A portrait of Abraham Lincoln had been mounted below the head lamp, and the locomotive was draped in black crepe. The crowd grew silent except for a few muffled sobs. The dim light from inside the last car allowed the spectators a final glimpse of the president's coffin as the train faded into the night.

"We'll go now," the guide announced. "We'll stay in the thick of the crowd. A few of the British came over to see the spectacle. We'll slip across the border with them. If I was a young rebel, I'd hide out in Canada for a few months."

"That's what I had in mind," Hemmings agreed. "Let the South settle down, too. My home is in Florida. Maybe I'll go home come fall. My war is over."

III

Durham Station, North Carolina
April 26, 1865

"The meeting is in that cabin. A local farmer named Bennet owns it and lets them use it. Of course, if he didn't, the army would take it anyway." Mike Flynn had talked their way past the army pickets and stood watching the building. "General Sherman and Joe Johnston have been in there for an hour. And when they come out, we'll know one way or the other."

He settled in the grass of the orchard and urged his two companions to the ground. All three wore dirty blue uniforms.

"Soldier, did you come to look at the trees or see history made?" Flynn asked a moment later.

Owen Wilson sheepishly turned his attention from the white and pink of the blossoms. The delicate scent lingered in the spring air, and if not for the uniforms, the rifles and the distant hum of two opposing armies, it would be an idyllic moment.

Bill Hunter was prone on the grass, his face a mass of ugly bruises. "Ow long, you thing?" The words came painfully through half-healed scabs around his mouth.

"What did he say?" Flynn turned to Owen to translate.

"He asked how long it would take."

"Can't understand a bloody word he says," Flynn confessed. "And how would I know how long they might be?"

"He was just asking," Owen replied. "Besides you claim to be privy to Uncle Billy's secrets."

"I don't know everything Sherman is up to but I do have connections. Either Johnston surrenders his rebel army on the same terms that Lee accepted, or the armistice ends and we'll have thirty thousand rebels to kill."

"Just kirl theem," Hunter whispered.

"That time I understood," Flynn said proudly. "Bill Hunter wants to kill them all, and the bloodthirsty bugger may have a chance. Sherman had a surrender tied up two weeks ago, but Washington said he was too lenient and rejected the deal. The government has a stronger hate for rebels since Lincoln was shot."

Flynn glanced at Hunter and saw him wipe a piece of bloody ooze from his face. "And that was what over two weeks ago?"

"Yath," Hunter answered.

General William Tecumseh Sherman had shared the grim news of the assassination with Confederate General Joe Johnston before telling his own men. And then, Sherman told his staff, Johnston broke into a cold sweat and freely began to discuss the terms for surrender. The Union army was harder to control. Raleigh could have joined the list of devastated Southern cities, but the troops were forcibly confined to camp.

Sergeant Hunter had been one of the few Union soldiers who dared to suggest that Lincoln had faults. Ten men had beaten him, smashing his teeth and jaw with a rifle butt. When the officers finally intervened, it was to administer more punishment. Hunter was tied to a wagon wheel and rolled about the camp before being dumped in front of a surgeon's tent. Hours later, Sergeant Hunter was demoted to private.

"Two weeks, and you ain't healed," Flynn observed. "Why did you do it, Hunter? Why were you so damn stupid?"

Owen too waited for the answer, his eyes drawn not to the battered face but to the sleeve where the sergeant's stripes had been.

"Goth the right to opinthon and freethom to thpeak," he told them, his defiance hardened by the slur of the words. "It's why we fought."

"You're like the damn negras," Flynn told him. "You have to learn there's a price for freedom."

Owen slipped down on the warming earth and watched the light breeze twist the blossoms. A few petals broke loose and drifted to the ground.

His thoughts flashed back through his time in the Union army. The young Canadian farm boy had been lured South by the offer of bounty money in 1862. Three years later, he thought of the friends he'd lost. The latest were Flaherty and Mulroney, two companions who were killed on the march through the Carolinas. Almost two months had passed, but he still woke from nightmares of the bodies swinging from the tree, an example of Southern justice. His lieutenant told him of the Union army investigation. A rebel prisoner claimed that the pair had been found in the kitchen of a plantation house, the white mistress naked and unconscious on the floor. And while the tall soldier watched, the shorter soldier mounted a house servant.

The lieutenant said there was no more to tell. The rebel prisoner would no longer be able to answer questions, since he too had been hanged.

On other nights, Owen had nightmares about the two Frenchman from Quebec who were blown apart in Georgia or about Jimmy and Mathilde, dead in Canada, but still victims of the war. He felt lost and unsure about his own future.

"Courier coming up." Flynn's words brought him back to Durham station.

The three watched as a gray-clad figure carrying a white flag swung from his horse to enter the cabin.

"Maybe the Confederates won't quit," Flynn suggested. "A bunch of rebels slipped out of Lee's camp and got away. And Jeff Davis is on the run."

The trio watched the cabin again for a few minutes in silence before Flynn spoke.

"Johnston's army is the largest, but there are bands of rebels in Alabama and across the Mississippi. The northern newspapers say the war ended with Appomattox, but we know better. If Sherman had allowed more reporters to travel with his army, we might be the heroes who ended the war."

The cabin door opened, and the courier emerged. He mounted and rode toward the rebel camp.

"What are you going to do if it's over, Hunter?" Flynn asked.

"Go 'ome." The answer came quickly.

"Go home," Flynn repeated slowly. "You might be wise to stay in the army until that face heals. You'd scare people at home. What about you, Wilson?"

"Don't know," Owen answered. He refused to consider the possibility that the war might end, forcing him to make his own decisions.

"Well, Hunter wants to 'go 'ome," Flynn said, imitating Hunter, "and I can understand that. But you claim you don't have a home anymore."

Flynn scratched his stomach before he spoke again. "Might want to think about another army. General Sweeney is looking for men."

"What for?" Owen was instantly curious.

"To free Ireland," Flynn told him, proudly. "Give some thought to the Fenians. One way or another we'll set the homeland free. We're already recruiting men."

"Dey're comin'." Hunter pointed to the cabin.

Two men had emerged. One wore a loose-fitting blue uniform and a large slouch hat. The other was hatless, his gray uniform well worn, but buttoned with military decorum to the neck.

The two officers shook hands while the Union guard begin to cheer.

• • •

Near Charlotte, North Carolina
May 2, 1865

There were too many campfires to count, a comforting sign. No Yankee scouting parties would dare to confront this many rebels. John Headley dragged a branch to the edge of the fire. The night was warm, but firelight would be welcome. Around him were remnants of the Second Kentucky, and it was only fitting that men who served under Confederate General John Hunt Morgan were here at the end.

President Jefferson Davis was in flight. His cabinet met sporadically as the last vestiges of the Confederate government moved south. Joe Johnston had come and gone several times before his surrender. Davis wanted the army split into small groups to continue the war, but Secretary of War John Breckinridge had urged Johnston to accept the latest Northern terms and the General agreed.

The Confederacy teetered on the abyss of history, staggered by body blows: the fall of Richmond, Appomattox, and the assassination. Davis had barely flinched when he heard the news of Lincoln. Secretary of State Judah Benjamin maintained a stoic calm, and it fell to others to quiet the soldiers who began a noisy celebration. Days later, they began to realize that there was little to celebrate. The assassin was a Southerner, and the single gunshot ignited Northern fears of a great Southern conspiracy. The knife attack on secretary of state Seward added fuel to the suspicion. Washington would look for revenge.

"You never asked how I got the idea to grab Andy Johnson," Robert Martin said quietly. He and had Headley had tried to kidnap the vice president several weeks before his inauguration.

"I thought you were just smart," John Headley laughed. He crumpled a newspaper and tossed it into the fire. Recent copies of Northern papers were hard to find, but there was no need to share the latest dismal news.

"Booth," Martin told him. "When he was in his cups in Toronto, he talked about a scheme to kidnap Lincoln. I thought it was brandy talking, but when we saw the vice-president and no guard, it all came back."

Headley watched the paper curl in the flames. "The paper said the hunt for Booth was concentrated in Maryland and Virginia. He's another mad rebel like the rest of us, I suppose."

"John," Martin said quietly. "We should forget we ever saw Booth."

"Agreed," Headley replied instantly, "and we won't be alone. Besides, there's a whole lot of forgetting going on. Another detachment was left behind yesterday to burn more records. There must have been something embarrassing in those files."

"What files?" an older Confederate lieutenant asked as he eased up to the fire.

"Some old records that were burned," Headley told him. He knew the face but couldn't remember the name.

"Probably trying to avoid questions," the lieutenant suggested. "I saw you heave that newspaper. Anything we should know?"

"You've heard it all," Headley told him. "Southern criminals and the like."

"Anything about Saltville?" he asked.

"Saltville?" Martin was surprised. "Why would anyone talk about Saltville?"

"Well, I hope they're not. We don't need that kind of blemish on the reputation of Morgan's cavalry."

Headley was mystified. "I don't know what you mean."

"Yankee papers were making a big to-do about a massacre after the fight there last fall and claimed we killed a hundred Negro prisoners. The papers made it sound like another Fort Pillow, when they said Bedford Forrest turned his men loose, but it wasn't. Some of the boys got out of hand, dragged Africans out of the surgeons' tents, and killed them. But it wasn't a hundred, and General Breckinridge stopped it real quick and then brought charges against one of our men. There weren't more than four or five killed, as far as I know. Yankees turned it into something it wasn't."

"The Yankees also have some explaining to do," Martin reminded him. "But the Yankees are winning, and the victors write the history. They can tear down the reputation of the Second Kentucky by claiming we were nothing but robbers and horse thieves or worse yet…murderers. At least the history books should note that Morgan's cavalry fought to the bitter end."

He stopped and caught himself before adding, "Whenever that may be."

Shouts in the distance interrupted the conversation.

"That will be Duke," the lieutenant told them. "He promised to talk to the men. I'll bring him over when he's finished."

It was three hours before General Basil Duke settled by their fire.

Duke was in his early thirties, but his dark hair was rapidly graying, and like the other men, his face was thin and his body, gaunt.

"It isn't often I meet with special service officers," he said, smiling. "And all the better when they are old friends with foreign experience."

"Canada is foreign in name only, General," Robert Martin said, taking his hand.

"It's good to see you. You remember John Headley?"

"Of course." Again, Duke extended his hand, but Headley saw a pained look cross the general's face.

"I'm afraid I have bad news."

Headley braced himself.

"It's a woman, Mary Overhall. I was told you were close."

Headley felt a tremor of fear. Mary was more than a friend, but he'd had no contact with her since she'd gone to scout a Union fort near Louisville six months earlier.

"She was arrested last fall," Duke told him. "She's as well as can be expected, but prison conditions can break a person. With the war winding down, she may be offered parole. Get word to her. Tell her to sign. She does us no good in jail."

"I'll try." Headley choked on the words. Duke's news cemented his plan for an early return to Kentucky.

Strains of music from a lonely harmonica drifted through the night air as Martin added another branch to the fire.

"What do you hear of the others?" Duke asked. "What of Tom Hines?"

"We saw him in January," Headley told him. "Since then, we've heard nothing. But Tom can take care of himself. Bennett Young was before the Canadian courts when we left. There's a rumor that Grenfell faces execution."

Duke grimaced and, as if struck by a sudden chill, moved closer to the fire.

"And you just came back from Canada?"

"Indirectly," Martin told him. "It took longer than expected. The country between here and Kentucky is infested with bushwhackers. We were on our way to Richmond when the city was evacuated, so we just followed the retreat. We gave our dispatch to the secretary of war, General Breckinridge, but he just laughed when he read it. Jacob Thompson had advocated a plan to open another Northern front, and that was not going to happen. So, we're hanging about and eating your food. But we're available for any duty. We heard that President Davis might try to slip off with only a couple of guards and we're willing to volunteer."

"That was yesterday. There will be no more special duties, no more orders." Duke sounded haggard but relieved. He reached into his pocket and produced two sheets of paper.

"Blank parole forms. Fill them out and you can move through the lines. Sooner or later, you'll be asked to take the federal oath of loyalty. You might as well if you intend to remain in this country."

"I'm going to stay," Headley announced. "I could go to Canada, but there's not much for me there."

"Eventually we'll need you in Kentucky," Duke told him. "It won't be easy to rebuild, but I'm going home too. I've decided not to surrender the Second Kentucky as a unit. We moved to Johnston when Lee surrendered and came to Davis when Johnston gave up. The men will take parole, but not the unit. I think it's the way General Morgan would have wanted it."

"It's come to that!" Martin murmured.

"Our war is almost over," Duke told him. "The cabinet is splitting up. Benjamin is striking off on his own tomorrow. Davis can't make up his mind. He may head for Florida and try to get away by boat or go overland to Kirby Smith and his army in Texas. I'll stay for a few days, as will Breckinridge and John Taylor Wood. Wood was a naval commander and a relative of Davis and he's become very important to the President. As to rank and file, I don't want one more man lost or wounded with the end this close."

Duke rose from the fire. "We're going to distribute the last of the Confederate funds tomorrow. It won't be much but might help some."

The general's aide hurried over with a horse, but Duke seemed reluctant to leave. "Please look me up back in Kentucky."

"We'll have a reunion," Martin suggested.

"It won't be very big," Duke answered sadly. "The Morgan family has taken a full share of the losses."

Martin silently cursed himself. He had forgotten that Duke was married to a sister of John Hunt Morgan. Morgan's famous cavalry raids were already a part of Kentucky history but his family paid a steep price.

"General Morgan is dead, of course," Duke reminded them. "The youngest brother, Tom, was killed on the great raid in Ohio. Kitty was a favorite sister, and she's in mourning with her husband A. P. Hill gone. We won't need a large room."

The next morning, Headley and Martin watched from the dusty street as the last of the Confederate cavalry rode off. The scant supplies that the Confederate pay would buy barely filled a saddlebag. The pair would have to scrounge on the return trip to Kentucky. The shopkeeper had been apologetic but could offer nothing more.

Morgan's unit filled the street with the traditional columns of fours. The horses that once had been the pride of the bluegrass state were as battered as their riders were.

Two elderly women sobbed and dabbed at tears as a rich voice carried strains of "My Old Kentucky Home" from across the street.

"Nice but sad," the storekeeper announced, blowing his nose and pocketing the piece of cloth. "But it's the wrong song."

Headley and Martin turned to face him.

"I like the music of Stephen Foster, but it might be more appropriate to sing something like, 'Hard times Come Again No More.' That's really all we can hope for."

IV

Montreal, Canada East
May 3, 1865

S arah Slater reveled in the attention. A gentleman doffed his hat and smiled, while another offered an arm to guide her across busy Saint Catherine Street. She suspected it was the pale-blue dress with the matching hat and the way her body filled the fabric. It wasn't her face. Only a hazy outline was visible beneath the veil.

She had discarded the black mourning clothes upon arrival in Montreal. Henry Hogan graciously welcomed her back to Saint Lawrence Hall. He asked no questions, not about her travels or the man with her.

"Mrs. Slater." The hotel manager smiled when he saw her. "I have an empty suite on the third floor." When she didn't ask about the presence of other Southern guests, he understood that she didn't want to know.

"The rooms are very private," he told her. "But please let me know if anyone bothers you. We've had a problem with Americans who refuse to register but wander the halls." The warning was clear. The hotel was being watched.

For three days, she and Mcgruder took meals in their rooms, enjoying their time without the danger of discovery.

Money was not a problem. Their cash was safely on deposit in a Montreal bank, and in a few weeks, the couple would be away.

Mcgruder suggested London, but she preferred Paris. Neither would need paying work for several years or longer if they managed their investments.

Sarah had been well paid as a courier. Mcgruder, from his post in the Confederate Secret Service, had seen to that. More cash had come from the clothes and medicine she had smuggled through the lines.

This morning, she had slipped from his arms and dressed quietly to walk the busy streets of Montreal. A year earlier, her servant would have followed a few steps behind. Sillery Fraser, a free black woman forced into service for the Confederacy, had become a friend and confidant. It was Sillery who had distracted a Yankee guard and saved the courier from prison in the weeks before the war's end. Mcgruder, as promised, had produced Sillery's slave-born daughter, and Sillery had planned a new life in the South.

Sarah's thoughts drifted from the past to the future. As she walked, she appraised the merchandise in shop windows. The settee in the furniture store might fit in her new home, as would the matching curtains and wallpaper. But the daydream evaporated as a reflection flashed in the glass.

A tall, well-dressed young man moved along the sidewalk with the air of one who owned the world, and though the image was blurred, she recognized John Surratt. He had been her guide between the lines as she crossed from Confederate to Union territory, and with each trip, she came to dislike him more.

She kept her back toward him, watching the reflection as he raised his hat to a pair of young ladies, who smiled and mouthed, "Bonjour." His hat and suit looked new or fresh from a cleaning. He moved only a few steps down Saint Catherine before turning up a side street.

"Scuse me, please." A chunky young man awkwardly brushed against her.

"Come on, Lou. Watch where you go," his companion chided him, "Excuse us, ma'am."

"I thought I saw Surratt." The voice of the man called Lou had a nervous quaver. His companion wore a tan, cotton duster, but Sarah's eyes were drawn to the blue pants and yellow stripes favored by American army officers.

"Better look sharp," the officer warned. "Stanton will hang you if we don't find him. He's spent a good deal of money on this wild goose chase. If we don't find Surratt, he'll think you were lying about him going to Montreal."

Lou seemed familiar, and Sarah tried to place him as the two men continued down the street. The memory returned as she walked back to Saint Lawrence Hall, and with it, relief that she had worn the veil.

Lou Weichmann was a boarder at Mrs. Surratt's Washington boarding house and a clerk in the War Department. He must have known of Surratt's role as a courier. The newspapers were full of stories of "a rebel nest" at the house on H Street and the frequent visits of John Wilkes Booth. Surratt's mother, Mary, had been arrested and was confined with others believed to be linked to the assassination, but Weichmann had not been listed as one of that group.

Sarah Slater swore silently. If they were looking for Surratt, they could also be looking for her.

Inside the hotel, she approached the manager.

"Mr. Hogan? Can you deliver a message?"

"I can send a clerk at any time."

"No! Can *you* deliver a message?"

Hogan considered for only a moment. "Of course. Where should I take it?"

"The Southern gentlemen are still in Montreal?"

"Mr. E.G. Lee is here along with Mr. Sanders, and I believe Mr. Porterfield could be found. Jacob Thompson appears to have departed."

She cursed silently. Thompson was the natural choice. She hadn't met Lee and neither liked nor trusted Sanders.

"Perhaps to Mr. Porterfield. Would you have a pen and paper?"

Hogan turned away as she scratched out the message.

"Surratt is being followed by Yankees. One is named Weichmann." She considered for a moment before signing S. Slater. She sealed an envelope and handed it to Hogan.

"A good choice, I believe, Mrs. Slater. Porterfield is well informed and a gentleman. I'll take it at once?"

"Thank you. And Mr. Hogan, could you send the shipping company brochures to my suite? I'm interested in Europe. We may leave sooner than expected."

• • •

Washington, DC
May 10, 1865

"That proclamation was premature," Stanton barked with all the authority the secretary of war could muster. "But he wouldn't listen. How could President Johnson declare hostilities are at an end when his own secretary of war warns it's not so? This won't be over until all of the rebels surrender, all of their leaders are in jail, and the chief offenders are on the gallows! That is the way it will be!"

He slammed his palms together as he stared at the nearby grounds of the White House. It took a full minute before he acknowledged the presence of the aide.

"What do you have?" he demanded.

"The woman—" The aide began.

"What woman?" Stanton was still seething, but the aide charged ahead.

"We thought we had the courier, Sarah Slater, but it's not her. It's another female who looks like Slater but uses the name Kate Thompson. We'll hold her at the prison. And there is that newspaperman, Sanford Conover, the one that you met last week."

"Yes, yes, I can remember what happened a week ago. He was a brazen fellow!"

And broke, the aide thought. The old man won't like this.

"Conover's sent another report from the Canadas with evidence of the Southern conspiracy. He has people who will testify to assassination plans and a man that will testify of a plot to blow the Croton Dam, the one at New York City."

"I know where the Croton Dam is!" Stanton was more testy than usual. "What does he mean by blow it?"

"Just as he says, blow it up, destroy it. It would have created a nasty flood, and since the dam holds the reservoir for the New York water supply, the city would have gone bone dry. No water for food, for cleaning; nothing to fight fires. And he says it's the sort of scheme the rebels were working on."

"Well, tell him to bring the witnesses. Judge Holt and his military commission can add it to the dossier when he convicts the Lincoln conspirators."

"You mean when he tries the conspirators," the aide corrected him.

"No, I mean when he convicts them! That's what will happen! Why do you think I ordered them hooded and separated? I don't want cock-and-bull stories spread about innocence and I don't want them to hatch some silly story to distract us. Now, Conover! Tell him to bring those witnesses to Washington."

"That's just it, sir." The aide hesitated. "He wants more money to cover expenses."

"We already paid him!" Stanton thundered. "No more!"

"Yes, sir."

"No, wait!" Stanton was reversing course. "Send him what he needs but warn him that these witnesses have to be good."

"Yes, sir," the aide agreed.

Stanton cocked his head as cheers erupted from the telegraph room. "What is all the commotion? If they've been drinking at lunch, there will be hell to pay!"

"I'll see what it's about."

But before the aide could move, the door swung open and a breathless corporal bounded into the room.

"What is the meaning of this outrage?" Stanton screamed, shaking his fist. "At least have the courtesy to knock."

"They got him, Mr. Secretary." The corporal gleefully waved a telegraph form. "Jeff Davis. Fourth Michigan captured his party near a place called Irwinville, Georgia."

"Captured...so he's alive," Stanton stammered.

"Apparently so. The telegram says captured." The aide glanced again at telegram. "Jeff Davis, his wife, secretary, and others. Where do you want him taken?"

Stanton had already considered the possibility. "Fortress Monroe. He won't get away from there! He can spend his last days ringed by walls of stone."

• • •

Near Saint-Liboire, Canada East
May 17, 1865

The horses struggled with the steep incline before finally cresting the hill. The valley below shone with vibrant shades of springtime green. As the carriage passed a farmhouse, a group of children raced alongside, yelling and waving, and then, like a dog that knows the limit, returned to their yard.

"People are friendly if you can understand what they say," John Surratt observed.

"I'm sure the priest at Saint Liboire can speak English," John Porterfield assured him. "And he'll probably be able to find others to provide conversation. You might improve your French."

"I've heard enough of it," Surratt told him. "I spent five days at that boarding house and the staff nattered away to each other in what they call French. I can speak the language, but not the way they do."

"I'm sorry, John," Porterfield told him. "But we had to hide you quickly. It took a few days to arrange for this location. It's out of the way, but you'll be safe. But you must be careful not to offend those who offer shelter. Don't complain about language."

"I sent a letter to my mother's lawyer," Surratt said, changing the subject. "I told him I'd come back and set things straight."

"We know," Porterfield admitted. "We've had a letter too. He suggests you stay quiet. And John, don't send any more letters. The federals have the note you sent home in April. It's why they concentrated their search around Montreal."

"But I should be doing something," Surratt argued. "The others arrested were all involved in the kidnap plot, except maybe Dr. Mudd. Booth was looking to buy land and that's when he met the doctor. I don't know if Mudd was involved in the Richmond line. The others, yeah, they were part of it. But Booth never talked of killing Lincoln. We were going to end the war by snapping up their president and carrying him off. We tried once, but Booth got it messed up. Booth thought we could nab Lincoln, but that day, the president was actually speaking at Booth's hotel and there we were waiting out on the road. Don't that beat all?"

A lonely road seemed the appropriate place for the conversation.

"Ma wouldn't agree with killing. She's very proper. She forced George Atzerodt to move out of our house. He was drinking and she wouldn't abide alcohol in the house. You see drink took my father. And she got angry when she heard that my brother, Isaac, was drinking and gambling and even dancing. She laid into him, and a few weeks later, he moved west. So, I never told her anything that would upset her."

Surratt hummed to himself for a few minutes as he gazed at the countryside. Then he began again. "The newspapers say they arrested Lewis Payne, or Powell, at my mother's house, and she didn't recognize him. That doesn't surprise me. Her eyes are really bad and worse when it's dark. There were nights I wasn't sure she could see her hand in front of her face."

"And your sister." Porterfield was curious. "Did she know what was happening?"

"Hell, no! Anna is a child. She was sweet on Booth, but a lot of women are. Or were."

"What about the other people at the boarding house?" Porterfield snapped the whip as the horses slowed on the ascent of another hill.

"No, they weren't the type to do anything. Now, Lou Weichmann was curious, but we didn't tell him much. I liked Lou. We went to the seminary together, but he's too cautious, always worrying about something. It took weeks to convince him to get us the reports on the federal prison camps, and the stuff he finally produced was really old and out of date. He didn't have any gumption."

"Then why do you think he's working for the federals now?" Porterfield asked.

"Lou? Working for Yankees?" Surratt showed surprise.

"Your mother's lawyer says he's going to be a witness for the prosecution."

Surratt slumped back against the cushion. "Lou didn't know anything! What could he tell them?"

"I wouldn't know. But he was in Montreal with a Yankee officer. That's when we moved to protect you."

"Don't that beat all, Lou working with the enemy."

The road crested a hill to reveal a village ahead.

"That will be Saint Liboire," Porterfield told him. "The priest will shelter you until the search ends or we move you somewhere else."

"You'll let me know about mother's trial?"

"Yes, of course." Porterfield snapped the whip, and the horses trotted toward the church. "I wouldn't worry. The lawyer said there was compelling evidence against the men, but the case against your mother is weak. So even if they convict her, she'd spend a few months or maybe a couple of years in jail. Even Yankees don't hang women."

Montreal, Canada East
May 20, 1865

"This is silly," Sarah Slater tried to explain. "I appreciate your coming but I don't believe I need a doctor."

"Well, let's just see." He smiled to reassure her. "I'm Montrose Pullen, a graduate of the University of Louisville."

"Oh, so you are from the South?" Sarah smiled. "And have you been in Montreal long?"

"Off and on for several years," he told her, opening his medical bag.

"I don't need a doctor," she repeated. "It was a simple faint and unfortunately it happened in front of Mr. Hogan. He summoned you."

"Yes, I've known him for several years." He placed his ear against her chest. "Breathe deeply," he instructed. "In and out, in and out. Your husband said you had been ill?"

"Oh, it's nothing; something I ate. The food repeats on me, but I feel better as the day progresses."

"I'd like to do a full examination," he told her. "Would you remove your clothes? Don't be modest, Mrs. Slater. I am a trained doctor."

"Yes, trained in Louisville, you said." She considered for a moment before she began to undo the buttons. "How did you get to Montreal?" Conversation, she thought, would make this easier.

"I was in the Confederate medical corps, sent originally to try to reach Johnson's Island. We were concerned with the health of our prisoners. The Union wouldn't give us access, and we had to rely on second hand reports. It was bad, of course, primarily because of the climate, stuck out in Lake Erie, and the poor conditions of the entire facility. The Yankees wouldn't spend money for proper barracks. I doubt it was planned abuse, just too many prisoners. The same sort of conditions we hear about at the Confederate camp at Andersonville, in Georgia."

She had opened the buttons on the top of the dress.

"Remove your clothes," he repeated and turned his back. "You can wear a dressing gown and when ready, lie on the bed."

"So, you've spent all this time in Montreal." She reluctantly slipped from the dress and underclothing.

"No, I traveled some. I was in France last year to buy medical supplies."

"My husband and I may leave for Europe in a few weeks."

He turned when he heard the bedsprings sag.

She looked into space as his hands pressed gently on her stomach.

"How are your menses?" he asked.

"My what?"

"Your monthlies."

"Oh." She paused. "I haven't been regular these last few years. I think it was the stress of travel. And I didn't have one last month. I had..." She tried to think of a genteel description.

"I had a nervous condition and was taking laudanum and wine. I fear I liked the medicine too much. It made my problems disappear, but I was living in a haze, and well, my husband took it away."

"Good thing," Pullen told her. "Laudanum can become an addiction."

His voice seemed to fall away.

"You should feel lucky Hogan summoned me," he told her. "I've made studies on the female anatomy and plan to specialize in female disorders in the future. It's a new medical field. We call it gynecology."

She felt fingers between her legs.

"I'm working on special instruments for this work. Pity! If I had known, I would have brought them today."

After what felt like hours, he removed his fingers. "OK. Sit up."

She lifted herself to the side of the bed and tightened the robe as the doctor opened the door. For an instant, she feared he was calling for medical students.

"You can come in now, Mr. Slater. You are planning to leave for Europe?"

"Yes," Mcgruder answered, his eyes focused on Sarah, the housecoat held tight to her body.

"I booked passage this morning. We'll go next month."

"Don't delay," Dr. Pullen advised. "Mrs. Slater will need extra rest. There are excellent doctors in London and Paris."

Sarah felt a sense of dread. Why would she need more doctors?

"There are good men I can recommend in both cities," a sober Pullen told them. "And you have to decide if the child should have French or British citizenship."

V

Quebec City, Canada East
May 1865

P aul Forsey had no problem finding a quiet corner table. The room was almost empty, and he wondered again why his British army friend had asked for a meeting at a lower town tavern.

"Bonjour," a waitress greeted him, leaning over the table to collect empty glasses and inadvertently offer a glimpse of ample breasts.

"That's it," he thought. "He enjoys the scenery."

The waitress moved off with a subtle swing of her hips.

"Brandy!" Geoffrey Ralston called, slipping into a chair. "Too much to see to notice me?" He wore civilian clothes; he'd left his army fatigues in the barracks.

Forsey blushed, but his eyes darted to the bar where the waitress bent in conversation. A peasant dress rode high to expose legs bare to the knee.

"Hah. I knew you would enjoy it here." Ralston laughed as the barmaid returned.

"We'll have another round in a few minutes, Francine," Ralston told her. Both men watched as she returned to the bar, but this time she slid onto a stool and turned away. Long black hair streamed down her back.

"Better scenery than watching clerks," Ralston told him. "It's why I thought we'd meet here. What news do you have?"

Ralston was a British army lieutenant posted to the local commander's office. As a friendship developed, he and Forsey shared privileged information.

Forsey reluctantly pulled his eyes from the woman. "There was a private letter from the legation in Washington," he began. "The American secretary of war has created a reign of terror. Anyone showing a hint of sympathy for the South is suspect. So the Confederates in Canada are afraid to go home, and each day more drift in. They're fighting among themselves—mostly over money."

"And the assassin?"

"Well, Booth's body was brought back to Washington," Forsey explained. "The search parties were told to take him alive, but dead men tell no tales. The man who was captured with Booth says others were in on the conspiracy—perhaps thirty-five others—but he can't or won't identify them."

"Probably all misguided Southerners," Ralston suggested.

"That's the way the story will be told," Forsey agreed. "But there are wild theories. One says Stanton wanted Lincoln out of the way. Now he wants quick convictions. He's set up a military tribunal to try the conspirators."

"A trial is a trial," Ralston opined.

"Not under American law. The military law won't allow defendants to testify or speak in court. Only the defense lawyers can speak, so the prisoners can't tell their own story. And there are a lot of questions—like why Booth left a note for President Johnson, suggesting a meeting. It makes it look like the new president was involved."

"So maybe the assassination wasn't a Confederate operation?" Ralston asked.

"No one knows. The Yankees hope the Southerners are behind it. Rewards have been offered for Clay, Thompson, Sanders, Cleary, Tucker, the whole slew of the group in Canada, and, of course, there's a reward for the capture of Jeff Davis."

"At least the threat of Confederate raids here has ended," Ralston told him. "Our garrisons have been quiet for the last two months. Things are almost dull."

"Yes, well, now the problem is smaller and harder to spot." Forsey glanced again at the barmaid before he continued. "American detectives are flooding across the border looking for anyone who might be remotely connected to the assassination. I think Macdonald and Cartier are looking the other way. Two prominent politicians don't want to be accused of hampering a murder investigation, even if our sovereignty is compromised."

"You mean Upper and Lower Canada sovereignty, don't you?" Ralston prodded. "The Confederation plan is falling apart. Prince Edward Island is out. New Brunswick voted it down. Nova Scotia is swinging in the wind, and if the question were put to the people, it would be defeated here too."

"It's not dead! The plan got a good reception in London. Macdonald is staying in England for a few more weeks, which shows that he's less concerned with American invasion. Of course, he'll also be sampling all the entertainment. His drinking is a problem but his chief associates try to overlook that issue and he really is running the show."

"He should come here!" Ralston laughed and signaled for another round. "He'd have lots to drink and from what I hear, he would be ogling Francine. Here, he could truly be the skirt-chasing 'old Jack' rather than the suave 'John A."

The waitress returned and repeated her earlier performance, swinging her upper body as she toweled drops of moisture from the table. She gave both men a broad smile.

"Macdonald needs a woman to keep him under control, but…" Forsey watched the hips sway back to the bar. "That one is too much for an older man. Not that he might not try."

He sipped on the brandy and waited.

"Do you hear anything about Fenians?" Ralston asked.

"They're here, but we don't know how many or what they're up to. Why?"

"I have my own private letters," Ralston announced. "Army friends in Britain warn of another dustup in Ireland. Our American cousins were allowing Fenian recruiters to sign men up before the fighting stopped. An Irish revolt is nothing new, but with experienced fighting men and modern weapons, the results could be different. It could be…rather bothersome."

"And, I suppose, the trouble could spread," Forsey offered. "I mean, the Orange Lodge hates Catholics and most Irish are Catholic…"

"And understand," Ralston cautioned. "This wouldn't be a plain old Saturday Donnybrook. With troops and supplies from the Americans, the Fenians could trigger a real war."

"So what will the British army do?"

"Nip it in the bud," Ralston confided. "Identify the ring leaders in Ireland and arrest them before real trouble starts. We should do the same here."

Forsey was thinking ahead. "But that still leaves the American Irish leaders and thousands of ex-soldiers across the border. How do you handle them?"

"Now that," Ralston told him, "could be a problem. I'm going to have another round and consider it."

"I can't stay." Forsey rose. "I'll leave you to ogle Francine. Perhaps you can improve English-French relations."

• • •

Washington, DC
May 27, 1865

"There you are! I've been looking for you!" Mike Flynn bent to peer under the wagon.

"The fellows said Owen Wilson would be catching up on his sleep. And I said I was going to wake him. Come on! Get out of there!"

Wilson lifted the straw hat from his face and rubbed blood-shot eyes.

"Must have been a quite a celebration last night," Flynn speculated. "I heard the boys spent the night carousing in Hooker's Division after the victory parades. It must have been a busy night for every bar and brothel. One look at you, and I know it's true."

Wilson crawled out from under the wagon. The bright sun burned his eyes, and as he rose, his stomach churned. He remembered going from one dive to another, the liquor coarse but cheap. An itch made him reach into his pants to scratch, and he thought of the woman. He hadn't really seen her. It was too dark. But it was fast, and as he wanted, just action—no questions, no talk.

The itch satisfied, he patted his pocket. The money was there, but not nearly as much as he had had yesterday.

What was called the Grand Review had been the culmination of four years of war and one final demonstration of the military power of the Union army.

The Army of the Potomac and the eastern regiments marched through Washington first. Thousands of men were fitted with new uniforms and marched in tight formation. But the next day, Sherman's army from the West paraded with the bummers, pioneers, and former slaves, as if to demonstrate that the war was anything but orderly or predictable. And when the parade was finished, the residents of Hooker's Division welcomed them, clean or dirty.

"Any word on moving on?" Wilson silently prayed the orders would be delayed, if only for another day.

"Nah, we'll probably be here for a while."

Wilson walked to the bushes to empty his bladder. He noted the steady stream and the lack of pain. The woman must have been clean.

"Some of the men from the Army of the Potomac are going home," Flynn told him. "The government of the apparently reunited States of America no longer needs or can no longer afford an army with a million men. General Sheridan is going to Texas to mop up what's left of the Confederates and patrol the

Mexican border, and there are Indians to tame in the West but that won't take a million men. The Eastern boys think political favorites and troublemakers will be let go first. Black regiments will be kept longer. The government will keep feeding them until they're sure there won't be any ruckus."

"And where does that leave the rest of us?" Wilson asked. He swatted at a fly that buzzed too close.

"I think by fall we'll be released," Flynn told him. "That's why I wanted to see you. Remember I talked about an Irish army?"

"Yeah." Wilson remembered hints of a bounty and paid travel, but the promises were vague. "The Finnegans." He deliberately corrupted the name, knowing Flynn was a true believer.

"Fenians, damn it! The name comes from the ancient defenders of Ireland, and we're all committed to giving the British bastards their comeuppance. My family starved when the potato blight hit. There was food in Ireland, but the British landowners made money shipping the crops to England. Whole townships starved. The only recourse was the poorhouse or emigration, and thank God my father chose the latter."

"So you should be happy in America." Owen laughed. "There's plenty to eat, a pretty blue uniform."

"I know you are joking," Flynn told him. "But I'm serious. The British are oppressing Ireland, and I won't be content until it stops. Thousands of us feel the same way."

"Why bother me?" Wilson asked. "I'm not Irish. I don't share your passion!"

"We need fighting men," Flynn said. "Men that know what's involved in keeping an army on the go. You were a bummer with Sherman. You learned how to collect supplies and live off the land. Think about joining us."

"The recruiters were only interested in men with a brogue," Owen told Flynn. "I listened, but they couldn't offer much."

"We'll offer more soon," Flynn confided. "And we'll have experienced men to lead us. 'Fighting Tom' will come with us as our secretary of war, even though he's still in the US Army."

Wilson conjured up the image of Thomas Sweeney on the march through Georgia with one arm of his jacket pinned up, the missing arm a legacy of the Mexican War. Sweeney hadn't let the handicap slow his long army career.

"Think about it," Flynn urged. "We can make things easier and maybe arrange a transfer to a soft job in Washington. Will you consider it?"

"I'd been staying here?" Wilson asked.

"At least for a few months."

"I've done too much traveling of late. It might feel good to stay in one place."

VI

Chatham, Canada West
June 1865

"Not much appears to have changed, but scratch below the surface and things are different." The black driver smiled to his passenger. "You folks had the war, and the waves sort of washed across the lake and onto our shores."

The freeborn Canadian black, Amos Baker, had been able to find work on both sides of the color line. He had no objection to Confederate cash and kept any thoughts about morality to himself. When Tom Hines needed assistance, Baker was ready. Even with the war's end, Hines offered business opportunities. The request for transport from Chatham to Lake Erie was easy work.

"Business appears to be brisk for the merchants of Chatham, just like last year," Hines observed. "The black community at Buxton looks as prosperous as it did last year, and the spring has come, like last year. What's changed?"

Baker shifted his weight, and the wagon swayed. "The former slaves who rode the underground railroad north are going south. There are fewer black folk in Chatham and in places like Buxton. That's not to say everyone will go. Folks like me will stay, and so will some of the recent arrivals, but a bunch of them want to find family and friends and are heading home."

"War uproots a lot of people and changes lives," Hines told him. "In parts of Kentucky, the houses are in ruin with only a chimney left standing. The gardens have gone wild, and whoever tended them is gone."

"It's not just Africans looking to go back," Baker said, bringing Hines's thoughts back to Canada. "The white folks who sheltered here are ready to go. They're just waiting to be sure it's safe."

"Maybe it's an opportunity," Hines said. "A fellow with a mind for business could pick up property at a cheap price if everyone is leaving."

"Yeah," Baker nodded. "A lot of property on the market means prices drop. If a man has the cash, he can pick up fine land."

"And you, Amos, do you have enough cash?"

"Could always use more, Captain, but Southerners were very generous. The odd jobs were very profitable."

"We might have more work," Hines told him. "We won't be able to pay as well, but it will be cash money."

"I'd be pleased," Baker told him. "Money is a little tight. Americans aren't buying the way they did when the war was going strong, and in a few months, they're planning to add a new tariff to goods shipped across the border. What we sell will be more expensive, so we won't sell as much. So any extra work would be welcome."

Baker guided the wagon off the main road.

"Eramosa has done well. He bought another farm. Good land and right next door to the home place." Amos pointed to a field where three figures bent to hoe weeds. Two, Hines saw, had removed their shirts and hats, while the third was fully clothed despite the spring heat.

The house showed no change; the red brick shone, the veranda was freshly whitewashed, and on the widow's walk, a Union Jack flew in a line of drying clothes.

"Eramosa must be out on Lake Erie."

"So you know the signal." The black man laughed and pointed the wagon toward the buildings. The British flag was a signal that all was well. Eramosa Willis lived in Kent County but had family connections in the South and had willingly helped the rebels. Like Baker, the farmer and fisherman was more concerned with cash than cause.

The three field workers began to sprint toward the road at the site of the approaching wagon. The one who was fully dressed outdistanced the other two.

"Brought a guest, Miss Erin," Baker sang out.

Hines peered into the shadows of the veranda, assuming the woman was working in the shade. Instead, she approached from the field.

"Welcome back, Mr. Hines."

The voice had the familiar timbre and the hint of Irish.

"Eramosa wasn't sure if you'd be in today or tomorrow. He'll be back this afternoon, and you are in time for lunch."

She lifted the cap to let the red hair fall to her shoulders. The cotton shirt hung to her waist and covered the top of heavy woollen trousers. Despite the rough male clothing, she was as pretty as Hines remembered.

"Amos," she asked. "Will you stay?"

"No, Miss Erin. I have business in town."

"I'll be in touch," Hines told him as he jumped down.

"And I'll be waiting."

After lunch, Erin sent the boys to the field and joined Hines on the veranda. She had replaced the rough field clothes with what she described as "ladylike apparel," and he again noted the trim figure and easy charm. Willis had good taste in a companion.

"I understand you are married. My congratulations," she told him.

"Thank you."

Nannie might not approve of him spending time alone with another woman. Southern reputations had been ruined by as much, but he reminded himself that the world was changing. And Erin was different. Her appearance concealed a tough and fearless demeanor. She had joined Willis on several of his wartime adventures.

"Will the new wife join you here?" Erin asked.

"Eventually, but for now she's safer with her parents. Kentucky is…well, let's say unsettled, and her husband's position is…well… let's say uncertain."

"And do you have work for Eramosa?"

He left the question hanging.

She rose to inspect the flowers in a veranda planter and removed a single blade of grass. "I ask for a reason. He's takes too many risks. He's always been headstrong but in the last year, he's pushed too hard. It's not just with you and the other Confederates. I've been along to see enough of that. It's in everything. He thinks he's indestructible. He's made enough to buy the next farm but he's not satisfied. On the lake, he takes more risks, overloading the new boat and challenging the elements. He's not content unless he flirts with danger."

"And what would you have me do about it?" Hines asked. "He's a man. He makes his own decisions."

"I know." She plucked again at the window box. "I've tried to talk to him."

She removed a flower, the petals half gone, and tossed it to the ground.

"What would you say if your wife asked you to be more cautious?"

Hines thought of the risks he had taken and those he would still take. "I suppose I would listen and be more careful," he said, hoping the lie was convincing.

"Of course, she is your wife. The two of you have that. Eramosa and I have a different arrangement. It suits us both. But I worry."

"If it helps, the war is over. Only a few loose ends to tidy up."

"If you need him, he'll go," she told him. "But because of you and not for any cause. He respects you."

"Don't worry," he said. "The dangerous stage of the war is over."

He hoped it was.

• • •

Toronto, Canada West
June 1865

The beat of a bass drum was as loud as the ragged chorus. The words were muffled, but the sound penetrated the hotel conference room.

"What is that racket?" John A. Macdonald demanded.

Forsey opened the second-floor window and leaned out. He counted five singers and the drummer ringed about the tavern door. A tall, stern-looking woman handed a sheet of paper to each man who entered.

"Temperance demonstration," Forsey said, slamming the window as the singers broke into another chorus.

Macdonald clasped his hands to his ears and swore.

"Forsey, go and—no. Bernard, you go. We need a meaner bugger. Go chase them away. Tell them the attorney general of Canada West will have them arrested for disturbing the peace. No. Give them a donation. Buy them off. Make their screeching stop."

His chief clerk shrugged and rose to leave.

"Bernard." Macdonald had more advice. "Send them to the *Globe* offices. I know George Brown shares their view. Tell them the printers are boozers! Just get them away! Forsey, we'll continue. Take notes until he's back."

Macdonald wanted the meeting finished quickly.

"Now, Gilbert, what's this latest American business?"

Gilbert McMicken was in his early forties. The rumpled suit suggested that he slept in his clothes. The hat in front of him was stained white at the headband from constant perspiration, and the fingers that picked through the file had accumulated grime from across the province. But Macdonald trusted McMicken and his frontier detectives. McMicken had quietly become the attorney general's eyes and ears in the final stages of the American war.

"The Yankees have whisked a few people to Washington," McMicken began.

"Kidnapped? Forcibly removed?" Macdonald wanted the details.

"No, not so far as we know. The Americans came with cash for the people they wanted and their offer was eagerly accepted."

"So we have no legal issues?"

"Not so far as I can see. At least, not yet."

"And are we glad to be rid of those who traveled across the border?"

"Yes, definitely. Godfrey Hyams is gone. He was the one who built up the story of the bomb factory."

"I remember."

"He'd go anywhere for money. The others, we're not so sure about. There's a Dr. Merritt from Cambridge or Windsor, depending on what mood he's in, and apparently a colored lady from the western district."

"I can understand why the Americans would like to hear from Hyams, but why the other two?

"Claimed to know of rebel plots," McMicken explained. "The New York reporter, Sanford Conover, convinced them to go. Although, for the life of me, I don't see why the Americans would send a reporter to collect them when there are trained detectives in Washington."

"But you will try to find out?" Macdonald suggested.

"My men are working on that now."

Bernard slipped back into the room, and Forsey realized that the singing had stopped.

"Did you blow the provincial budget?" Macdonald smiled. "Well, it doesn't matter. It's quiet again. And Gilbert, unless there's something else, we can let you go."

"Er, one more thing, Mr. Macdonald. The Fenians."

"And what have they done? My colleague, D'Arcy McGee, sees them as all talk and he's the cabinet minister with the strongest Irish connections."

"Talk it may be," McMicken said, rubbing the hat brim between his fingers. "But my man in New York says they claim seventy thousand members in these provinces."

"Seventy thousand!" Macdonald sputtered.

"That's the number he heard," McMicken answered meekly. "I'll let you know when I have more."

"Thank you, Gilbert." Macdonald smiled as the detective left the room. "I wish I had more like him. We need an ear to the ground. A few more could infiltrate the camps of all of my opponents."

Macdonald walked to a decanter. He poured a liberal portion, and took a deep drink.

"Ah!" He spat the liquid back into the glass.

"Water. They sent water! Forsey, go to the manager and ask him—no, wait. Let's finish this business first. It shouldn't take long."

The glass was abandoned, and Macdonald's mood turned sour.

"Do we have an interest in the case of the British mercenary? *The London Times* seems to have set off a storm with the series of articles on his trial and conviction. Perhaps he doesn't deserve to hang."

"George St. Leger Grenfell." Bernard supplied the name. "He did spend time in the province but he's a British national. Surely, London must mount the defense and carry the case to the Americans. We didn't ask him to become involved in an attempt at revolution. It shouldn't concern us."

"I agree," Macdonald told him. "But the *Times* has a large following here. People may be aroused by the coverage and this petition urging Washington to commute Grenfell's death sentence.

Lord knows the Americans are suspicious. A few of them may believe Grenfell was acting on orders from London and not realize he was acting on his own. However, we have enough on our hands. You're right—let England handle it."

"The Americans obviously think he's guilty," Bernard assured him. "They wouldn't welcome our input."

"Enough, then." Macdonald returned to the table.

"Any correspondence from the Maritimes?" he asked Bernard. The chief clerk shook his head.

"So we wait." MacDonald grimaced. "I warned them to get the Confederation arrangements through the legislatures before any elections, but they wouldn't listen. London is eager for the union, but suddenly the Eastern colonies develop cold feet. They'll feel the sting when the free trade agreement with the Americans ends. The Maritimes will soon need us and our markets."

• • •

Detroit, Michigan
July 1865

"A prediction from Washington," a merchant from Chicago called as he waved the latest newspaper. "Four will be hanged for the murder of the president, and the others will spend their lives in prison. The legal system has done the job, even if many of us feel they all should all be hanged. Now the country needs to get back to business."

The words were greeting with cheers by the five hundred delegates gathered for the first North American Commercial Convention. Representatives from the British colonies and the Northern states were united in a bid to improve business conditions. They parted company on how.

"I wish American politicians would listen to us," Joseph Howe, who had journeyed from Nova Scotia, muttered.

"Don't take it personnel. They don't listen to their own people either," an Ohio foundry owner laughed.

Howe chuckled but grew serious as he continued. "The end of the reciprocity agreement, and the higher tariffs is a political reaction to something that wasn't true. The senators and congressmen think the British were too close to the South, but thousands of our men fought in Northern armies. Many a night, I worried about my own son serving with General Sheridan. British blood flowed on your battlefields, but their sacrifice is forgotten. The leaders in Washington are ending a trade agreement in retaliation for a misunderstanding."

A New Yorker wasn't buying the argument.

"The rebels were always comfortable in the British colonies. How about those bandits that raided Vermont?"

"Now, as to Saint Albans," Howe said, having anticipated the question, "we in Nova Scotia felt it was an act of piracy and murder. But as to the right of asylum, is there a British subject who would give it up? No. We retain the right of asylum, but it doesn't mean we sympathize with rebels. Bennett Young claims to have acted under the orders of his government as a partisan ranger, so give him asylum for now and let the courts decide."

J. W. Porter, the former American consul in Montreal, forced his way to the front. "Why don't you give up completely?"

"Face it! Without reciprocity, the British colonies will wither away. In months, a few years at most, their representatives will beg to join the United States." Porter said. "Oh, they preach a fine sermon of a new Northern Confederation, but the business between those little provinces won't compensate for the loss of American trade. And there's no general agreement among the provinces on the terms of union. Even Mr. Howe is opposed. Do you deny it? Do you?"

"No, I don't deny it." Howe scowled. "Confederation is a bad deal for Nova Scotia, but make no mistake. We won't be joining your republic. But we can be neighbors and we can still do business together."

VII

M ike Flynn had worked more magic with his army connections. In mid-June, Private Owen Wilson was reassigned to
light duty in the arsenal guard. What was known in Washington
as the "old arsenal" had been converted to a prison, and the
Lincoln murder conspirators' trial was underway inside its walls.

"The testimony is taken in secret," a private assigned to the
actual courtroom had explained. "We can't say anything about
what we hear, but since you are joining us, I'll tell you what's happening: nothing. The lawyers spend the time arguing."

The private waited. If Wilson wanted news, he would have to
pay. A flask was soon passed, and the courtroom details poured out.

"There was a fellow—name of Conover—a newspaperman.
He said he'd been all over Canada...infiltrated the rebel cir-
cles...but the judges didn't hear much from him cause all they
did was argue. And the prisoners, all you hear when they enter
the room is the clank of chains. The men have handcuffs and
ankle shackles and are under hoods, so all you see are two eyes
and a nose and a mouth. Must be uncomfortable as hell, but I
guess they deserve it."

Wilson's duty, as Flynn had promised, was light. On many
days, the lawyers and spectators were gone by the time his shift
began, but the guards posted to the courtroom continued to

pass on testimony. More evidence emerged of the plot to abduct Lincoln and of the other attempts to bring terror to the North and disrupt the Union war efforts.

"Guilty as sin, or most of them are," one amateur lawyer pronounced.

"The men who conspired with Booth are done. They'll swing. But the Surratt woman may be innocent. It comes down to who you believe. One fellow, the tavern keeper, claims she ordered "the shooting irons" the day of the assassination. But he's a drunk. And young Mr. Weichmann seems to think she was involved, but he may be trying to save his own hide. Maybe she was sweet on Booth and under his influence? Females can be easily swayed."

Despite the drama of the courtroom testimony, Wilson lost interest. The months in the army had hardened him to thoughts of justice or compassion, and at night, even alcohol could not erase the long list of bad memories and nightmares. Lost friends haunted his sleep. Mornings found him in a pool of sweat and surrounded by the flies that thrived in the filth from Washington streets and canals. Somehow, he dragged himself to the guard-house and managed to escape close scrutiny by the arsenal officers.

But one morning in early July, he awoke to the sound of hammers, saws, and a loud shout from a gruff sergeant.

"Get your ass in gear. We've four people to send into eternity."

Wilson steeled himself for what was to come, as the grim parade passed within a few feet of his position. The prisoners were led by the freshly dug graves and four rough, wooden coffins, while near the gate, a lone guard watched for any courier who might carry a last-minute reprieve. Washington lawyers had launched a flurry of attempts to win a reprieve for Mary Surratt. The rumors created a buzz of conversation among the few spectators considered lucky enough to witness the executions.

Owen tried to focus above the courtyard and on the sentinels atop the prison wall, but something drew him to the faces of the condemned.

A priest read quietly to Mary Surratt. There was David Herold, the young man who had fled with John Wilkes Booth; George Atzerodt, whom Booth had selected to attack Vice President Johnson but who was too drunk to act; and finally, the muscular rebel who had attacked the Secretary of State Seward. His name was Powell or Payne, but no one seemed to know for sure or care. On the gallows, he appeared completely calm, a half smile playing across his face as he had a mumbled conversation with the executioner, the aptly named Christian Rath.

Suddenly, something seemed familiar to Wilson and he remembered a young Confederate prisoner at Gettysburg. The prisoner had been helping at the hospital when Owen took his friend Jimmy for medical treatment and the same man now stood on the gallows. The doctor at the Gettysburg hospital was another Canadian, Dr. Solomon Secord and he had warned that men like Powell had been warped by the war. Wilson now saw that Secord had been right.

Rath cast a final glance toward the gate, but there was no courier and no reprieve. The executioner had his orders and could wait no longer. Hoods were dropped over the heads of the prisoners, and the nooses were slipped into place. Rath paused for only a moment before he opened the trap door beneath them.

Silence descended on the prison yard. Again, Owen tried to look away but found his eyes drawn to the bodies of the three men and the woman twisting in the air. After several long minutes, all but one was still. Powell continued to twitch until Rath finally descended from the scaffold, threw his arms around the prisoner's legs, and jerked.

• • •

On Lake Huron
July 1865

"There's the light, so we're making good time," the tall man said with a laugh. "And once we pass the lighthouse at Point Clark, we're only a few hours from Kincardine. You will find the town has grown."

"Everything changes." Dr. Solomon Secord turned his coat collar up against the wind. The summer breeze could be cold on a Great Lakes steamer. He felt no need to talk, but the man beside him was pressing for conversation. Bill Caters was a lumber agent with designs on the forests of Bruce County, and if all went as planned, he would soon move his family to the area.

"You left in '61?" Caters had poked and prodded until he began to learn the doctor's story—or what the surgeon was willing to share.

A lung condition had convinced Secord to leave Canada West and try for a recovery in warm Southern air. He never expected that the air would soon be filled with gun smoke. When the Georgia militia discovered Secord's medical background, there was no choice. He must serve with the Southern army or face arrest and prison.

The next few years were a haze: Battles like Antietam, with the dead and wounded stacked around the makeshift hospitals; and Gettysburg, with three days of fighting and a never-ending stream of casualties. And when General Lee began his retreat from Pennsylvania, Secord decided he had no choice but to stay with the wounded, even if it meant becoming a prisoner of war. So for weeks, he tended the men and watched the lingering pain of those for whom he could nothing. As the summer progressed, more wounded recovered or died, and there was less need for the surgeons. He became a true prisoner and was moved to Fort McHenry but through a quirk of fate, for only a few weeks. When a careless guard fell asleep, the doctor slipped into the night.

"I don't understand why, when you escaped the Yankee prison, you didn't come home," Caters prodded again. "Why on earth would you go back to the South?"

"These things are hard to explain," Secord told him. "I'm not sure I understand myself. Any damn fool could see that slavery was doomed. But I grew to respect the Southern people. So when there was no one to smuggle medicine back through the lines, I went. When my lungs began to act up, they moved me to administration work in the rebel hospital system, and that was as bad as the carnage of the battlefield. We didn't have anything to work with. There were times we had to use the same bandages again and again. It was an utter mess!"

"But at least you survived. Bruce County can use you. You are feeling well enough to resume your practice soon?"

"Oh yes," Secord assured him. "But I need to start slow. I've had better food and better living conditions as I made my way north. But I still have the odd bad day."

"Kincardine will be delighted," Caters said, smiling again and pointing to the lighthouse in the distance. The warning light grew stronger as the evening dusk approached.

"We're making good time, but it will be dark before we get there."

"Day or night, I suspect I'll find my way," Secord said. "The thoughts of peace and tranquility and old friends kept me going through the bleak times."

"I wonder, Doctor, if there might be a way to boost your income until you are back on your feet?"

Caters knew an economic slowdown was taking hold in the provinces. But the slowdown, prompted by the end of the American war and the higher tariffs expected on shipments across the border, must eventually pass. The winners in the next business cycle would be towns that could offer services for a growing population. Communities with doctors would be more attractive.

"What did you have in mind?" Secord was intrigued.

"An area where your expertise would be put to good use. The province is fitting out new militia units. Several of us are working on a plan to form a Bruce Regiment. The workload would be manageable. You'd only have to inspect the men, make sure they are healthy…perhaps treat the odd sprain, that sort of thing."

"Excuse me, gentlemen," a crewman said as he slipped passed, holding a lantern. "We'll be lighting the stateroom lamps in the next few minutes, and supper will be served in the main cabin." Secord turned to watch as the sailor made his way along the deck.

"Why do you need a militia?" Secord's tone was measured as he fought for control. "The Americans appear to have satisfied their blood lust. The Indians here are under control. What worthy opponent would you attack or defend against?"

"Well, I…I…" Caters stammered before he pulled his thoughts together. "Look, the government is making the money available. There will be money for uniforms, weapons, and paid drills. We might as well have our share."

Secord was silent and Caters started again.

"Maybe the government knows something. There's been talk of Irish rebels called Fenians. The British may have them under control in Ireland but there are probably more of them here. The Irish may cause trouble in Canada. We need to be prepared to stop them."

Secord shook his head. "More boys playing soldier. Please, God, this time may they survive to become men."

"Think about it," Caters suggested.

Secord removed his hands from the ship's rail and rubbed his head.

"I'll do it. I need the money, but you may not like my style. I'll do the examinations but I'll have my medical equipment by my side. Each man will see where the amputation might be, perhaps at the ankle, at the knee, or up the thigh. I can show them where a bullet will enter the stomach, and when it does, how many hours they have left. Or I could have my tool to remove shell fragments from the brain. That will make them think! I'll show them that it's not all guns and glory, and make them see the gore. And I'll tell them how, even if they escape mutilation, they may be changed forever."

Again, he rubbed his head, as if trying to force dark thoughts into a deep inner cavity. "It's you who might want to think about it. Those would be my conditions."

• • •

Charleston, South Carolina
July 1865

"That woman is back again," Sergeant Edwards hissed. "The good-looking one who could pass for white if it weren't for her African child."

"Have her wait, Sergeant." Major Martin Delaney leafed through the newspapers that had just arrived. Delaney was one of the few black officers in the Union army and a man who took intense pride in his color. He had recruited former slaves for the Union ranks before moving to the Freedmen's Bureau to help oversee the efforts in the conquered South. The New York newspapers contained the first details of the executions of the Lincoln conspirators, but reluctantly he set the papers aside and retrieved the woman's file.

Sillery Fraser claimed to be a house servant from Richmond who had relatives in South Carolina. She had found her daughter but was still looking for other family and had filed a claim for the forty acres of land former slaves hoped to receive. Delaney willingly championed the idea. He felt the land abandoned by former Confederates should be forfeited, and if he had his way, other white, and rebel landowners would be expelled. But title to land given to blacks would be subject to challenge, and who knew what a white judge might decide in the future. Delaney already had met his share of deceptive whites. The number who claimed to have been secret Unionists and abolitionists was astounding. Most, he suspected, were really ardent rebels. And who knew what secrets remained hidden?

The Fraser woman presented another challenge.

Allowing a claim in a woman's name could open the floodgates to other female applicants. And there was something more, something suspicious about her story. "Bring her in," Delaney ordered.

He let her stand in front of his desk for several minutes before he looked up.

She was well dressed, too well dressed, he decided. The clothes could have come from a high-end shop in the North. And, as Edwards noted, she could pass for white, but the child beside her was obviously of African heritage. The child was silent. Her tiny hand grasped her mother's dress.

"There's a problem, Mrs. Fraser," he began. "We need evidence of a Mr. Fraser."

The woman stiffened before she answered flatly, "There is none."

"There is a child." He tried not to judge or even acknowledge the girl. Slave marriages often ended with the sale of a husband or wife, and each might find a new partner on the next plantation, but he doubted the woman in front of him had spent much time in the slave quarters.

"Yes," she said. "I found her. She had been sold away. But the father is gone. I don't know where."

"Well, perhaps we should look for him and if we can't find him, you could join with one of our fine black soldiers. We need a man's name for the documents."

"I don't want a man or a partner," she told him crisply. "I want my land."

"I doubt that's possible."

He expected tears but received an angry glare.

"At least provide us with rations." The frustration grew in her voice. "Other former slaves and even white refugees get rations each day, but there's been nothing for me or for my child."

"You don't appear to be starving, and we can only afford to help the destitute," Delaney told her. "You wear fine clothes. How did you come by them?"

"A gift from my former mistress."

"Mrs. Fraser," Delaney said, abruptly rising from behind the desk. "There's something about your story that I don't like. When you are prepared to be more forthright, I might help...so come back when you are ready to tell the truth and not before." He waited but saw only the hostile stare.

"Sergeant, get her out of here!"

A dozen black faces watched from the waiting area as Edwards escorted Sillery Fraser from the office.

"Miss Sillery," a gray-haired Negro burst out, stepping forward. "Remember me? I'm Douglas. I worked at the Spotswood Hotel in Richmond and helped you and that nice Confederate colonel when your lady was sick. You had those Secesh officers eating out of your hand."

"No, you must be mistaken," Sillery snapped and at the same time slapped Edwards's hand from her arm. She pushed the child in front of her. "You have me confused with someone else."

Delaney watched as the woman hurried into the street before he summoned the gray-haired man to enter his office. "What do you know about that woman?" he demanded.

"She worked for one of those rebel ladies that used to cross the lines to Canada and back," Douglas explained. "I worked for Miss Elizabeth Van Lew and she worked for the Union. People said she was a spy but all I know is Miss Van Lew sent messages to General Butler, and knew a whole lot that she told the Yankees, all about what was happening in Richmond these last few years. Miss Sillery and her mistress disappeared when the war ended. But I doubt Miss Sillery had any choice in what she did. She may look white but she was just another slave."

He looked at Delaney and returned to his original mission. "But those of us who risked everything for the Union should have a reward."

"Yes, yes," Delaney scratched out his signature on a paper on his desk. "Protect this document. It's your property deed."

On the street, Sillery wiped her sleeve across her face to hide the tears.

"Come, Shasta." She tugged on the child's hand, "We'll go to the boarding house. Mommy has things to do."

• • •

Johnson's Island, Ohio
July 1865

The guard, Travis Beattie, put his best effort into the performance, waving his arms to act out each line of the poem.

"The blissful scenes of childhood gone,"
Leaves but the view so dreary."

He wiped an imaginary tear from his eye.

"To rest the aching eyes upon…"

He took a deep breath for the grand finale.

"The prison on Lake Erie!"

The performance was greeted by silence from the cell.

"It was written by one of your rebel friends," Beattie said as he peered through the bars at the man stretched on the cot.

"The poet was from New Orleans. Called himself Asa Hartz, also known as Major George McKnight. You like that?"

There was no response.

"Ah cat's got your tongue. Well, I'll miss you. You were a wonderful captive audience."

The ring of keys jingled in Beattie's hand before he finally turned the lock.

Bennet Burleigh watched the door swing open, fearing another trick. The guards had grown bored as prisoners were released from the former Union prison camp. Taunting was a favorite pastime.

"Come on. You don't want me to come in and get ya," Beattie snarled.

Burleigh pulled himself to his feet. He was weak, but the prison cough had faded with the warmer temperatures, and in recent weeks, he had been allowed outside for exercise. "Where are we going?" he asked.

"Shut your trap!" Beattie rapped a wooden baton against the iron. "I'll do the talking. Grab your coat."

Burleigh reached to collect the jacket, the only possession he had been allowed to keep.

The constables in Canada West had taken him by surprise one bright day almost a year earlier. The first of the cannon built in the Guelph foundry had already been sent north, where John Yates Beall was to arm his Great Lakes raider. Burleigh had just loaded a second weapon on a wagon for shipment when the police arrived. A scruffy civilian, a man the local constables called McMicken, took charge, and as Burleigh was led away, McMicken mounted the wagon and drove in the opposite direction.

Later, the authorities in Toronto questioned Burleigh only about the raid on Lake Erie, the failed attempt to seize the American gunboat, the *Michigan*, and free the Confederate officers imprisoned on Johnson's Island. The matter of the cannons, molded in Canada and destined for rebel forces, seemed to be ignored, as if Canadian authorities preferred to believe they never existed. The American lawyers, too, had concentrated on Johnson's Island and the two ships seized on the lake when they argued for Burleigh's transfer to US authority. The British finally agreed to extradite him, and in a finally irony, Burleigh was confined in the prison on Johnson's Island."

"Pirates hang, but first we'll show you an Ohio court!" Beattie told him and pointed toward the open door on the cellblock. "The American justice system won't be as lenient as the Canadian courts. Jee-siz, I can't believe it. The Canadians tossed the case out on technicalities three times before they finally gave you up. But we have you now, Burleigh, the last of the 'Lake Erie pirates' and probably the last prisoner on Johnson's Island. Maybe someday you'll go home to Scotland…but probably in a pine box."

Burleigh almost tripped on the sill of the outer door. After the darkness of the cell, the bright sun burned his eyes, but he squinted beyond the waiting guards to the parade square and buildings around it.

Three thousand Confederate officers had once packed the earth to a fine powder. Now the barracks were empty and from their appearance, could have been abandoned years earlier and not in the weeks since the end of the war. He thought of the sea of uniforms, of butternut and gray, and the failed attempt to set the men free.

Beattie interrupted his reverie and called to the civilians who loitered near the gate. "He's all yours. The government of the United States won't waste more money on him. Trot him off to a local jail. The state of Ohio can pay for the hanging."

VIII

Quebec City, Canada East
August 1865

The lone bell began to peal as the coffin was carried from the cathedral. The family members followed, the politicians a few steps behind.

The funeral for the Premier Sir Etienne Taché brought rare silence to the old city. Taché had witnessed the fight to transfer power from colonial administrators to elected representatives, seen the cut and thrust of years of provincial politics, and finally the push to unite the colonies.

The pallbearers slowly lifted the remains into the horse-drawn hearse, and the cobblestones echoed as it rolled away.

John A. Macdonald, George Brown, and Georges Cartier, the principal figures of the coalition and the drive for Confederation, watched.

Macdonald finally spoke. "Good-bye to our gallant knight." He gently slapped his hat against his thigh. "The work was too much for him. He looked ghastly when he spoke to open the Confederation debate last February, but how were we to know he was only a day from a major illness?"

"He wouldn't have changed anything," Cartier told them. "Illness wouldn't stop him. He saw that speech as a great honor."

The men began to move toward the street, walking in the direction opposite to that of the carriages that followed the hearse.

"And now," Cartier asked, "has the governor general called on you, Mr. Macdonald? It seems only natural that you would become the next premier."

"No," Macdonald began to explain, "Viscount Monck and I decided, out of respect for Mr. Taché, that the decision should be delayed until after the funeral."

"We are still a coalition."

Brown's interjection carried the hint of anger that always lay just below the surface. Macdonald cast an uneasy glance at the two men.

"The choice of a new prime minister should be made by the coalition," Brown declared. "I would suggest we meet later this afternoon. I'll come to Macdonald's office at four o'clock."

Brown stormed off, leaving the other two to wonder if the tolling bell also signaled the end of the political truce. The three men had worked together for over a year, breaking the stalemate in the legislature, and setting the stage for the Confederation accord.

The governor general rearranged his schedule to attend the meeting and was the first to speak. "We need a new premier, and there should be no delay. The legislature returns in a few days. I've offered the post to Mr. Macdonald. He's next in line. He has the experience and the support of the house."

"He does not!" Brown exploded. "We have a coalition with shared power, but Macdonald is a Tory. He does not have the support of all my Reformers."

"What would you suggest?" Cartier asked. "And be honest. Is this your way of demanding the job? Or is it something more? You and Macdonald have an uneasy alliance. Is this your way of simply blocking him?"

"No, and I resent the implication," Brown snapped. He turned and appealed to Monck. "I would not accept the position. I cannot accept Macdonald and I can't accept Cartier. The appointment of any one of us would destroy the coalition. If the coalition fails, Confederation fails with it. Any signs of friction will give added strength to the opposition movement in the Maritimes and produce new opposition at home. We've come too far to fail now."

Brown swung to face Macdonald. "And you know it to be true."

He waited, but there was no reply.

"I've said all I intend to say," Brown announced and stormed from the room.

"Petty jealousy," Cartier said as the door slammed. "His nose is out of joint because he wasn't offered the position."

Macdonald remained silent. It would be the governor general's decision.

Monck rested his head in his hands for a moment before speaking. "Be that as it may, he does have a point. Macdonald is a natural choice but not at the risk of destroying the coalition. We must avoid all the fractious party nonsense. Mr. Macdonald, please be patient. Your time will come, but for now I'll ask Sir Narcisse Belleau to accept the position."

"Belleau." Cartier slumped in his chair. "He's a fine gentlemen but he's another very old man."

"Oh, agreed," Lord Monck replied. "He'll be a figurehead. Mr. Macdonald will have to take on most of the responsibilities, as he did with Taché, and when Confederation is approved, Belleau must step aside. A new nation will need a new leader."

• • •

Lake Erie, Canada West
August 1865

"So you have work for black associates but nothing for a white man?" Eramosa Willis was smiling, but his tone indicated that the question was serious.

"I needed Amos Baker," Tom Hines told him. "If you were black, you could have had the job."

The two men sat in the wheelhouse of the new fishing boat, the first of what Willis hoped might become a fleet. The craft was larger, better equipped, and replaced the little boat that he lost during the abortive raid on Johnson's Island.

"Baker went to Montreal," Willis prodded. "I could have used a trip."

"I wish you had gone in my place," Hines replied. "Playing nursemaid and companion to the family of Jeff Davis is not my idea of a good time."

"Don't you like children?" Willis chided.

"When they're well behaved, but little Jeff isn't," Hines told him. "Besides, there was no real danger. The boy can't be more than four or five. If you ask him what he likes to do, he'll say "Whup Yankees," but after his father was captured, the Yankees convinced him to sing a song for his mother, and he gave a rousing chorus of "We'll Hang Jeff Davis from a Sour Apple Tree."

"A song from a little boy was the reason to move them to Canada?" Willis was skeptical. "They'd be better off in Richmond or Savannah or Charleston."

"Not really. The head of the household is the Confederate president and in prison," Hines reminded him. "And the Yankees are making up the rules as they go. It's not safe for ordinary people in the South and certainly not safe for famous families."

"So you watched them as they rode the train?" Willis asked.

"The family didn't know I was there," Hines told him. "Relatives of Mrs. Davis met them in Montreal."

"And Baker," Willis persisted, "what was he doing?"

"Watching luggage." Hines smiled. "Like the other black porters. That's why I used him. The family was worried about one trunk, afraid it might be stolen. We needed someone in the baggage car. When we got to Montreal, it was taken to a bank vault. Must have been valuable, although I don't think it was money. Maybe sensitive papers."

"And you came back to tell me of an easy job I missed?"

Willis was smiling but Hines detected something more.

"What's bothering you?" he asked.

"Did Erin talk to you? She's got the damn fool idea that I should be more careful. Did she talk you out of taking me?"

"No. I didn't need you. But I need you now."

Willis was leaning back, rocking his chair on the two rear legs, but at the mention of work, he sprang forward. "Where are we going?" he asked.

"London." Hines smiled. "The one in Canada, not the one across the water."

Willis sank back in the chair, the disappointment obvious. "Been there!" he spit. "Know it well."

Hines chuckled. "I do too. When I passed through in the spring, someone thought I looked like John Wilkes Booth. Nearly the same thing as happened in Detroit. I had to move quickly."

Willis's frown turned to a smile. "There *is* a similarity, I suppose, but a closer look and you can see the difference. Anyway, count me in. What are we doing?"

"We're going to stop a man that wants to kill President Johnson."

Willis began to laugh. "Four months ago, the Confederates killed a good president, and now they want to save a poor one."

"Forget what you may have heard," Hines said, allowing the anger to rise in his voice. "Booth made his own decisions. Richmond probably knew about the kidnap attempt, but Jeff Davis wouldn't approve of murder."

Willis was curious. "So somebody else approved it?"

"Signals may have been crossed. Maybe Booth thought he had authority. We'll never know now. Booth can't talk."

"The Americans won't give up," Willis told him. "Detectives, newspapermen, you name it, are swarming around the province. I'm surprised they haven't tried to grab you."

"They may yet. And that stands for my associates. But are you still interested in the work?"

"Yes, of course. Tell me what you want."

"We have to find Isaac Surratt."

"Surratt...a relative of the woman they hung for the assassination?"

"Isaac is the older brother. He was fighting in Texas. He blames Andrew Johnson for the death of his mother. The other members of his unit took up a collection, told him to go to Washington and kill as many Yankees as he could. And Isaac knows how to use dynamite."

"Why would he go to London?" Willis asked.

"We don't know. The information came from friends in Washington who heard it through federal detectives. It may be a wild-goose chase, or Surratt may be staying there with Southern refugees."

"Why is anyone worried about a lone nut?" Willis was perplexed. "Surely, there are guards at the White House."

"Oh, there are, but with explosives, he could blow up half the capital."

"And why worry about their president? I would think you'd be happy to see him gone."

"Johnson talks tough," Hines explained, "But he may be more sympathetic to the South than first thought. Besides, another assassination would rile the Yankees, and we're in no position to fight back."

"And if we find him?" Willis asked.

"We'll have a conversation. Warn him about the danger that exists for his brother and sister and make him see reason. We'll make him change his mind."

"And if we don't find him?"

"You'll be paid!"

"I guess I'm in." Willis stood and walked to the wheel. "But I don't want Erin to know. She'd worry. And it isn't just our business that bothers her, Tom. Things are happening in the province. There's bad blood between the Catholics and the Protestants, and this Irish-Fenian business is upsetting a bunch of folk. Less she knows, the less she'll worry."

• • •

Quebec City, Canada East
August 1865

Paul Forsey wiped the sweat from his forehead as he entered the tavern. The Quebec City summer was at its peak, and the buildings steamed from heat and humidity.

Francine offered him a winning smile and a demonstration of her growing English vocabulary. "Mr. Paul will have the brandy?"

"No, beer today."

"I bring the…bare."

Her long hair was damp, and perspiration rolled down her throat to stain the top of her dress.

"Lovely, even in this weather," Forsey told Ralston as he slid into a seat at what had become their constant meeting place.

"I'll have a 'bare' too." Ralston giggled and slipped an elbow into Forsey's ribs.

"Oh, grow up," Forsey chided him. "I'm sure you've have a good look at all of her. At least her English has improved. Your French hasn't."

"Don't need it," Ralston assured him. "Queen's English is good enough, although if I knew more French, I could talk business with her relatives."

"You aren't getting serious about her, are you?" Forsey was incredulous. "I mean, she's a striking woman, but how would it look? Your superiors would write you off for going native. No more promotions, no more advancement."

"Does it matter? I can't afford to buy another commission. My army career is stalled. Perhaps it's time to consider a new line of work. Maybe marry and settle down."

Ralston's eyes followed Francine as she worked.

"You can't be serious. What about her family? They'd expect you to become a Catholic and trot you off to Mass with all the other Johnny Baptistes or have you painting that symbol they like…the maple leaf."

"I'd be happier in Quebec City than in a godforsaken British outpost in India."

"Don't be rash," Forsey urged. "I know the frustration of waiting for promotion, but you don't see me giving up…or going native."

"Leave it! I'm thinking out loud." Ralston turned his attention from Francine to the clerk.

Forsey wiped his brow and grimaced. "This heat is insufferable."

"You seem anxious." Ralston said.

"The heat; the French; summer in Quebec City; long, tedious letters to copy; taking notes on long conversations that could be completed in half the time; too much work and too few clerks. The Americans have the right approach. Their government apparatus grew by leaps and bounds during their war."

"Ah," Ralston said, smiling. "Our clerk wants to learn from the Americans, who reduce the size of the army but keep the clerks. See here. I suspect you do marvelous work, but consider where it leads. Each clerk begets another clerk, and all they do is write letters and reports for each other. Each department grows and becomes more expensive. Sandfield Macdonald, the opposition politician, was right in arguing against creating another level of government. Each will fight over jurisdiction. Is it your bridge or ours? Will you collect the tariff or will we? That's where it's taking us."

"An active government does spread money around," Forsey reminded him. "Look at the work the civil war created. If you want a really strong economy, perhaps you need constant war or the fear of one."

"That's fine for my present business, but who knows what the future holds?"

Ralston waved his glass and smiled at Francine. "Her cousin speaks both languages. He'd be a valuable man for government but he's quite content. He hires out his horse and carriage and offers tours to the visitors."

"He will feel the pain when the government moves to Ottawa."

"Oh, I don't know. People will come to see the sites of old Quebec. He squired John Taylor Wood around last month."

"Wood, the Confederate privateer, the man related to Jefferson Davis?" Forsey asked.

Ralston smiled. "Yes, one and the same. He has an interest in a shipping firm in Halifax. Money was not a problem. The cousin was paid well. And what do you think he wanted to see?"

Forsey waited patiently.

"The Plains of Abraham. After four years of war and his escape from the South, he should be thinking of peace and quiet. But no, he wanted to see the battlefield where Wolfe beat Montcalm, and I can imagine what he was told. Wood probably came away with stories of terror and English barbarity and heard all the excuses for the French defeat. I'll bet he got an earful."

"Is Wood still here?"

"No, he went to Montreal. Probably looking for orders from the Southern government in exile. Or, with his connections, maybe he brought instructions."

"Probably met with E. G. Lee," Forsey guessed. "The general's cousin seems to be in charge of any Confederate business that is left. But there can't be much to do. Maybe they just deal with refugees."

"And spread propaganda," Ralston added. "They write letters to American newspapers. I liked the one where Beverly Tucker said President Johnson should explain his relationship with John Wilkes Booth. Ha! Fat chance of getting an answer to that one."

"The Americans aren't giving up on the assassination," Forsey told him. "John A.'s detective has been nosing around. A newspaperman called Sanford Conover keeps finding witnesses to tie the planning of the assassination to Canada. Gilbert McMicken says the witnesses are liars and probably rehearsed and well paid. One of them claimed he had warned a justice of the peace in Canada West about the plot, and the JP refused to act. Well, the JP says that was a lie. And McMicken claims that Conover worked with both Confederates and Yankees. He also uses another name, Charles Dunham."

"Sounds like a very accomplished liar," Ralston suggested. "And a man who has found a way to part the Americans from their cash by telling them what they want to hear."

"Enough of Conover." Forsey slapped his glass on the table. "What about more important things. General Grant paid a quiet visit to Quebec City. Did you see him?"

"Only a glimpse," Ralston told him. "Grant paid a very informal visit, but he apparently assured the governor general that the American army is being reduced. That should ease the fears of an early war with the Americans."

"Welcome news," Forsey conceded. "But I don't like the idea of the top American general coming to inspect our fortifications."

"Wouldn't worry," Ralston told him. "The army has a way of showing guests what the army wants them to see."

"So if there's no American threat, we'll need fewer troops," Forsey reasoned. "Perhaps you should consider another line of work. George Brown says the officials in London were eager to see the Confederation plans proceed but less enthusiastic about paying for defense. They might prefer that we become an independent state."

"Wouldn't that be rich?" Ralston chuckled. "And about as stable as an African or Latin American nation. No, you need the kind, guiding hand of the British crown. And as for troops, well, London is worried about the Fenians and wants the militia prepared. Better to have a little war in Canada than a big war across the Irish Sea."

"McGee says they are a joke," Forsey told him. "He says Fenianism is a foreign disease. I presume he means an Irish disease."

"Don't count them out," Ralston warned. "If they can't take Ireland, they can raise hell with other British possessions. I think this new country would be a nice, fat target."

IX

Spotslyvania County, Virginia
August 1865

T he latest job that Mike Flynn had promised would take only two days was well into day three. The stifling summer heat forced a stop every hour to rest the horses that pulled a US Army wagon. Owen Wilson dozed in the wagon, sprawled across burlap bags of cornmeal, and had fashioned a shelter above his head with the blue Union tunic.

Through the clouds of dust, he had seen evidence of the war damage. Fields grew high in weeds, and once-thriving farmsteads were seldom more than blackened ruins.

"We should be there soon," Flynn said, breaking the silence. "Let me do the talking. There are things only a few of us know."

With the heat and a lingering hangover, Owen simply grunted and closed his eyes.

Only minutes later, he felt the buckboard stop and heard another voice.

"Are you Flynn?" a slow Southern drawl asked.

Owen shifted to the front and saw a short, stout man with a shotgun by his side.

"And you were expecting someone else?" Flynn asked.

The shotgun rose slowly so any discharge would pepper Flynn's upper body.

"Put that damn thing down," Flynn ordered and stepped slowly from his seat. "There's just me and a helper. The meal is in the bags, and I have a roll of greenbacks."

"This way." The shotgun dropped to the man's side as he pointed up a dirt track.

"Bring the wagon. We're going to the other side of that little hill. And stuff that damn blue jacket somewhere it won't be seen. People around here don't care for anything Yankee."

From the crest of the hill, Owen saw a small open meadow and several figures working with shovels and handcarts. The guide directed them to a small shack where another man sat watching.

"He says he has the cash," the guide announced.

"Willie! Simon!"

The man rose from a rickety chair and motioned toward the field. Two hats bobbed up, and for the first time, Owen noticed the black faces. Something white was tossed into the cart before the pair began to move toward the waiting men.

"Go back to the main road, Stumpy. I'm not expecting any-more company today, but keep a watch."

"Whatever you say, Major." Stumpy and shotgun sauntered off as the major studied the two guests.

"Guns?" he asked.

"No. We ain't armed," Flynn assured him.

"No, you ass. I mean you came for the guns."

"Oh, yes. That we did." Flynn shifted nervously. "I'm to pick up a load of Spencer repeaters."

"Well, the Yankees who dropped them sure don't need them anymore." The major laughed. "As soon as I check the cash, you can load up."

"You called, Boss?" The Negros and their cart had arrived.

"Yeah, dump that load and then come to unload this wagon. You," he said, pointing to Owen, "help them push while Mr. Flynn and I have a word."

Owen joined the pair to push the cart around the side of the shack and to a large, open pit. At the edge of the hole, the men lifted a cover from the top of the cart and pushed upward to dump the contents. A loud clatter was followed immediately by the buzz of flies as a host of insects rose into the air. Owen waved his hand across his face to ward off the swarm, stepped forward to glance into the pit, but quickly jumped back. A human skull teetered on a small mountain of bones, some bleached white by the sun, others with bits of skin and flesh still attached.

He fought a rising sense of nausea.

"Just bones, Mister." One black laughed. "A lot of them around here. From what they call the 'Wilderness Battlefield.' Northern and Southern boys all mixed up together, but at least they ain't fighting no more. Must be hundreds of bodies, and most of them aren't buried deep."

Owen stepped farther from the pit and again waved at the clouds of flies.

"We stir up the flies when we dump, but they'll settle when they find fresh feed."

"And you rebury the bones in this pit?"

"Rebury? Hell no!" The black laughed. "Major has us dig them up and then he sells them. Yankees want bone meal for fertilizer or for their china, so he calls them horse bones and collects a few cents a pound. Major knows how to make money, and he's paying us to help. We're free now, so we get paid. A few weeks ago, we gathered lead, the pellets from the bullets. That was better money, but we've picked up most of the spent ammunition, so now we concentrate on bones."

Owen stepped farther away, the flies following as he stopped and leaned against a tree.

"If it helps any…a few of them get proper burial," the black offered. "We sent off a skeleton this morning. Wife had come to reclaim the body of her man and had a Yankee officer with her. He made us call him Colonel Hurley…made us stand up straight while he read some words over her set of bones."

"But he wasn't really her friend," the other man said, laughing. "He gave money to the major. And the major had plopped one of those belt buckles with the name of an army regiment on the bones. So Hurley says, 'There's the proof, ma'am...the Seventeenth Michigan. This will be your man. And she didn't even notice the horse bones where his leg should be."

Owen braced himself against a tree to compensate for shaky legs.

"But she was happy. She thinks her man will get a proper burial. And that Colonel Hurley was happy because he got paid."

Owen waited by the tree as the two men returned to the cabin. Minutes later, they began to carry rifles from the shack. The canvas that had covered the bone cart was soon tied in place to hide the weapons.

"Wilson, get over here," Flynn called. He stood by the major with a bottle in his hand. "Better take a good snort. It will be a dry day on the road." He waited as Wilson drained the bottle.

"And Major, I'm not supposed to say much, but these weapons will be put to good use in the fight to free Ireland."

"Rather see them used against Yankees." The major shrugged. "But do what you will. We may find more, so make sure your friends know where to find us."

Owen climbed into the wagon and flicked the reins to start the team, but then changed his mind and pulled the horses to a stop. "Uh, Major," he called. "The black boys said a man named Hurley was here today. Would his first name have been Levitus?"

For the first time, the major smiled.

"Oh, so you know the colonel. He can be a bit arrogant but he gets the job done."

Memories flooded Owen's already overloaded mind: Hurley leading the burial detail at another battlefield, at Antietam; the story of Hurley murdering one of his own men at Gettysburg; and the trip to Canada where his unauthorized search for deserters had pushed Owen's friend, Jimmy, over the edge. Jimmy had killed himself and his companion, Mathilde.

"Will Hurley be coming back?" The memories and Owen's thirst for revenge had never faded.

"Funny you should ask," the major replied. "Said it was his last trip. Guess he made enough money with the body-retrieval service and plans on moving on. He didn't say where."

"Yee-hah!" Owen abruptly lashed the team, almost sending Flynn flying from the wagon.

"Now what in hell has got into you?" Flynn demanded as he grasped the seat.

"Just shut up," Owen snarled. "Don't say another damn word."

• • •

Near Charleston, South Carolina
September 1865

Sillery Fraser bolted the door. The ramshackle cabin was a hundred yards from the road, nestled on the edge of small forest. Barely visible in the day, it faded into the lengthening shadows as night approached. An old blanket hung over the lone front window to reduce the chance of anyone seeing her lantern. To reduce that risk further, the wick was cut low.

A band of Negros had passed by earlier in the evening, men and women flaunting the rules called the "black codes." She knew what to expect next. White men who called themselves "regulators" would come. Most were former rebel soldiers trying to reimpose their authority.

The Africans had appeared to be far gone on whiskey, the first black mark against them. And since they were several miles from the nearest plantation, they would be guilty of moving about at night without permission, and the regulators could claim that men and women together provided evidence of "gross vice."

The transition to freedom had been bungled, and Sillery wondered how after four long years of war, the American leaders had failed to plan for the aftermath. Millions of the newly freed lived in conditions that were as bad as slavery.

The ambitious blacks tried to adapt, tending gardens and a few acres of field crops. But the harvest was approaching, and crops appeared poor. And she suspected that when the men tried to sell their cotton and rice, shady white buyers would complain of poor quality and offer low prices.

Other former slaves took a different view of freedom, refusing to work for black or white, moving aimlessly, looking for something, but not knowing what.

She tensed at the sound of hoof beats, the regulators beginning a night of sport. A few men would wear the old gray or butternut, and a few youngsters would be along in training for the future.

As the horses passed, she tried to lose herself in a New York magazine. The pages were filled with advertisements for the latest fashions, labor-saving devices for the Northern lady, and announcements of ships sailing for European ports. She read it on nights when she needed to dream, a habit she'd learned from Sarah Slater.

During the war, Slater had posed as a Southern belle. Sillery's presence as a maid added to the illusion. The two women had slipped repeatedly through the lines of the opposing armies, carrying messages between the Confederates in Montreal and the Confederate Secret Service department in Richmond, but Sillery was no volunteer. In exchange for her work, the Confederates guaranteed the safety of her slave-born child. Mother and daughter had been reunited until conditions in the South had forced the latest separation. Sillery had enrolled the child in a new black school and left her in the care of a black family in Charleston.

She found that she missed her daughter less than she expected. Shasta was a delight but she was as demanding as a mistress. At times, Sillery questioned her own motives. Was the separation a selfish step, or was the child better off in the care of others? Finding the cabin had been a stroke of luck. It was too dilapidated to produce any envy from others seeking shelter. Her cache of coins was smaller than it was when she left Richmond but large enough to make her a wealthy woman in the South Carolina of 1865. The coins and a few other valuables were safely hidden in a compartment of her carpet bag. The lonely shelter allowed her time to think. She must decide if she would remain in the South or perhaps move north. She had fond memories of time spent in Canada. Shasta was probably best in the care of friends until Sillery was settled.

In the distance, she heard a dog bark and concentrated as the sound came again. Most tracking dogs had disappeared, killed by the slaves they once pursued. A bloodhound with a slit throat was a sober message for a former white master.

She tossed the magazine aside and picked up another. It was a special issue published in the North during the war and aimed at black freedmen. She flipped through the pages, finally turning to an installment of a serialized novel. With shock, she saw that it was written by Martin Delaney. She would read it completely before her next meeting with the Yankee colonel at the Freedmen's Bureau but she glanced at the final sentence.

"Woe be onto those devils of whites."

And almost certainly, she knew, he would extend that admonition to those who were part white.

She froze at a distant gunshot and then a volley. The regulators had found their prey but with luck, they would be too drunk to hit anything. The blacks would be defenseless. She doused the light completely and sat in the darkness, waiting and listening before beginning to doze.

Sarah Slater and Dan Mcgruder were with her again at the Spotswood Hotel in Richmond.

"Yankees are at the door," Slater hissed. "Get ready to run. Sillery will distract them."

The image faded as the cabin door collapsed.

The handheld lantern and the blue arm of a federal uniform were no dream.

"I'll handle this." The voice came from behind the lantern. "The rest of you wait outside. Send out pickets. Keep looking for rebel scum."

A Union officer held the lamp high to survey the cabin. "Are you alone?" he asked.

She nodded and forced a soft, "Yes."

He held the lamp close to her face.

"What's a white woman doing out here?"

"My husband..." she stammered trying to remember her latest story.

"Your husband what?" he demanded.

He held the lamp so close to her face that all she could see was the bright flame.

"Maybe your husband was one of those Secesh bastards we just killed?"

"No, no." She thought frantically. "My husband died of fever over a year ago. We hid here to escape rebel conscription."

The light was a thin red spot in front of her eyes.

"Maybe!" The officer would need convincing. "A woman shouldn't be out in the sun without a hat," he told her. "Your face has turned as brown as a soldier's."

He wrenched her hand into the light. "And a woman shouldn't be grubbing around in the soil. Look at what you've done to your hands, all dirty and calloused."

"A woman has to survive," she told him.

He set the lantern on her table. "Bet you're still white underneath." His voice had changed. "Be nice to me. I got a whole troop of black soldiers out there who haven't had any sport with a woman, much less a white woman, in a long, long time. You'd be a mighty fine reward for a hard night's work. Be nice to me or meet the rank and file."

In the dim light, she saw a gritty smile.

Two gunshots interrupted the proposition.

"Now what the hell is going on," he said, storming to the door.

"Think it's rebels!" a voice shouted.

"Goddamn!" The Yankee officer rushed back to his men.

Sillery didn't wait. The carpetbag by the rear door was packed, and in seconds, she was in the woods. The thickets would hide her until morning. She now knew that she would leave the South.

X

On Lake Erie
September 1865

E ramosa Willis gave a slight pull to the wheel to bring the boat closer to the wind. He wished he could afford a small steamer, but that was out of the question. The sails would have to provide power for a few more months.

The day's catch had been good, but the American market was drying up. The end of the free trade agreement was months off, but buyers were rejecting the Canadian-caught fish and larger supplies at home were driving prices lower.

Over Erin's objection, he had dismissed two of the orphan laborers, and only her favorite was left. Rufus was standing in the prow, scanning the lake for anything that would take him away from the heavy work ahead.

If it weren't for Tom Hines, the financial picture would be bleaker. First, there had been the fruitless hunt for Isaac Surratt. They had found Southern refugees in London and other small cities across Canada West, and more were trickling in each day, but there was no sign of Surratt or dynamite.

The other job had been more productive, an easy sail across the lake and passed the former prison on Johnson's Island, where men were already scavenging the lumber. The barracks were little more than ghostly shells. Willis had tied up at the dock in Sandusky, Ohio, and waited. Just after dark, Tom Hines and another man slipped aboard and into the lower cabin. The return trip to Canada was two hours old before they emerged.

"Oh, the Canadian fisherman," said a voice with a Scottish accent, "I remember him from our cruise when we seized the *Philo Parsons.* Let's hope this trip ends with more success."

Bennet Burleigh reached out to take Willis's hand.

"There was you, the boy, and the pretty red-haired woman. We didn't really have much time to get acquainted. Mr. Beall, God rest his soul, wanted to keep your presence a secret. And I believe it worked. The detectives who questioned me asked if there were any Canadians involved, so I lied and said no."

"I thank you for that," Willis replied. "Perhaps I can return the favor."

"Simply forget you saw him." Hines laughed and joined the conversation. "Mr. Burleigh will soon be the object of a man-hunt, though the jailer was well paid to look the other way. But the Americans may not look too hard. They're losing interest in Confederate raiders. He will leave us to return to Great Britain, and you can count on his discretion."

"Am I the last one?" Burleigh asked Hines. "Or do you have more men to rescue from American justice?"

"There's one more," Hines answered. "George St. Leger Grenfell is being transported to a prison off Florida after his death sentence was commuted. We'll try to make contact and see what we can do. The lawyers think Bennett Young will be released in Toronto. The Americans are losing interest in him, too. Like the Lake Erie raid, Saint Albans will soon be forgotten, as will Beall's attempt to arm that other ship."

"The *Georgian,*" Willis offered.

"Never saw her," Burleigh announced. "But I did make cannon for her."

"The cannons are at the bottom of Georgian Bay," Willis explained. "Mr. Denison decided to dump everything as the war was ending."

"So another souvenir of the Confederate period will disappear," Burleigh said, smiling. "Perhaps it's for the best. Let the deeds of our Secret Service slip away."

A shout from Rufus brought Willis back to the present and the work on the lake. The youngster was pointing ahead. The boat was racing through the water; it was a far cry from the ponderous bulk of the *Georgian* and her dead weight. Willis made a mental note to contact George Denison. Denison was a Southern sympathizer but if anyone knew of paying work, it would be the militia officer and his upper class associates in Toronto.

Erin would approve of that, he thought. Perhaps she was right, and he had taken too many risks, but she had no legal claim on his life, as he had no claim on hers.

The boy was yelling again and pointing to starboard.

Willis lifted a spyglass from the shelf and scanned the water but saw nothing.

He thought again of Beall, Burleigh, and the other rebel raiders. Willis had been angry—locked in the cabin on the return trip to Canada after the Lake Erie raid. The rebel raiders had not trusted him to see the torpedo mines sown at the entrance to the Detroit River. The mines must have sunk to the lake bottom. He had not heard of any ships damaged by mysterious explosions.

Rufus shouted again and continued to point. Willis scoured the lake until he too saw a small metal drum lift with the action of the waves and wash toward the boat. He only had time to read the faded lettering of "Confederate States of America" before the boat hit the cask.

He had an instant to wonder how Rufus was able to fly before the blast reached him. In mere seconds, the wreckage from the flaming boat began to sink beneath Lake Erie.

Port Stanley, Canada West
September 1865
"Bill, the woman is back, the one that lived with Willis."

The fisherman swore softly as he slashed the skin to gut the latest catch. Above his head, a faded sign read, "Munson's Fishery." He cleared the stomach in one easy motion before rinsing the fish and tossing it into a waiting barrel.

His wife pointed up dock to where the young, redheaded woman waited.

"I'll speak to her." Munson climbed from the boat.

"Still looking," Erin said, trying to smile. "I've been along the shore from here to Port Dover, but no one has seen any sign of them. It's not unusual for Eramosa to disappear for a few days, but it's two weeks now."

Munson cleared his throat to speak, but Erin was ahead of him. "I don't have much money left, but I wonder if we might take another look..."

Munson shook his head sadly. "There's no use." He watched her face begin to tighten as he spoke. "Look, I was off west this morning and saw the crew from the fishery at Port Glasgow. Well, there's no easy way to put this. They found a body last night. They think it was a kid, not a grown man."

"Rufus." She struggled to get the word out. "Rufus, one of the boys, was with him."

"Yeah, well, a few pieces of wood were floating near him but that was all."

"Can you give me directions?"

"Miss Erin. It's not something a woman should see. The body is only half there, just the top half, like it was blown in half or something."

"Can you give me directions?" she asked again.

"Yes. But stay with us tonight and leave first thing in the morning. The remains are in an icehouse. A few hours won't make a big difference."

"No, I'll go tonight!"

XI

Washington, DC
September 1865

"We can still use you," Mike Flynn told him.

"With this?" Owen Wilson patted his leg.

He had come through the war with a few minor scratches only to take a vicious kick from a nervous stallion. For a few days, he had been unable to walk. An army doctor assured him that nothing was broken, but weeks later, the leg remained stiff and tender. He had worked through a crutch and a cane and tried to rebuild his strength, but while the pain subsided, the limp remained. It might heal, the doctors advised and reminded him he was lucky compared with other soldiers who were missing arms, legs, eyes, and other body parts, or locked away in asylums.

"We figure they'll keep you in the army another couple of months anyway," Flynn told him. "Keep working on the leg. When the release papers come through, the Fenian brotherhood will still sign you up. There's a hundred-dollar bounty. You know what that is?"

"I'm familiar with the concept. I collected a couple of payments from the Union army."

"You deserted and signed up for a second bounty? Ain't you brave. Men were hung for that."

"Well, I wasn't, but keep your mouth shut."

"You seem to have a lot of secrets."

"Just never mind. What else do I have to know?"

Flynn needed a moment before he replied. "Well, for six dollars you can buy the personal gear and a weapon. Be sure to do that. It's how we outfit our army."

"Like the guns we collected in Virginia?" Wilson asked.

The two men were alone in what had once been a crowded army barracks. The rapid discharge of the American troops left rows of empty bunks.

"We won't need the Spencers," Flynn explained. "In fact, I already sold them and turned a nice profit for myself. Our army will have new weapons because we have the right connections at the highest levels here in Washington. But I can't tell you more than that. At least not until you've taken the oath and been properly sworn in. Have patience for a few more weeks. And if I keep quiet about deserting, you can keep quiet about my gun profits."

"Agreed!" Owen smiled. "But one more question. You are not sending me to Ireland?" The chance to leave North America had seemed a welcome opportunity. A new start might be what he needed.

"No, the Irish rising is delayed. The Brits got wind of it and broke up the leadership. The bastards actually broke into a newspaper office and seized all the papers, including our membership lists. Raiding a newspaper office shows what they think of freedom."

Wilson was tempted to remind him of the uproar that ensued when American authorities had raided newspaper offices during the war and of the editors sent to prison for defying the Lincoln administration, but Flynn gave him no chance.

"So, our Irish expedition is off for now. But there will be big doings in North America, and hasn't Mike Flynn taken care of you? Without me, you wouldn't have witnessed history."

"Don't start on the hangings," Owen warned. Flynn had demanded repeated descriptions of the final moments of the Lincoln conspirators.

"Well, I mean you know where the bodies are buried," Flynn continued. "That's a government secret because the authorities are afraid the rebels will try to dig them up and distribute parts of them as sacred relics."

Owen stared into space, refusing to be baited into another description of the four graves or watching the jailor spread a thick layer of quick lime over the bodies to speed decomposition. A small bottle had been placed inside each coffin. "When the bodies decay, we'll know which is which," the jailor announced as the soldiers leaned on shovels. "Inside each bottle is a piece of paper with the felon's name. It might seem a waste for this lot, but we follow the regulations."

"The rest of the conspirators have been sent to the Dry Tortugas," Flynn explained, "a big prison off Florida and miles out to sea, so there's no chance of escape. Some Confederate criminal is with them. A fellow named Grenfell. It turns out he was British and was supposed to be hung, but the English kicked up such a fuss that the sentence was commuted to life in prison. See, the English will go overboard for a well-bred toff and leave the children of Ireland to starve. Well, the Americans have put one over on them because from what I hear, Fort Jefferson is the same as a death sentence."

Flynn could be tiresome, but for Owen, the Fenian opportunity was too good to ignore. He knew of discharged soldiers who had returned home, but many more wandered the streets of Washington, spending nights in Hooker's Division and days wherever fate took them. A place in a new army would keep him away from that.

• • •

Montreal, Canada East
September 1865
The rooming house was a hovel. An open window looked onto an alley, the dumping ground for the waste from other nearby

buildings. John Surratt closed the window to reduce the foul smell, only to notice a missing pane of glass. With luck, in a few hours he would be gone.

The summer had passed slowly. The priest at Saint Liboire had policed his every movement, and like a prisoner, Surratt was allowed an hour of exercise outside and only at night.

In early summer, John Porterfield, one of the Confederate operatives had returned with shocking news. Despite last-minute appeals, Surratt's mother had been hanged as an accomplice of John Wilkes Booth. Surratt had wanted to hear no more that night and for hours sat silently in a dark recess of the parish church. It was two weeks before he could control his anger. Later, Porterfield had told him that the evidence had been stacked in favor of the prosecution via innuendo, hearsay, and outright lies.

"And Lou?" Surratt asked.

"Weichmann," Porterfield sneered, "gave evidence and is now assured of a government job…as long as he lives."

Surratt was shocked into silence.

"But he may not live long. We'll be looking for him," Porterfield promised. "Even if we don't find him right away, he'll always have to look over his shoulder."

"Anna, Isaac?" Surratt had memories of the quick anger his brother so often displayed and the sister who was little more than a girl.

"Anna is at the house on H Street with friends to watch over her," Porterfield explained. "We don't know where Isaac is. He left Texas. The federal detectives looked for him in Canada, and so did we, but we couldn't find him. Can you think where he might go?"

"No," Surratt told him, "I have no idea."

"We need to get you away," Porterfield had said. "We think you would be safer in Europe. The Canadians are under pressure from Washington. If they find you, you'll be turned over quickly."

Surratt had spent the next few weeks waiting. Finally a carriage had brought him to the Montreal rooming house. The bag waiting in the room contained new clothes and a new identity, and Porterfield had promised to provide enough cash to allow Surratt to make a clean break with the past. He tensed at the sound of the footsteps outside the door. It was just one person, he thought, but he pulled the small revolver from his pocket.

Three taps, a pause, and two more was the agreed-upon signal.

"Damn near time!" he opened the door to find Porterfield. "You went all out on lodging." He motioned to single bed and the lone chair in the room.

"I'm sorry, John, but this is the best we could do. Your picture has been splashed all over the city. Even with the beard and the dyed hair, someone might recognize you."

"And what about my new clothes," Surratt said, running his hands over the rough fabric. "I suggested a purchase at Gibbs, the store with the best clothing in Montreal, but what do I get? Cheap goods made by some poor sot or maybe an apprentice. He had the nerve to add his name to the coat. Let me assure you, I know about these things. This Patrick Whelan is a damn poor tailor."

"Outfit yourself in England," Porterfield suggested. "I have two hundred dollars and a ticket for the passage. You know where to go in London?"

Surratt nodded. He would ask for more cash as soon as he arrived.

"Will Jacob Thompson be there?" he asked. "He ran things here during the war. I would like to see him again."

"That's not likely." Porterfield almost laughed. "Thompson made it to Europe, but there's an issue with funds. Perhaps he feels the Confederacy should provide compensation for his damaged property in Mississippi or his expenses in Canada, but whatever the reason, we think he has Confederate cash that he refuses to surrender. And please, don't try to approach anyone else. The British may accept refugee's like Confederate cabinet members, men like Judah Benjamin, but they won't be pleased to see you. The best thing is to disappear. You will be a wanted man for a very long time."

Surratt responded with a cold stare.

"Good luck, John!" Porterfield rose to leave and extended his hand.

"No." Surratt brushed it aside. "I'll take the money and ticket but I won't consider any of you as friends. What I do now is for me."

"A fellow named Donnelly will come tomorrow," Porterfield told him. "He'll take you to the boat, and by tomorrow night you will be safe on the Saint Lawrence."

Surratt slammed the door to leave Porterfield in the half-light of the stairwell.

And we'll be rid of a major headache, Porterfield thought. An ungrateful bastard and a drain on the now meagre Confederate funds.

• • •

Chatham, Canada West
October 1865

She shifted slightly as the train whistle sounded a warning where a country track met the railway line. From the rail cars, Tom Hines glimpsed a farmer fighting a team of horses at the crossing, but in mere seconds the train roared through and the wagon lurched forward.

Nannie stirred but left her head against his shoulder. She had fallen asleep as the train left Windsor, the result of the long trip from Kentucky and their first night together in a new country. As his wife stepped from the Detroit ferry, Hines understood that a new life was truly beginning.

The whistle sounded again as the train began to slow. He nudged her gently and watched her come awake.

"Where are we?"

He pressed his fingers to her mouth. "Chatham," he told her, "and a surprise."

Nannie was reticent but eventually shook the hand of the black man who met them.

"Amos is a friend," Hines explained. "I could always count on Amos Baker."

Baker offered a reluctant smile. "Take you to the hotel, then?"

"Hell, no! Take us out to Eramosa and Erin," Hines said with a laugh. A few months ago, he would have refused to utter their names, fearing that Union detectives might be among the passengers at the station. The end of the war eliminated the danger.

"Maybe I should take you to the hotel," Baker suggested again. "Let the little lady have a chance to freshen up."

"Why not head out?" Hines began before he caught the expression on Baker's face. "Or perhaps it would be better to rest. Whatever you think, Amos."

"That would be best." Baker seemed relieved.

Hines made certain that his new wife was comfortable before he returned to the street.

"You don't know?" Baker asked.

"Know what?"

"We aren't going to the lake. Eramosa is dead. Or at least we're pretty sure he is."

For the first time in weeks, Hines felt a rush of dread.

"What happened?"

"He and the boy, Rufus, went out on the new fishing boat and never came back. Weather was fine and no other fisherman saw anything."

"Are you sure he didn't disappear for some reason? Maybe new business?"

"That's what I thought," Baker answered. "But Miss Erin said no. She had a feeling something was wrong. She looked herself. She spent a week on a rented boat going up and down the lake, walking the beach for miles, and asking questions of fishermen, sailors, or anyone that might have seen them. They found the body of the boy a couple of weeks later. It was pretty beat up, but Erin said it was him. We ain't found Eramosa."

Hines was stunned. He stood silently and leaned against a wall. He had planned the surprise for all of them, a night free of war or fear of discovery.

"Is Erin at the house?" he asked.

"No, that's the other sad thing. Eramosa had cousins who are legally his next of kin, and very proper types. They didn't care for him or the woman who lived with him…in sin."

Hines could guess where the story was leading.

"So they told her to get out. That she was a servant and wouldn't be needed and gave her an hour to pack her things. She came to Chatham. Times are getting hard with business dropping off. But I got her a bit of cash and put her on the train. She thought some of her relatives might be on the Niagara Peninsula and guessed she'd see if they were still there. I haven't heard from her since. She always was independent."

"And nothing can be done?" Hines asked. "Eramosa was independent, too, and didn't want to be tied down, but he and Erin had a special relationship. He wouldn't want this to happen to her."

"I know," Baker told him. "I went to my black lawyer and he went to a white lawyer, but property goes to the next of kin. That should be Erin, but the law don't see it that way."

"I wanted Nannie to meet them," Hines explained. "She and Erin are very different in many ways, but the spirit is the same."

"What do you want to do?" Baker asked.

"Let Nannie sleep," Hines decided quickly. "Take me to the depot. I'll get tickets for the morning train."

"And then?" Baker asked as Hines swung up beside him, and the wagon rolled down the street.

"On to Toronto," Hines told him.

"Might follow along in the next few weeks," Baker said. "Business is real bad now—for blacks *and* whites. I may start over somewhere else."

"But I thought this was home."

"As you are about to prove," Baker told him, "home is where you make it."

• • •

London, England
December 1865
The thick fog dampened the sounds of the shod hooves and carriage wheels on cobblestones.

"We're here." Dan Mcgruder spoke softly to Sarah and pointed through the window at the top of a hat. A short, rotund man opened the door and slipped into the seat opposite them.

"Tell the driver to move on," he ordered. "Even with the fog, someone may be watching."

Mcgruder tapped the carriage roof and the carriage moved slowly forward.

"You look well, Mr. Benjamin." Sarah lifted the veil to smile at the former Confederate secretary of state.

"As do you." Benjamin's attention was drawn to the pronounced swelling of Sarah's stomach. "Both of you. Or should I say the three of you? I recall a time when women went into confinement on the approach of a child, but things change, and this is 1865."

"I'm sorry to bother you," Mcgruder began, "but we didn't know where to turn."

"You might be surprised by how often I've been approached since I arrived in London in September. I thought my duties with the Confederacy were finished, but little matters keep popping up."

"I tried to reach Mr. Thompson," Sarah told him. "But he's off on a European tour with his wife. It must be expensive."

"Ah, yes...expensive," Benjamin repeated. "From the tone of the question, you've obviously heard about the dispute with Mr. Thompson and the missing funds. His case is settled, and I won't say more. And as for the Confederacy...it's bankrupt. We're hard-pressed to find money for the president's lawyers. I'm strapped, too. In fact, I'm going back to school. I find a certain appeal in becoming a London barrister, and for the record, aspiring lawyers are not well paid."

"No, it's not us," Sarah assured him quickly. "It's Surratt. I thought I was done with him, but he's shown up in London. He had the gall to approach Dan."

"Yes, he's become a nuisance," Benjamin agreed. "But the matter is in hand. We have an engagement for him in Rome." He chuckled before continuing. "An ideal appointment for a good Catholic lad is with the troops of the papal guard. He's to leave soon. And, what's amazing is that the arrangement was set in place by me, a Jew."

"I fear he will tell the authorities where I am," Sarah admitted. "We were never friends, and my name did surface at his mother's trial."

"Ah, Mr. Holt's inquisition." Benjamin smiled. "He made a fine case out of supposition at the trial of the so-called Lincoln conspirators. There were the tantalizing hints about people like you and others, right up to Mr. Davis and myself. Most of it was preposterous."

"I told her not to worry," Mcgruder interrupted, "but Surratt makes her nervous."

"I wouldn't be concerned," Benjamin told them. "In his defense, he does feel misled. Our people in Canada thought the mother, Mary Surratt, would be pardoned. They thought the execution announcement was an attempt to smoke John from hiding and didn't tell him of the verdict until after the execution...

But if he takes our advice and stays quiet, the Yankees may well forget him."

"And forget me," Sara added hopefully.

"You will be lost in the swirling fog of time," Benjamin assured her. "I suspect this will be the last time we meet. The Confederacy thanks you for your efforts, Mrs. Slater, and you, Colonel Mcgruder, but I'm afraid that is the best we can do."

Benjamin tapped on the roof of the carriage, and it slowed to a stop. "I'll walk from here. And Mrs. Slater, the old gentlemen used to say that a woman's name should be in a newspaper only three times: when she's born, when she marries, and when she dies. You've had the misfortune to be named much more often. I hope the colonel gives you a new name and another chance."

"He already has," Sarah said, laughing. "We're now known as—"

Benjamin waved his hand. "I don't need to know, but I do wish you well." He tipped his hat and stepped into the fog.

XII

Journal of Paul Forsey
Quebec City, Canada East
January 1866

*T*he end of another year signals my final months in this old city. My workload has increased as the government prepares for the move to the new capital, and Ottawa will be bleak compared with the attractions of Quebec City.

We are told that space will be at premium, but I have a chance of an accommodation in the house that Macdonald is renting. The danger of discovery makes it impossible to bring the confidential papers I have collected over these last few years, but through Geoffrey Ralston's French companion, I have found a place to store them. Francine will keep them safe.

The American war is fast becoming a memory. The government workload now centers on the plans for the new nation, even if the Grand Confederation Scheme has been delayed. And, the pessimists have found another worry. The Irish republican or Fenian threat appears to be growing. The British army appears prepared and has ordered extra training for the militia.

• • •

The Niagara Peninsula, Canada West
January 1866

Erin took extra care as she washed dirty plates and cups. The china was used, well used, but the hotel owner had already docked her pay, claiming a cup was chipped.

"Erin Brady. Irish! Best settle for room and board," Vera Hoffman had announced when Erin applied for the job at the tavern. "Maybe a monthly wage when you prove yourself. Your type won't get a better offer."

Any offer had been welcome. The family she had hoped to find had moved on or died off.

The Hoffman tavern was a half-day's ride from the major hotels at Niagara Falls and it offered travelers a break en route to the interior of the province. Today, three customers picked silently at their food and watched as a pair of British officers settled their bill.

"The Brits come here often, Miss?" one man asked as soon as the soldiers were gone and she began to clear the table.

"I'm new to the Niagara," Erin said, "but the owner said patrols come by often." She carried the plates to the kitchen, but washing could wait. Instead, she dropped into a chair and poured a cup of coffee. The customers' conversation drifted into the kitchen.

"There are more of them every time I come."

"Those were British regulars," another answered. "The militia are different, a seedier lot."

"The commanders will want to know how many we saw."

"They asked us to find out how Canadians felt. Let them send someone else to count the troops."

"I can't believe it!" a third man with a deep voice joined in. "We offer the people a chance to do something for the homeland, and they laugh."

"Maybe conditions here are better than we thought?" the first man offered.

"Nah, they're cowards—Irish emigrants afraid to risk the little they have. And the fools are putting faith in men like D'Arcy McGee. They think he's such a fine man and a great politician. I told them how McGee claimed that the Irish are hated and live in filth and squalor. And a man had the nerve to tell me that McGee was referring only to the American Irish."

Erin heard the tinkle of a glass being refilled.

"But did you see his face when I told him that McGee is nicknamed 'Darkey' because of his skin and his black, curly hair. He's no better than a Negro!"

"Our agents will have to do a better job of persuasion," the second man said.

"Let's hope we have better luck in Toronto and Montreal. Factory workers are treated like slaves by lazy English owners. And in Montreal, the French will rise to join us. I have no doubt. They hate the English as much as we do."

"But what of weapons?" The third voice was lower, and she strained to hear.

"I've seen no place where I would leave a revolver, much less a crate of rifles and—"

The conversation stopped abruptly as the tavern door opened.

"Don't let me interrupt, gentlemen! I'm the owner here and delighted to have you stop by."

Erin thought she heard Mrs. Hoffman sniff the air. "I have new staff. Are you well served?"

"Oh, yes," the first man responded for the trio.

"Bring any complaints to me. The new girl may be pretty, but we have to light a fire under her to keep her working."

Mrs. Hoffman nodded to the men and made her way to the kitchen.

"They're good looking," she whispered to Erin. "Big, sturdy boys. Girl like you should be paying attention. Pay more attention to them, and they may come back. And by the way, the coffee comes off your pay."

Erin returned to the main room as the men prepared to leave. "Can I get you anything else?"

"Not this time, Brigid." The man with the deep voice pushed a coin across the table. "But we'll be back soon with something for all of your people."

She did her best to curtsey and smile.

. . .

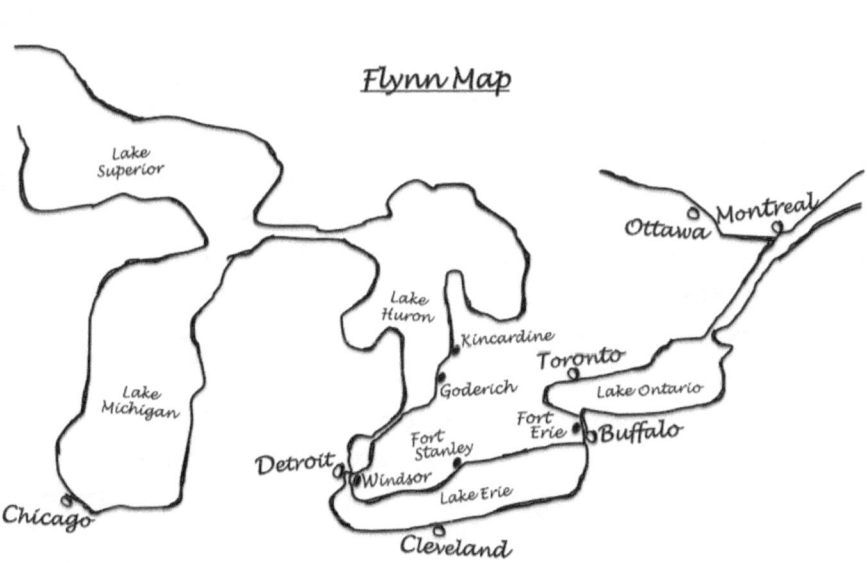

Buffalo, New York
January 1866
Owen Wilson struggled through the wind-whipped snow and finally found the entrance to the dilapidated warehouse on the Buffalo waterfront. Inside, armed men watched with suspicion

until Mike Flynn descended the stairs to confirm Wilson's identity and lead him to a small second-floor room.

"All right Wilson, you've sworn the oath. I can tell you what's ahead. The objective is across the river."

Owen was more concerned with the heat from the stove than the fiery zeal of Fenian rhetoric. Winter had been slow to arrive but was now pounding Buffalo. The cold affected the muscles in his leg, and the pain was back.

Flynn rubbed a glass with a dirty rag. "Hang the great coat by the fire. Let it dry while we talk."

Flynn had reappeared in the early December with discharge papers for Union Private Owen Wilson, proof, he said, of the power of his connections. He produced one hundred dollars in bounty money and another six dollars to cover the purchase of a rifle and other gear from surplus Union army material.

"I'd have cut orders sooner if I had known you were familiar with what they call Canada West. We need scouts," Flynn told him. "You'll be well paid and you can pose as a traveler seeing the sights. But I have to ask a few questions. The powers that be wonder about your loyalty. You were born and raised in Canada, and they kind of—"

"I have no loyalty except to those who pay me," Owen interrupted. "I have no family or friends left. I don't commit to causes unless there's money on the table. The British haven't offered to pay me. Your Fenian friends have."

"OK. That's what I thought." Flynn appeared embarrassed. "I had orders to ask…so I guess we can push ahead. Have a look at this."

He pulled a leather map case from under the table and spread the contents on the table. The map showed the lands around the lower Great Lakes.

"I don't have to warn you," Flynn said, suddenly remembering the need for secrecy, "you can't talk about this outside of this room."

Owen rubbed his leg and looked at the bottle.

"And go easy on the grog," Flynn warned. "Don't have to be cold-water temperance. Just be careful." He smiled before adding, "But men like us can handle our alcohol." He poured a deep measure in each glass.

"We've a bit of friction in the organization," Flynn admitted. "Here in Buffalo is what's called the Senate wing. We're ready to take action. The others, the dissenters, seem content to just talk and raise money. They may come around eventually, but we're not going to wait. We're going to invade Canada."

"What on earth for?"

"Because we have nothing else to do." Flynn broke into laughter at the surprise on Owen's face. "One of the boys wrote a charming little marching song."

He tapped his foot and began to sing.

We are the Fenian brotherhood, skilled in the art of war,
And we're going to fight for Ireland, the land that we adore.
Many battles we have won, along with the boys in blue,
And we'll go and capture Canada because we've nothing else to do.

"There!" He made a bow.

"Wait and get serious. How does the invasion of Canada set the stage for Irish freedom?"

"I'll come to that, but first have a look at this." Flynn pointed to the map. "Our secretary of war is General Sweeney. Remember? They used to call him the armless sleeve when he marched with Sherman. Well, he's plotted two campaigns. With ten thousand men, he plans to cross the ice and seize the provinces in the next few weeks."

Owen shivered at the thought of crossing Lake Erie ice in the face of a howling blizzard.

"But planning is taking longer than expected," Flynn continued. "If Sweeny doesn't collect enough men soon, he'll opt for a different strategy, and that's what the map is about."

"See here—Chicago. Come spring, we'll load the men on boats and come up the lakes to capture places like Goderich in Canada West. It's one those godforsaken Canadian villages, but there's a good harbor. From there, we'll strike across country to where we can cut the main line of the Grand Trunk Railway. At the same time, more men will be crossing Lake Erie and landing under the very guns of Fort Stanley."

Owen took a closer look at the map. "No, Port Stanley is a fishing village. There's no fort."

"No fort? Are you sure?" Flynn asked.

"I'm certain."

"I told them Canadian experience would help. I'll send the word along. Anyway, the regiments will march inland and—"

"Why march when there's a railroad at Port Stanley?" Owen interrupted.

"A railroad?" Flynn studied the map. "There's no railroad."

"It's a small line," Owen told him. "But it's been there for ten years or more. It connects to the Great Western at London."

Flynn bent closer. "Ah, this is an old map. I'll pass that along, too. At any rate, with the southwestern part of the country cut off, we'll push troops from Buffalo and seize the Niagara Peninsula while other units strike into Quebec. So we need you to scout out this end of the province. Look for locations we might use, maybe tell us what the local people are saying."

"And the British will calmly stand by and watch when you invade?" Owen asked.

"Well, the major British posts are in the cities," Flynn explained. "Canadian supporters can overwhelm them. Besides, many of the British soldiers are Irish and will join us. The English won't be able to send reinforcements because we'll control the waterways and railroads."

"Do you understand how big this country is?" Owen was perplexed. "Sherman could repeat the march through Georgia and not see all of it."

"Ah, but the people will be with us," Flynn assured him. "Almost a third of the population is of Irish descent. And there's the French. They'll rise, too. Canada will soon be under the green flag with the golden harp."

"And then what?" Owen was curious.

"Well, we can make a deal with the British. We can give Canada back if they leave Ireland."

"And if they don't bargain or decide to fight?"

"We have the United States," Flynn told him smugly. "Washington will recognize us. If it comes to a full-scale war, American armies will fight by our side."

"And Sweeney will start all this with ten thousand men?"

"Actually, with a summer campaign he'll want maybe twice as many, but men are there. The fellows who were recently discharged from the Union army are bored."

He laughed again. "Because they've nothing else to do. It's that simple!"

• • •

Halifax, Nova Scotia
January 1866
Joseph Howe cast an approving glance around the print shop of the *Halifax Morning Chronicle.*

"I like to see people work hard, and in the newspaper industry, nothing makes them work harder than a change in control. An owner steps in to shake up the staff and put a new stamp on editorial policy."

"There will be a change," William Annand, the owner smiled. "And starting immediately. The former editor drifted from my principles, and I warned him. He didn't listen. If he wants to push Confederation, let him buy a press and risk his own money."

"William, we've been able to work well together over the years," Howe reminded him. "In the legislature, in government, in campaigns, and now this new challenge. People must understand this union is a bad arrangement, a hybrid of nothing. The delegates should have picked the best parts of the American and British systems, but the Quebec resolutions are a hodgepodge and especially bad for Nova Scotia. We'd lose our independence—and not to the imperial government but to the upper provinces."

"I have space in the next edition of the *Chronicle*," Annand told him. "How quickly can you deliver on the columns?"

"Right away." Howe smiled. "The first of my letters will be in your hands tomorrow. I've played on 'Confederation' in my headline...I call it 'Botheration.' But make no mistake, the arguments won't be amusing. I'll rip the agreement to shreds but I warn you, it won't win friends in the Tupper government."

"I'm not worried," Annand told him. "We get more revenue from commercial printing than from government contracts. The paper will survive."

"Watch the revenue," Howe warned. "The end of trade reciprocity means hard times. The Americans are no mood to do us favors. Most of them would prefer to add another ring of

Northern states. Let's hope they pin their hopes on annexation and a peaceful conquest."

"Why wouldn't they?" Annand asked. "Surely, with their war, they've had enough bloodshed."

"It's this Fenian business," Howe cautioned. "What if the Irish are more than talk? And what if an American army comes with them?"

XIII

Montreal, Canada East
February 1866

D'Arcy McGee drew closer to the fire. A slight cold had developed into something more, and his doctors recommended rest at home.

"The world becomes a darker place when one is ill," McGee announced as Paul Forsey delivered the latest cabinet reports.

"The newspapers are full of gloom." McGee motioned to the stack of publications beside him. "Spring is far away. My doctors say I must reduce my consumption of alcohol, and who knows what lurks in these files."

Forsey tried to think of something positive. "We miss you at the legislature."

"Do you, now," McGee answered and abruptly pointed to the rows of books that lined his den. "Reach up and grab my poetry...the third shelf...*Canadian Ballads and Occasional Verses.*"

Forsey retrieved the volume.

"Look at the back of the shelf," McGee ordered. "There's a bottle. Pass it to me."

He followed instructions and waited as McGee took a deep pull.

"Have a nip and slip it back," McGee ordered. "My wife pays too much attention to the physicians and their admonitions on liquor."

A quick sip was enough for the clerk.

"Do you enjoy poetry?" the little man asked. "Or do you prefer serious reading—and I mean beyond government reports."

"I don't read much for pleasure," Forsey confessed.

"Ah, but you should. Take my book with you. You are a recent immigrant?"

Forsey nodded and was pleased that the minister remembered. He had left England five years earlier.

"Get a better sense of Canadian history. Start with something like Cartier."

McGee flipped through the pages and began to read:

From the seaport of Saint Malo, 'twas a smiling morn in May,
When the Commodore Jacques Cartier to the westward sailed away.

"My cabinet associate, Georges Etienne Cartier, was a distance relative of Jacques. The French see themselves as the only true Canadians, the *pur-lain*, pure French stock, but remember the 'habitants' are immigrants like the rest of us."

He closed the book before he suggested, "And perhaps another nip."

This time he took a deeper pull.

"Is the cabinet quieter with Brown gone?" McGee wiped a sleeve across his lips.

"It is, and Macdonald rests easier."

McGee began to laugh. "I'm sure he does. He and Brown were like dogs fighting over a bone. But Brown should have been part of the recent delegation that went to Washington. He has a grasp of the trade issues. And the fact that he wasn't included suggests that Macdonald was scheming, again. After that, Brown felt he had no choice but to resign, and Macdonald was happy to see him go."

Forsey glanced toward the bookshelf.

"By all means." The gracious host motioned to the bottle. "Leave it out but if you hear my wife coming, put it back quickly". The room was quiet for a few moments. "Are you content as a clerk?" McGee asked quietly.

"Government offers steady work," Forsey answered, "and a chance for advancement. The chief clerk, Mr. Bernard, feels I've been of service in preparing for the move to the new capital. He's offered me temporary accommodation with him, Macdonald, and Mr. Brydges."

"Brydges of the Grand Trunk Railway." McGee shrugged. "Macdonald and Cartier are too close to the financiers. Money is always welcome but comes with a price. The railway men want something in return, and very few politicians will resist them."

Forsey took another sip from the bottle.

"Will you be content to always do a politician's bidding?" McGee asked. "Don't you want to leave a mark on the world? A clerk is nameless, faceless, and has no opinion. Are you content with that?"

"For now." He wished he could share his plan. He had already decided that McGee would receive sympathetic treatment when he wrote his book.

"Someday you may change." McGee drummed absently on the arm of his chair. "You may find you want to be important. It's difficult for a clerk. Now—"

McGee stopped suddenly. "Put the bottle away," he hissed. "Quickly, man."

The bottle and book were barely on the shelf before the door swung open.

"Mr. McGee, time for dinner," the woman said, smiling.

"Ah, Molly, you haven't forgotten me. I'll come directly after I thank Mr. Forsey for his pleasant conversation."

McGee's face broke into a broad smile, and he winked. "Come again and review more *dry* history."

• • •

Toronto, Canada West
February 1866
The Heydon Villa was warmed by the sound of Southern voices as George Denison welcomed old friends to his home. "Let the young people go to the parlor," he called. "General Breckinridge and I will join you in a few minutes."

Denison puffed on a cigar but carefully flicked the ashes away, fearing a smudge on his new uniform. "What do you think, General? Is it well tailored?"

He stood ready for inspection. "Our troop will wear this uniform for the next season, plus long, dark overcoats and bearskin bonnets, tall ones. And, my men will be well trained, in formations, even in responding to little things like special bugle calls. It may be a ceremonial display, but we are the Governor General's Guards. We'll be better drilled than the other militia units."

"The men will look splendid," Breckinridge agreed. His own gray uniform had been retired during his flight from the South, and he had no desire to replace it. Breckinridge had made a harrowing escape across the swamps of Florida to Cuba, to England, and finally to the British colonies. The former Confederate secretary of war was a recent arrival in the growing Southern community in Toronto.

"Any news of President Davis?" Denison asked quietly.

"Nothing of import," Breckinridge replied, "although he is allowed exercise now. The shackles, the ball and chain, have been removed."

"Ghastly business. No way to treat a man."

"His health is suspect," Breckinridge continued. "Light bothers his eyes, and the Yankees keep a lamp burning at all times."

"Scandalous," Denison interjected. "And that book, rushed into print by his prison doctor. That shouldn't be allowed."

"I tell myself that," Breckinridge admitted. "But since I have begun to tutor the young men here, I remind them of American law and freedom of speech. The system has been damaged severely in the last few years, and we must restore it. Well-trained young lawyers will be needed. Tom Hines has a good mind. Bennett Young is a more indifferent student."

"Oh, I'm aware of Young," Denison said, chuckling. "I've introduced him to the British court system."

"He and Hines study at the University of Toronto by day and I lecture them on American law at night," Breckinridge explained. "Imagine, a year ago, I supervised the War Department of the Confederacy and now I teach law to a pair of refugees."

"Maybe you could advise us," Denison suggested. "Our politicians are making a hash of things."

"No, I'm a realist. No Canadian party would be comfortable with me, a former Confederate and a former American vice president under a charge of treason. I must be content with what I have. But if you could get a message to your leaders, it would be appreciated."

"Of course. What message?"

"That we appreciate the refuge," Breckinridge told him.

"Your government had the power to order deportation. I suspect that in several cases, deportation would have led to prison or execution. So the sanctuary is welcome. We try to live quietly and we won't forget the kindness."

Denison took a puff on his cigar. "I'll pass it on gladly."

"And I have to thank you personally," Breckinridge continued, "both for assistance during the war and now. Gatherings at Heydon Villa mean a great deal to our young men and women. They feel part of society again."

The room had cleared, and in the neighboring parlor, some-one began to play the piano.

"One slight word of caution." Denison moved closer. "The city, in fact the whole of the country, is on edge over this Irish busi-ness. Each time Fenians are mentioned, the Protestant Orange Lodge puffs itself up. And Brown's *Globe* newspaper doesn't help. He was quieter when he was more active in government and had other things to occupy him. Now he has the time to hatemonger with an anti-Catholic bias. Mind you, I'm no papist. I don't like the Roman church or priests, but I don't want the country torn apart by religious zealots."

"I'm not sure I understand." Breckinridge was puzzled.

"Tell your people to be careful. Saint Patrick's Day may bring serious street demonstrations. The men can defend themselves, but the women, well…Mrs. Hines, for example, is pregnant."

"Is it that serious?" Breckinridge asked. "Other refugees are thinking of moving here. Should I advise them not to come?"

"I don't mean to frighten people, but tell them to keep their eyes open."

XIV

Ottawa, Canada West
March 1866

Winter had returned. A few mild days melted much of the ice and snow, turning the streets of the capital to a quagmire. But then, an early March storm, heavy snow and strong north winds, began to lash the city.

With each step, Paul Forsey sank through snow into the mud and sand below. A sharp freeze would firm the ground, but it would be hours before the muck would be firm enough to support man or beast. He glanced to the upper floor of his temporary home. Bernard's room was in darkness. There would be no questions about the completion of the work that the chief clerk had assigned at the close of normal business. Bernard had disappeared into the gathering storm, leaving his junior clerk at the mercy of the files and the elements.

But Macdonald was wide awake. A lamp burned in the window of his ground-floor study, showing two men in conversation. Sixty-three Daly, know as the Quadrilateral was a few blocks from the parliament buildings. Macdonald had leased the home and then overcame his almost constant financial woes by renting space to associates.

Forsey almost slipped as he climbed the steps, recovering his balance only to slam against the door.

"A burglar, sure as you live!" Macdonald's shout carried above the wind. "And a damn noisy one at that. The door is unlocked, Mr. Forsey. When you have removed the winter attire, join us by the fire for a cordial."

Moments later, he was introduced to Macdonald's companion.

"Meet a railway baron," Macdonald said with a laugh.

The decanter on the desk between the two men was almost empty.

"C. J. Brydges," the guest said, introducing himself, but he remained seated. "And 'railway baron' is usually reserved for those who own the lines. I ensure the trains run on time."

"Far too modest, Charlie." Macdonald chuckled and motioned to an empty chair. "As for Mr. Forsey, he's a government worker who understands the need for discretion and will gladly exchange future silence for a warm place on a cold winter night."

"That I will." Forsey rubbed his hands in front of the fire before accepting a glass.

"Mr. Brydges is instructing me in the fine art of railway construction," Macdonald explained, "and how iron and steel can bind a nation."

"Oh, you must be speaking of the Intercolonial Railway." Forsey smiled knowingly. "The new railway link to Halifax. Has there been a decision on the route?"

Brydges ignored him but fixed his gaze on Macdonald. "He can be trusted?" he asked.

"We'll soon find out."

Brydges cast a long glance at Forsey and shrugged. "Eventually, money will be found to finance the link to the Maritimes, but prepare for a long battle to shake it loose. With the end of the American war, the military feels the need is less urgent. And the turmoil in the European money markets means investors will be hard to find."

"Railway investors are always nervous," Macdonald countered, "and often spread whispers of money trouble. The Great Western and Grand Trunk have teetered, and a couple of smaller lines have failed. But there's always someone greedy enough to try for a fortune."

Forsey sipped at his glass and studied Brydges. The man was only in his early forties but with his railroad experience, he had the respect of leaders in the colonies and Great Britain.

"True enough." Brydges smiled. "And sometimes all it takes is a little encouragement. The value of land rises when the railroad grows through. A small station or the promise of a construction contract whets an appetite. But you need more than just individuals. Think of the coal in Cape Breton. Toronto and Hamilton need the energy to fire their factories. Imagine trainloads of coal—Canadian coal for Canadian plants. Offer the people a promise of new jobs to get them excited."

"And we do need a link to a British port. The Grand Trunk reaches the ocean at Portland, Maine," Macdonald reminded him. "The Americans may be quiet now but they covet our territory. The defense rationale may be less urgent but it is still real."

"The Americans are looking west, not east." Brydges rose to lift the poker by the fire. "Troops are already protecting the construction crews on their Union Pacific route. In a few years, the rails will reach to California."

He pushed the poker into the fire.

"And the Americans are generous with railway contractors. Washington promises loan guarantees and land grants. The railways will eventually sell thousands of those acres. The land will bring settlers, who will eventually push north. Why, the first squatters are already moving into the Hudson Bay lands, and those sodbusters put more faith in Washington than in Ottawa."

Brydges stepped back as the flames rose.

"Someday you may need to carry troops to the West. So John, don't just think about the East. Think about a British line running to the Pacific. Imagine all those acres ripe for the plough. Why, even little British Columbia might find a way to raise money to build a railroad. Just imagine...a Canadian Pacific."

Macdonald smiled.

"And imagine the millions of dollars for railway contractors. There's the business for a young man—a rosier future than that of a government clerk."

Forsey leaned forward, but before he could speak, Brydges continued. "Public servants can be very important. A file can be placed on the right desk or a letter might disappear. But that would come later. For now, you have to build the interest. Make sure the right people are in the right offices. Make sure the right politicians are elected."

"Oh, that's under control," Macdonald assured him. "Our friends in the Maritimes will get what they need and not just moral support. But in addition to cash, the leaders will want a safe railway link. We'll push the issue in London as part of the Confederation package. The western dream will come later. There's ample time for prairie settlement."

"When you get to England, don't overlook pride and vanity," Brydges suggested. "A small gesture can go a long way. Mount Brydges is a tiny community on the Great Western line, but it is named after me. Maybe someday it will grow to a major center. Promise to name some towns after the British gentry—especially those with money to invest. It may be only a whistle stop in the wilderness, but the great lords and ladies may never come to check."

"But if they do, they must find our lines are well built." Macdonald offered a condescending smile. The existing Canadian railroads had been faulted for shoddy construction and a constant stream of accidents.

"Get us the money, and we'll do the proper job." The smile on the railway man's face grew tighter. "But it won't be easy. Everyone will take advantage. I swear, farmers drove worthless old cows onto the track when we opened the Great Western. And when our engines killed them, they sued for compensation. If a poor, dirt farmer can smell the cash, think of what other scoundrels will try."

"But it will be worth the effort." Macdonald rose and swayed slightly. "It's time for bed, and no charge for accommodation, Mr. Brydges. A free night under my roof."

"Hah!" Brydges laughed. "I'm already helping pay for the lease on this house and I provide free political advice. Someday I may expect a reward."

"The pleasure of my company," Macdonald answered and began to extinguish the lamps.

"Uh, Mr. Macdonald?" Forsey rose. "Might I take a lamp? I have a few files in my room that need attention."

"Of course." Macdonald lurched to the stairway. "But don't work too hard."

"No worry on that." Forsey laughed as he began to plot the outline of his chapter on railroads.

• • •

Near Saint John, New Brunswick
March 1866

"Hello, Mr. McReady! Come and meet the next premier of New Brunswick?"

Leonard Tilley smiled and waved from the sleigh. His assistant stepped down and beckoned to the figure beyond a split-rail fence.

"Does it look like I have time to meet anyone?" McReady shouted.

A mixture of snow and mud covered the barnyard and the cow that was lashed to a post. A rope dangled from two tiny legs, a calf reluctant to leave the womb. McReady tugged gently on the legs but with no success. He took a deep breath, wrapping the rope around his body, and pulled much harder. With a burst of blood and mucous, the calf emerged and dropped to the ground. The farmer quickly slipped the rope from the cow, allowing the mother to reach the newborn.

Tilley stepped from the sleigh as the farmer crossed the yard. McReady's hands were covered with blood, but he wiped them on his pants and reached across the fence.

The premier had no choice but to take the hand.

"A safe arrival." He watched as the cow roughly licked the newborn.

"Yeah, been working on her for over an hour." McReady was gruff. "What did you want?"

"There's an election coming," Tilley's assistant explained. "We thought people might like to meet Mr. Tilley, and he could answer any questions."

"Think spring is close?" McReady asked. "That's the most important thing to me. And I'm running low on feed. Do you know where I could get some cheap?"

"Well, no—" Tilley began.

"Then what kind of questions can you answer?"

"He can explain the new Confederation agreement," the assistant interjected again. "You must have some questions about the new country."

"No, not really." McReady turned to watch the cow.

"We're going to build a railroad," Tilley offered, "to connect the Atlantic with places like Montreal and Toronto. Your produce could get to more markets."

"Or other people will ship their goods into my market," McReady retorted. "I don't care for railroads. My granddad built a good stagecoach business and the Saint John-Shediac railway put him out of business."

"Is there anything about Confederation you like?"

"Well, I guess not really. The plan appeals to politicians and not us ordinary folk. I don't see much for farmers, or mechanics, or tradespeople."

"Aren't you concerned about defense? United colonies will be better able to defend your property. The Irish may want this country."

"That might be," McReady agreed. "But take a look around here."

Tilley took note of a ramshackle house and barn and the few cleared acres surrounding the homestead.

"Do you really think the Fenians want this?" the farmer asked.

Tilley knew when he was beaten. He shook the bloody hand once more and returned to the sleigh. His assistant continued an earnest conversation with the farmer.

"You have his vote!" the assistant said, smiling, when he returned to the sleigh.

"What did it take?"

"He wanted twenty dollars, but I got him down to ten. I'll pay him when he votes."

"At least our money woes are past." Tilley's voice grew muffled as he burrowed under a blanket.

"I've telegraphed Macdonald for extra funds, told him every dollar helps, and he's come through on all of our earlier requests. He thinks I made a mistake with the election last year, but when I win next month, he'll eat his words."

XV

T he tinny doorbell announced another customer. A young woman glanced quickly over the gloves near the door before moving to the rear of the store. Two tough-looking men appeared at the front window. One shaded his eyes with his hands to peer through the glass.

"Can I help you?" Sillery Fraser dropped a dustcloth and moved toward the customer. The bell would alert the owner, who expected every shopper to be greeted and pampered with friendly service. Sillery waited a moment, but there was no sound from the rear of the store—the familiar pounding of heavy boots, a sign Donald Smith might come to supervise a sale. After only a few weeks, she had come to loathe the owner and his constant advice on what had been done right or, most often, what had been done wrong.

"No, I'm browsing," the customer replied, lifting a bonnet from a hatbox but glancing back toward the street.

"We have several styles." Sillery pointed to the freshly dusted boxes. "All styles and all prices." She repeated Smith's slogan and tried to decide what the young woman would want. Smith could sense a customer's desires and expected his employees to learn the practice.

"Yes, I see." The woman moved to the brooms propped against a wall and glanced once more toward the door. She shifted behind a display as another of the men peered inside.

"Perhaps you have something in mind?" Sillery asked.

"No, not really." The voice quivered as if she was afraid to say more. Instead, the women bent to silently inspect a package of needles.

The front door opened and banged shut. The customer's hands began to shake.

"What is it?" Sillery whispered. "Are they following you?"

The woman was attractive, in her early twenties, and judging by Smith's rules, well-to-do. Her hands were soft and showed no sign of exposure to heavy work.

"Yes, I think so." The accent gave away her Southern birth.

"I was at Mass and when I left, the men blocked the sidewalk. One of them called me a stinking Catholic and told me the Orange Lodge would be coming for me and my Irish kin. I'm not Irish, but they followed me and kept drawing closer. That's why I came in here."

Sillery felt instant sympathy. The memories flooded back of young, white men insulting blacks on the street in the South. Only weeks ago, it had happened to her if she walked with her daughter. It made her decision easier. Her daughter remained with friends in Charleston, South Carolina, while she began another new life in Canada. Shasta would join her when she was settled.

The former slave had been able to pass for white and told a carefully constructed story of a loving husband, dead of disease while serving with the Union army. And with each telling, she emphasized that he joined to preserve the union and not to encourage black liberty.

"The back door," she told the woman. "Go down the alleyway and make your way to Queen Street. Those hooligans won't see you go."

"Thank you." The woman glanced back toward the front. The men were standing in the doorway and laughing.

"I don't want to involve my husband," she confessed. "He'd want to settle the affair right away, and that could only lead to trouble." She took a deep breath. "I can handle myself in a scrape but I'm going to have a baby and well…"

"Don't worry. I understand." Sillery led her through the stockroom, hoping Smith wouldn't notice.

"My name is Nancy Hines." The woman found her voice. "I thought Toronto was safe but now I'm not sure. The good Father says there have been threats against the church. And he's worried about the Catholic men, too. They may take matters into their own hands. It's not just the Fenian business. There's bad blood between Protestants and Catholics, and it's so sad because we are all Christian."

"There's bad blood everywhere, but you'll be safe now, Mrs. Hines."

Sillery watched until the woman turned the corner onto the main street at the end of the alley.

"Mrs. Fraser."

She hadn't heard Smith approach.

"I don't approve of personal visitors and certainly not visitors who are shown out the back door. That's something I would expect from the shanty Irish or Africans. You will do well to remember that."

• • •

The Thames River, Canada West
March 1866
The steamboat with Owen Wilson aboard left Chatham early on a Sunday morning. The air hinted at spring, and along the bank, the first green shoots had begun to show. The Irish brotherhood had ordered him to survey the western portion of Canada West.

Money was no object, and he had opted to take the steamboat from Chatham to Detroit. The ship moved slowly along the shallow Thames River, through prairie farmland and swamps and passed a country church where rowboats and canoes were pulled unto the bank.

"The faithful will be hearing the good word," a fellow passenger said, edging closer. "The church is called Saint Pierre. The local French cling to their old ways and their old language."

The speaker identified himself as Paul Dalby, a commercial traveler selling hand tools. "I prefer the steamer," he explained. "The train is best for winter, but this time of year with the promise of spring, there's more to see on the water. Did you see that?"

Owen scanned the reeds and grass where Dalby was pointing.

"Muskrat," Dalby announced. "Good eating if they're cleaned right. In fact, nothing like a good feed of rat! Every community has a special delicacy, and I am expected to sample each dish. You don't win business insulting local tastes."

Dalby continued to scan the reeds.

"Someday these swamps will be drained, and it will be excellent land, but today it's easier to trap or to pasture cattle on the high ground. When the river floods, much of this land is under water. It's why the railway line is built so high."

The track of the Great Western was a few hundred yards from the river. Smoke from the tall stack and a telltale stain across the sky signaled the approach of a locomotive. Both men watched as the train moved closer.

"Heard about the Baptiste Creek wreck?" Dalby asked.

"Can't say as I have," Owen replied and waited.

"Happened back in '54. The railway wasn't really completed, but they were running trains, and one was on the wrong track. See that creek? That's where it happened…Baptiste Creek. The wreck took fifty-four souls to their maker."

Dalby turned slightly, and Owen saw what he thought was the sign of the cross.

"Many more injured, of course, and some never recovered."

"Did you know someone?" Owen had noted the change in mood.

"No, but I heard the stories. One of the survivors became a famous general in the American war. It was Meagher, Meagher of the sword and the Irish Brigade. He had been convicted in one of those Irish rebellions but escaped to North America. He was very heroic, pulling people from the wreckage."

"What was he doing up here?" The reference to Meagher peaked Owen's interest.

"Passing through, I guess." Dalby was trying to remember. "No one ever offered an explanation. He didn't stick around because he could have been arrested. The British had a warrant on his head. I suppose he could have been meeting Irish revolutionaries. He was close to our D'Arcy McGee at one point, but they had a falling out. The Irish do fight among themselves."

The river began to bend through a widening swamp.

"Lighthouse Cove is ahead." Dalby pointed to the top of a tower visible above the trees.

"We're about to enter Lake Saint Clair. The Americans burned the first lighthouse during the war of 1812, and the locals fear it could happen again. The Fenian business has people on edge."

• • •

Halifax, Nova Scotia
April 17, 1866
The beat of the drums was growing closer and making it harder to control the legislature at Province House.

"Mr. Speaker." The provincial government leader, Charles Tupper, rose to his feet. "Might I suggest a short adjournment? We could reassemble in an hour."

The members were out the door before the speaker could give his approval.

In the streets, people lined the sidewalks as the British regiments marched toward their warship.

"Every available man," Tupper explained to the clutch of supporters who surrounded him. "The HMS *Duncan* is ready for the troops. The Redcoats should confront the Fenians at Campobello in a matter of hours."

"An impressive site," the member from Pictou said, joining the conversation.

"And three more British men-of-war are on the way. Ten thousand of the local militia have been called to duty, with another two thousand in reserve. The Irish will never know what hit them. I hear there are hundreds of them across the border in Maine… armed, drunk, and ready for a fight, but one look at British steel and they'll fade away."

The long lines of battle-ready Redcoats continued to weave through the streets in a massive show of power.

"And it's a happy coincidence in timing." Tupper's mind remained in the legislature and on the vote supporting the principles of Confederation. "We've delayed until now, but the Fenians help our cause. There's strength in unity. Our union measures will definitely pass the house."

"So we'll finally vote on the Quebec resolutions?" another member asked.

"No." Tupper was emphatic. "Or at least, not yet. The resolution will endorse what I call 'a scheme of union' and leave the door open to negotiate better terms. New Brunswick and Mr. Tilley are on the same course. Joseph Howe and his anticonfederation campaign ruined any chance of immediately passing the Quebec measures, but we'll have union and have it on our terms."

"Mr. Tupper," a member asked as they returned to the legislature. "What will happen if the Fenians defeat our men?"

"Not going to happen! The rabble will run at the first sign of the Redcoats."

XVI

Ottawa, Canada West
April 1866

"This would have been a good site for a fort. Place cannon here and fire right up the river. Turn the other way and rake the town below."

Paul Forsey spun at the sound of the voice. The man must have picked his way silently through the blocks of stone that still littered the construction site of the parliament buildings. The workmen were gone for the day. The new arrival appeared to be in his forties, with a sprinkling of gray through his hair and beard. Steel-gray eyes appraised the clerk.

"And a good location for our quiet meeting." The man stepped forward. "The envelope in your pocket is addressed to Fides. That's me."

"I'll need some identification." Forsey tried to add gravitas to his words and then silently cursed himself. Fides was a secret operative, and no one, not even McMicken or Macdonald, would admit to knowing his background. He was unlikely to confide in a mere clerk and messenger. The envelope contained cash to fuel more secret detective work of the new frontier constabulary. Fides had surfaced in the United States at the height of the scare over Confederate raiders and stayed on to infiltrate the ranks of the Irish republicans.

"Perhaps this will prove my identification." Fides opened his coat to expose a holstered revolver.

"Yes. That will do very nicely."

"I could have approached earlier," Fides said as he sat down on one of the large stone blocks. "Office workers stand out on a building site. It was obvious you wouldn't know a hammer from a saw. The envelope, if you please."

Forsey fumbled and almost dropped the package. He quickly returned the hand to his pocket, hoping Fides didn't notice the shaking.

The detective paid no attention, instead ripping the paper to expose a single sheet and a thick wad of American dollars.

He thumbed through the stack and quickly scanned the note while leaving Forsey to shiver in a cool and pungent breeze. Ice still floated on the Ottawa River. A winter's worth of night soil had been transported from the outhouses across the city. The reek would continue until the ice melted and the human manure sank to the river bottom.

"I'm to go to the Western District," Fides announced and slid the cash into a coat pocket. "Take a message back to Macdonald. Tell him that if the Fenians are going to act, it will be in Canada East, or Canada West or maybe both. They've made a laughing stock of themselves and failed on the East Coast."

"I'd heard they were retreating." Forsey had seen the news reports from the Halifax papers.

Fides quickly corrected him.

"Retreating! Their men never advanced. It was more like a grand skedaddle! First, they were going to invade and then they run. The few hundred that showed up were all cowards."

"I didn't really understand," Forsey confessed. "But you were there. Campobello is just a speck on the map. Who would want it?"

"It was to be a prize, my young friend."

Fides didn't seem to mind the cold or the smell and instead took several deep breaths.

"You should have seen their faces when the British regulars starting pouring off the HMS *Duncan*. The Redcoats were all battle-hardened veterans. One look and the rabble ran."

"But why Campobello?" Forsey persisted.

"If they could control a small territory, they could set up a base for privateers. Imagine a fleet to terrorize the sea routes to the British Isles."

"So is the threat past?" Forsey thought of the months of tension with the rumors of raids, like the frontier attacks and demonstrations predicted for Saint Patrick's Day that never came.

"Don't be in too big a rush." Fides cautioned. "Their organization is split in two factions. One group has taken action and failed. The other is better organized and more dangerous. We hear of caches of arms along the border. We just don't know where or when they might use them."

"But surely we're stronger too," Forsey persisted. "The militia is in better shape than it's been in years."

"If farmers, shopkeepers, and schoolboys can become soldiers. It took years of war to finally turn the Americans into fighting men. The militia here has never heard a shot fired in anger."

"But we have more resources," Forsey reminded him, "and we're bringing the other colonies on side."

"Don't put much faith in the fighting strength of New Brunswick and Nova Scotia," Fides said, laughing. "The vote for union came only when it appeared that the Fenian hordes were at the gate. Besides, how many men would they send and how long would it take them to get here without the railway link? And just watch, Nova Scotia is still waffling."

"But the legislature in Halifax is on side," Forsey told him.

"Don't listen to the legislature," Fides advised. "Not all of the leaders, not all of the best men are in legislatures. The best fighting volunteers in Nova Scotia weren't even British citizens. Did you know that the Southern Confederates were ready to turn out? John Taylor Wood offered to step forward…Wood and a dozen ex-rebels. Those men know how to fight and would have been valuable, but I doubt the legislature will admit they made the offer."

Forsey knew the offer would appear in his inside story of Confederation.

"And does Macdonald know of McGee's latest problem?" Fides asked.

"Yes, the drinking and the money woes."

"Oh, more than that. The man is a target. Killan, the leader of the Fenian operation in the East, used to work with McGee. The men who oppose Canadian Confederation think McGee exaggerated the threat with Killan's help. So no matter what happens in the next few months, McGee is in for trouble,"

"I'll tell them."

Macdonald would be surprised to learn the clerk was able to collect key information and might reward him with a larger role in the ministry.

"Now turn toward the river," Fides ordered. "Spend a few minutes appreciating the scenery. You don't need to see me leave."

• • •

Toronto, Canada West
April 1866
"Why not wait for a few months? We'd all like to go home but not if it means prison." John Breckinridge let the question hang.

"It's my wife," Tom Hines explained. "She had a scare and is frightened. She misses her family and with a baby on the way, she'd like to be where she knows everyone."

"I would advise against it." Breckinridge hoped his tone was close to the old voice of command. His time in Toronto had been spent in what he considered final administrative duties, answering letters and requests for information—a far cry from leading troops or supervising the Confederate war department.

"But more of our prisoners have been released," Hines reminded him. "Sam Davis has arrived. The Yankees didn't press new charges against him and they could have hung him as a spy."

"And we got him to sanctuary in Canada the minute he was released from Fort Warren. His commander at the Andersonville prison camp was hanged. Sam wasn't there long but former prisoners have long memories. The Yankees could still come after Davis. Someone could come forward with more trumped-up evidence of abuse."

"Headley is out," Hines argued.

"But only after weeks in prison," Breckinridge cautioned. "And don't forget the time his new wife spent behind bars. Besides, he's not well known. The newspapers weren't full of stories of him plotting revolution in Chicago. You became famous. And look at Robert Martin. He's still locked away. The Yankees don't know the half of what he was involved in. Let's hope they don't find out!"

Hines twisted in his chair and looked out the window. A teamster was waving his whip over a reluctant team. The wagon had slipped into a mudhole, an early spring hazard on the streets of the Toronto. Summer promised dust and months of inactivity.

"I'm bored," Hines confessed. "You've been kind in instructing us in the law, but I can only study so long. I need to be doing something, to find a job. There's very little money."

"We all have to economize," Breckinridge agreed. "But maybe that's a solution. I'm moving my family to cheaper lodging, a summer house at Niagara-on-the-Lake. We can make the journey across Lake Ontario by boat in only hours. The town is devilishly close to the border with New York State, but British troops guard the river. Bring Mrs. Hines. Bennett Young and Sam Davis will be joining us, and there's an excellent chance we'll see General

Early. Senator James Mason may come. He could teach you a thing or two about diplomacy."

But Hines, he saw, was reluctant. "All right, try this," Breckinridge offered. "Leave the wife with us. She'll be safe. You can mount a scouting expedition to Kentucky and Tennessee. Read the mood before you decide."

Hines began to show more interest.

"We do need to know the true state of affairs in the South," Breckinridge explained. "Look around and report back." Letters were one thing, but Hines was trained to observe. His impressions would be important.

"Nannie would probably enjoy a break from the city," Hines admitted.

"She'll love it," Breckinridge told him. "On the hot summer days, there's a cool breeze from the lake. The town is small, but we'll find something to entertain her. You will consider it, then?"

"There's nothing to consider. I'll go."

"Good! Good!" Breckinridge smiled broadly before he sobered. "We can't be as liberal with the cash as we once were, but you won't have to be a destitute refugee."

"One other question." Hines rose to leave. "Is there any more on Grenfell? He was taken to the Dry Tortugas, but I've heard nothing since."

"His is a difficult case," Breckinridge admitted. "He crossed Edwin Stanton and the American secretary of war has seized more power than he should. The pressure from Grenfell's English relatives and their upper-class connections convinced the Yankees to commute the death sentence, and that, too, upset Stanton. He had Grenfell sent to the New York penitentiary." Breckinridge smiled. "But perhaps he had memories of you and General Morgan escaping a Yankee prison and changed his mind. At any rate, Grenfell was shipped to Fort Jefferson. It's almost inaccessible, miles off the Florida coast, and a frightful climate with the heat. We know he's there but nothing more."

"Is there any chance of release?" Hines asked. "He's an old friend and was with me in Chicago when he was arrested. There was no time to send a warning. I'm not really sure he wanted to be involved. He said he was feeling old and often talked of going home. But I could always count on his advice. Is there any chance the Yankees will have a change of heart?"

"Doubtful," Breckinridge confessed. "The other prisoners at Fort Jefferson were convicted in the Lincoln murder. The Yankees won't give them up even though the testimony against them was mostly a pack of lies. Conover, the man who coached the so-called witnesses, is in prison himself."

"Perhaps there's another way to help Grenfell," Hines suggested. "We should at least get word to him so he knows he is not forgotten."

• • •

The Niagara Peninsula, Canada West
April 1866

Owen Wilson brought the horse to a stop and studied the heights of the Niagara Escarpment, the rocky barrier that rose to dominate the landscape. Guns on the heights could command a clear field of fire. An army on the heights would hold the best defensive position in the region.

He was about to deliver his report to the Fenian commanders and later brief them on what he had found in the last few weeks. His experience with Sherman's army had been put to use in finding the best ground for a camp or for a fortification, a site to use as a base for a lightening raid or to withstand an attack. In his saddlebag were rough maps, but he wondered if anyone would pay attention. The Irish leaders believed that the local population would rise to overthrow the existing government. It might happen, he thought, but it was very doubtful.

Only in Toronto had he found a small pool of rabid Irish intent on delivering their new homeland from British domination. Agitators offered reminders of British rule, the great migration, the need to rid Ireland of oppressors, and the dream of a return to the homeland. But in many cases, the arguments fell on deaf ears.

Only a few appeared ready for action; most offered only half-hearted support.

"Ireland is a hard land," an aging Paddy told him. "We can grow enough to supply a man and perhaps a woman on the little farms but we'd be hard pressed to grow enough to feed a family. But God will supply! Get the English out, and we'll have a go at it. I'd be prepared to go back home."

"There are lots of us," another supporter added, "but more men are finding jobs. They're not as easy to arouse because their lives are settled here. And hundreds more are in the countryside, clearing the bush. A few will join the cause, but the youngsters don't seem to care about the old country."

Flynn had been convinced that Fenian squads were drilling across the province. Owen had found only one. Thirty men practiced a rough march on a muddy field near Maidstone, deep in the Western District. But after half an hour, the majority of the troop slipped away. Their befuddled commander could only shrug and watch them go.

"Find the Irish," Owen had been ordered. "Find our people."

A community on Lake Erie's north shore called Tryconnell, or "Little Ireland," appeared to offer promise. Mills and houses were spread along a road with a sharp descent to the water but a long pier that extended into the lake. The pier, which was built to move wheat to Ohio during the Civil War, could easily handle ships filled with men and equipment.

"But we're different here," a local explained. "Our people come from the North of Ireland. We're British. Our Saint Peter's

Church is Anglican. You may find some Romanists about, but not many Fenians."

A few miles away, a British survey crew marked the outline for a camp of volunteer militia. "We'll be ready if the Irish come," Owen was told.

It was the same story in other towns and cities. A few men were ready to rally to the cause, but thousands simply went on with their lives and hoped for peace.

He expected to find support from the Catholic priests, but the church hierarchy had its own issues with the promise of a secular Irish republic. The church could lose power. Priests read the letters from the bishops and urged their flocks to remain loyal to the crown.

He turned the horse to the west. He would make one more stop. His report could wait a few more hours.

• • •

Hoffman's Tavern, Canada West
April 1866
Erin Brady delivered a special smile to the man who had become a regular customer. He had been coming often, always alone, and always choosing a table in the back corner. His clothing suggested that he was a farmer, but no one could remember seeing him before the last few weeks. His beard was only a few weeks old, she guessed, and light brown but with the first hints of gray. Above the beard, the face was weathered by sun and wind. The slight limp offered evidence of a hard life. His eyes followed her as she returned to the kitchen. Green eyes, she thought, and he's handsome in a rugged sort of way. On a whim, she added an extra portion to his food, straightened her skirt, and smoothed her hair.

"You've come by often. What attracts you?" She set the plate in front of him and then refilled his glass. The alcohol always disappeared quickly but today he picked slowly at his food. The absence of other customers meant there would be time to talk.

A half smile, perhaps a hidden secret, was his first sign of reply. "I'm looking for farm land. The features are not as harsh and rough as in the backcountry. Have you lived here long?"

"Oh no, only a few months. Born in Dublin. My parents had me just before they emigrated."

"So you have family?"

The question was innocent and natural but produced a storm of emotion. She had refused to speak with Eramosa about her past; the painful days as she watched two brothers and her parents die. The Irish disease, the authorities called it, as they set torches to what was deemed a house of pestilence. Cholera would send thousands more of Toronto's poorest to unmarked graves. An aunt had raised Erin for a few years before she too died. By then, she had been old enough to find her own way.

Meeting Eramosa had changed the course of her life. There was an instant of remorse, of guilt, as she smiled at the customer, but she knew that Eramosa wouldn't agree with a young widow pining a life away.

"All gone," she told him, "carried off by the angels."

"I'm sorry." She read the sympathy in his eyes. There was something more as well, something hidden.

"Oh, it's all right. I'm Erin Brady, spinster on the census records."

The half smile changed into a full grin.

"Owen." He seemed to need time to remember his name. "Owen Wilson."

"Well, how ja do, Owen Wilson," she said and extended her hand.

His was rough, calloused. She hoped hers was less raw.

"Can you join me?" He pointed to a chair.

"It's a slow day. I might as well." She primly settled across from him, a position from which she could also see if Mrs. Hoffman returned.

"If you are Irish, you've heard of the Fenians?"

"Oh and they've been by but went away disappointed," she told him. "Serving girls in Toronto may buy the twenty-dollar bonds to finance their cause, but not me. If I had the twenty dollars, I'd spend it another way."

"They plan to invade Canada," he told her.

"Hearsay," she scoffed. "The Americans were supposed to invade and never came."

"So you're not worried?" he asked.

"Why? What would they want with Hoffman's Tavern? Or for that matter, most of the district? There's really nothing of value unless they want to farm. No, if they come, which I doubt, they'd pass right by."

"I hope so, Miss Brady."

She smiled at his politeness and watched as he began to spoon the food from the plate.

"I've been to the states." He looked up briefly. "And I've seen the Fenians. Ex-soldiers are not always polite to a lady. If you hear they are coming...leave."

"I'll consider your advice, Mr. Wilson, but if they come, the British soldiers will turn them back."

"Armies aren't easy to control," he said, trying again.

"And you know from experience?" She wanted to learn more about him and not discuss some foolish Irish experiment.

"Yes, ma'am."

"The American war?" she asked.

"Yes, ma'am. Served under General Sherman in Georgia."

"I noticed the limp. A wound?"

His meal finished, Owen was content to watch as she spoke. Her red hair was pinned back and if loose, it would fall below her shoulders.

"Hah! No." He laughed. "Wrong end of a horse."

"I have to go." She rose abruptly as a rickety buckboard rolled toward the front door. A matronly woman clutched the reins in one hand, a whip in the other.

"But please come again. We'll talk more."

"I'd like that, Miss Brady. I'd like that a lot."

"Come and take a room," she suggested. "We could get to know each other and I could show you the area. Perhaps you would find the ideal farm."

XVII

Quebec City, Canada East
May 1866

"The government, she uses a lot of paper."
The French teamster watched as Forsey closed a packing case, the last of the files to be moved to the new capital. The junior clerk had been summoned back to Quebec City to help with the transfer. Over the coming weeks, the elected representatives and other government workers would begin to move to Ottawa.

"And *sacre bleu*, the bitches are hay-vee!" He grunted, clutching the handles and weaving to the stairway and the half-loaded wagon below.

The papers were sorted into three piles: those that could be destroyed, those that would be needed when the legislature reassembled, and a third and smaller pile destined for his private collection.

C. J. Brydges had arranged a special train to carry the files, a few politicians, and selected staff to the new capital. The railway executive continued to do all in his power to befriend the ministers.

Macdonald hadn't been seen in several days but was to be on the special train. Bernard explained that the attorney general was "indisposed" and that after the events of the last few months, all of the ministers needed rest.

Militia units stationed along the border had finally been sent home. The fears of a Fenian invasion had peaked with Saint Patrick's Day and the defeat of the raid on Campobello, and an uneasy calm had settled over the colonies.

Forsey reread a letter sent from the archbishop of Toronto before moving the envelope to his personal file. The archbishop had offered to cancel the Saint Patrick's Day parade in exchange for the cancellation of the Protestant Orange parade in July. Macdonald had rejected the idea, knowing he would need the Orange vote in Canada West.

"She's 'ot!" The teamster was back.

"Then work faster and get out of the heat," Forsey sneered. "Besides, this is the last set."

"You leave soon?" the teamster asked.

"Yes, tonight. Quebec City will become very quiet. All the federal employees will soon be leaving."

"Oh, we don't worry," the teamster said, smiling. "Me, I can't read but I listen. The new Quebec parliament will be here. No more worries about the English. We will be independent. Our members will think only of Quebec. And they will all speak our language."

Forsey turned to stare. The man was probably right.

The new provincial legislatures would deal with only local matters. Macdonald was still working to ensure that the new federal government would play the dominant role. The French leaders insisted the new arrangements meant that the Quebec legislature could now deal with the issues most important to the Quebecois.

"I take all the cases?" The teamster motioned to the last bag.

"No. I'll take the last one." He ushered the man from the room and gathered the last of his papers. He would have time to see Francine and leave the latest collection. His private files would be safe in Quebec City and well away from any prying eyes.

• • •

Buffalo, New York
May 1866

The appearance of the ramshackle warehouse hadn't changed, but inside, the atmosphere was charged as the Fenian organizers studied the scout's report from Canada West.

"We should have sent an Irishman! Our people probably thought he was a spy and wouldn't tell him anything. Flynn, you should have known better. Don't even bother taking this trash to the leadership. The idiot delved into history. No one cares about Meagher anymore. And, contrary to what he thinks the people will flock to our banner when we invade."

As far as Owen Wilson could determine, the speaker was but one of dozens who claimed a connection to the Fenian leaders. It was obvious his report on Canada West would be disregarded.

Flynn stood and stretched and motioned Wilson to leave the room.

"Nothing we can do," he whispered to Wilson. "But never mind. There's other work for us in the days ahead."

"I did try to find them—" Owen began to speak when they reached the hall.

"Don't matter!" Flynn interrupted. "Remember the US Army. General says the men are there…they must be there! Besides, I wasn't counting on the Canadians. Maybe they'll see the light when our men cross the river."

Owen rubbed his leg. The pain had returned with the wet spring weather, and he was limping badly again.

"So what now?" he asked.

"Weapons and planning," Flynn told him. "Like the old quartermaster corp. Food, ammunition, you name it. We'll be moving material close to Buffalo as the day for the invasion approaches. We have the ammunition. Food won't be an issue. The men can live off the land."

"Don't count on that," Wilson warned. "The farms across the river are small. And the livestock supplies are tight. Cattle and horses were sold to the American army in the last few years. The army offered cash, and any extra stock was sold."

"We'll manage," Flynn told him. "We'll have to."

"How many men?" Wilson asked, thinking of what Sherman's army consumed in a day.

"That's a problem," Flynn admitted. "We aren't sure. There's a little issue with funds. There's no cash to transport the men across the lakes from Chicago, so the regiments are making their way east by train. We'll have more than expected when they arrive in Buffalo, but the more the merrier."

"So the main landings will now be on the Niagara and at Port Stanley?"

"Well," Flynn hesitated, "here, for sure. The leaders aren't quite so sure about landing men under the guns of a fort, especially after hauling the boys across Lake Erie on barges. The men might be seasick and have trouble taking the fort."

"But there's no fort." Wilson's voice rose in frustration. "I told you...it's *Port* not Fort Stanley."

"And I told them," Flynn answered. "But it's like the early days in the Union army. The officers know best. Besides, if there's no money for ships at Chicago, it's unlikely there will be cash for ships or tugs or barges in Cleveland. My guess is we'll see most of the lads' right here."

"When?" Owen asked.

"Couple of weeks." Flynn, as usual, was noncommittal. "So we want you to disappear again. Work your way one last time around the Niagara Peninsula, but pay special attention to the guns of Fort Erie."

"It's a village. There's no fort there, either," Wilson reminded him. "All that's left of the old fort is a pile of rocks, a bunch of debris. The British haven't used it in years."

"I'll tell them, but they want to know what's over there, and you're the best man to find out. Now, get on your way. I have other men coming that need my advice."

• • •

Niagara-on-the-Lake, Canada West
May 29, 1866
"Mr. Breckinridge, a young gentleman to see you."

The maid came with the rental of the house and was feeling her way with the new tenants.

"Who is it?" Breckinridge asked.

The girl was young, probably not much more than twenty, a farm girl, and eager but lacking the experience of a well-trained domestic. The black servants of the past were more reliable.

She waited silently, shifting on her feet until she remembered the rest of the process. "His name is...Haynes." She hesitated. "Young fellow, a little man. He's in a hurry, with his horse all lathered up."

"Thank you, Evelyn, and in the future, the name will be enough. I don't need the description."

Breckinridge had hoped for a quiet morning. The growing Confederate community looked to him for guidance on everything from living arrangements to education for their children. "Show him to the veranda," Breckinridge ordered.

Evelyn made a poorly executed curtsy and dashed from the room.

Breckinridge glanced to his daily journal. Former rebel General Jubal Early was expected for the afternoon. Early had just arrived, and the meeting would last for several hours, so he must make short work of the uninvited guest.

The home, known as the Captain's House, stood on a small rise where the Niagara River flowed into Lake Ontario. The veranda was cool despite the first heat of summer, but best of all for Breckinridge, it was economical. The Confederate funds were quickly disappearing. He found the visitor gazing across the river to the stone ramparts of the American Fort Niagara.

Breckinridge broke into a broad smile when he saw that Haines was Tom Hines.

"The view is better on a day when there is no wind." Breckinridge laughed and pointed to the fort. "When their flag hangs limp."

But Hines had no time for small talk.

"We're leaving," he announced. "Nannie is already packing."

Hines was tense, in marked contrast to his usual behavior.

"Why? What did you find?" Breckinridge sank into a veranda chair and motioned Hines to take another.

"No, I won't stay." Hines began. "First off, the conditions in Kentucky and Tennessee are as expected. The Yankees are doing all they can to make our people uncomfortable, but the worst may be over. The work to rebuild will take years but the job is started, and it's safer there now than in Canada West. That's why I want to get my wife away."

"What do you mean safer?"

"You are sitting beside a powder keg."

"Tom, it's hot air," Breckinridge tried to reassure him. "Colonel Denison of the Canadian militia is by frequently. He says the government spies are thick as fleas in the Fenian organization. Nothing happens without them knowing, and aside from a few parades and speeches, nothing is happening."

Hines shook his head.

"He hasn't seen Nashville. Hundreds of men are ready to move north. This is more than talk! Most are ex-soldiers, some from Meagher's Irish Brigade but a few Confederates, as well. The fellow in charge is a former Union officer, name of John O'Neill. He was an Indian fighter before the war and then led a colored troop. Now, the Yankees used the Negros as cannon fodder, so O'Neill isn't afraid of shedding blood. The second-in-command seems to be a shady Canadian called Henry, or as we learned in those Toronto French classes, *Henri*...Henri Le Caron. This fellow sticks his nose in everywhere and has a reputation as a busy body. Four to five hundred men were ready to board the cars when I left, and more are coming. I can only vouch for what I saw, but there may be thousands on the way."

"Preposterous." Breckinridge pulled himself from his chair. "The American government will stop them. Washington, the army, someone will stop them. President Johnson has enough on its hands without a war with Britain."

"That's another thing," Hines said. "And you would know better than I do, but *President* Johnson," his emphasis was sarcastic, "does come from Tennessee. O'Neill was working as a federal land agent, and you don't get that job without political influence. He probably knows Johnson. Anyway, the men are being told that the Americans will sit back and watch."

"A dangerous game." Breckinridge walked to stare out over the lake. "It really could bring war."

"Those men know how to fight," Hines reminded him. "Once they get a toehold they would be hard to dislodge. And if the US lets them, they can move reinforcements and supplies across the river."

"Denison says there are only a few British regulars on the Niagara Peninsula." Breckinridge was thinking aloud. "Plus some militia. Regular troops would have to be moved from around the province. I'd think twice about fighting British regulars, but trained Americans will roll right over the local militia."

"I have to get Nannie away," Hines told him. "We leave tonight to get clear of the border as fast as possible. If it was just me, I would stay for the fireworks, but with the baby coming…"

"Oh, I understand." Breckinridge began to consider the safety of his own family and the Southern community. "But if we stay quiet, we should be all right, and we're probably safer here than in the cities."

He looked back toward Fort Niagara and the cannons on the walls.

"What did you hear of artillery?"

"Nothing specific," Hines replied, "but the Irish bought surplus rifles from the federals, so they probably have cannon."

Breckinridge had a vision of burning houses and streets filled with frightened refugees.

"We don't know how the Fenian leaders feel about Southerners. They might be happy to turn us over to the Americans. Men like Early, Blackburn, Porterfield and me have a special problem. Our names have been blackened in the last few months. Washington might pay to get us."

Hines weighed the options. "So you either go inland or stay and hope the British can stop them, and I'm sorry but I won't be here to help. I did take the loyalty oath back in Kentucky. And there's an offer of a job. It's not much pay—working for a newspaper—but enough to tide us over until something better turns up."

"Again, I understand," Breckinridge assured him. "If I was you, I would go."

Hines hesitated as he reached the door.

"It was pleasure serving with you, General. Perhaps we can look forward to discussing the finer points of law back in the blue grass…or…if you need me, I can return when Nannie is safe."

"Thank you, Tom. Let's hope that won't be necessary."

As Breckinridge watched Hines ride off, he thought of what must be done.

First, he'd send for Denison and pass the warning to the Canadians.

XVIII

Buffalo, New York
May 30, 1866

T he Fenian camp was a scant hundred yards from the Niagara River. On a normal night, the river road would be quiet. Tonight it was congested, filled with men, creaking wagons, and horses that felt their day's work should be done. Only the river was normal, the current gathering speed before the great fall a few miles downstream. Owen Wilson sat close to the flames, relieved that the night was warm and there was no need for a larger fire. He was to cross with the first wave of the Canadian invasion, one of a dozen advance scouts of an army rumored to be thousands strong.

"You are not Irish?" a voice that obviously was, asked as the speaker stepped into the firelight.

The men called him Sergeant Regan, but there was no sign of rank on the new green blouse or on the battered Union army cap. Only the blouse and the black belt identified him as part of the army of the Irish Republic.

"I'm not sure what I am," Wilson admitted.

A few months ago, it hadn't mattered. The brotherhood provided money and shelter. He felt no patriotic zeal and certainly no keen allegiance to either the British or the Irish. But for first time, a woman made him think of a future that extended beyond the next day. On the last visit to Hoffman's, he prolonged the stay and Erin slipped away to guide him through fields, forest trails, and along the limestone ridge. He didn't speak of his army experience, and she spoke only of the last few months, but a bound was growing.

"You sound like a Northern Yankee," Reagan said, settling down by the fire. "Not a fire-breathing, Negro-loving New Englander, more like a Pennsylvanian or someone from Ohio."

"I was raised in Canada West."

Reagan studied him across the fire. "And you're having second thoughts about going home in company with us. Put it behind ya lad. Too late for second thoughts. Tomorrow or tomorrow night is when we're going."

"That's what everyone thinks," Owen agreed.

"This fight is different." Reagan pulled a cigar from his pocket and lit it from an ember. "The men don't show the emotion as they might before a battle in Virginia. There, we knew we were facing another deadly army. Here, we'll march in and take over."

"Don't count the British out," Owen warned. "The militia may not be up too much, but the regulars know a thing or two."

"Ah, a fight is a fight," Reagan boasted. "A bunch of the British regulars were recruited in Ireland. They may join us. But I've fought Irish, like the boyos on Marye's Heights at Fredericksburg, Confederate Irish, and they whipped us good. But we came back and won the war."

"You were at Fredericksburg?"

"I was there," Reagan said, puffing on the cigar, "with the Irish Brigade. I was one of the few that got away unharmed. Rebel guns were on the heights and the graybacks were sheltered behind a stone wall. And we knew what was coming. But it wasn't like tonight where we see the peaceful candles burning in the windows across the river. The night before Fredericksburg, the undertakers made their rounds. Greedy bastards measured men and took deposits in advance for embalming and caskets. You don't see that here!"

At a nearby fire, an amateur musician blew on a Jew's harp while his companions cleaned and oiled weapons.

"Of course," Reagan continued, "some of this bunch are barely off the boat. Came out during the last year of the war, touched New York City, and were shanghaied into the army. One youngster told me proudly he was given twenty dollars when he signed, but the going rate was seven hundred dollars or more. The rest of the money disappeared in a crimp's pocket. Boy didn't see much fighting but saw a lot of country."

"We all did," Wilson reminded him.

"True enough." Reagan rose.

"I'll check the camp. I have to meet another new officer. He's supposed to be a fighter and a real stickler for discipline. You won't meet him since you and the scouts go over in a few hours."

"We're off on a fool's mission." Wilson made no attempt to hide his contempt. "There aren't enough horses on the other side to mount many men. We may have to seize trains if we want to move inland."

"Don't worry," Reagan reassured him. "If worst comes to worst, we'll march."

Wilson watched him disappear into the night and emerge in the light of the neighboring fire. He turned back to the river and watched more lights begin to glow. With luck, the letter sent to Hoffman's Tavern had arrived, and she had taken his advice to leave.

Two hours later, Sergeant Reagan stood in front of his new commanding officer.

"I'm a late arrival, Sergeant, but don't worry about that. I know a thing or two about fighting."

Levitus Hurley wore a fresh Union-blue tunic, but there was no indication of rank.

"For the record, Sergeant, our leaders consider me a captain, but during the late war, I was a major. I saw action and lots of it. Bull Run, Antietam, Gettysburg. I was in the midst of some of the dirtiest fighting and I learned a few things, and that's why I wanted to see you privately. My actions may be unorthodox, but they work."

Reagan was baffled by the conversation.

"When we form a line of battle," Hurley continued, "designate two men as runners but stay with the front line. The runners will bring messages back to me. I will be in the rear and send my orders forward. You won't have to worry about a lack of instructions because someone was killed and took all the ornate battle plans to hell with him. Do I make myself clear?"

"Perfectly, sir," Reagan answered. He had seen officers blown to bits as they advanced in the front line. Brave men, but perhaps Hurley had the right approach. Too many times the units had fallen into chaos for lack of command.

"And one more thing," Hurley said, rising from behind his desk and walked to a wall map. He pointed to the Canadian shore.

"Once we are across, be very careful. Canadians are a devious lot. Don't trust them. I tracked bounty jumpers, cowardly deserters over there during the war."

"A bad bunch, the bounty crowd," the sergeant agreed. "We kept an eye on bounty men in case they snuck away. We couldn't trust them."

"Precisely, Sergeant!" Hurley smiled. "That's all. You are dismissed."

"Begging your pardon?" Reagan had half-turned toward the door.

"Yes."

"Those bounty jumpers? Did you catch them?"

Again, Hurley smiled.

"A partial success. There was a fire, so it was hard to identify the bodies. But I'm sure I got one and his woman. The other one is probably still hiding somewhere in Canada."

• • •

Ottawa, Canada West
May 30, 1866

"Another telegram from Denison," Forsey said, ripping through the flimsy paper.

"Oh, not again." Bernard's usual calm was wearing thin. "Doesn't the man have anything to do? Does he want new uniforms, repeating rifles, or has he heard an Irish accent?"

Forsey scanned the message.

"He's had a warning from an American. The Fenians are massing in Buffalo and will soon cross the river. He wants the militia assembled and all available troops sent to the Niagara."

"And does he think he is in charge?" Bernard barked. "McMicken sent no warning and he would know. We've just released the last of the militia after the March scare, and the auditor general is raising concerns about questionable spending. No bloody way will Macdonald order them out again because of a vague warning. Besides, we know Denison. I don't think he has an American friend. His friends were Confederate. File it!"

"But what if he's right?"

"Let me remind you that you are only a junior clerk," Bernard snapped, "and with our new government taking shape, we may reassign a few people."

The three hundred and fifty members of the civil service faced an uncertain future. A complete reorganization of existing departments was underway, and positions would have to be found for staff from the Eastern colonies. Jobs would go to those who were best connected, and legislators from Canada East and West would protect their favorites.

"Bernard!" The loud slurred voice sounded from Macdonald's office. "I have a meeting at the Rideau Club and will be out for the rest of the day. This will be a day to celebrate, since both Nova Scotia and New Brunswick have endorsed union. You may tell anyone who asks for me that I am busy... very, very busy."

They heard the sound of a door slamming and footsteps weaving along the corridor. A horse and carriage waited at the entrance to the east block.

"And that's another reason to file it!" Bernard shrugged. "He's in no condition to make decisions. Besides, the warning is from Denison. He's hot air."

• • •

Buffalo, New York
May 30, 1866

The street along the Buffalo waterfront was filled with men, but most were wandering aimlessly. The former Confederate officer in plain clothes blended easily into the crowd.

"Better watch where you are going, my friend," Sam Davis said, steadying a man who backed off the wooden sidewalk into his path.

"Mighty sorry," the man answered as Davis placed a hand on his back. "Lost my balance, but one good turn deserves another."

He worked a small bottle from a pant pocket and held it to his mouth before offering it to Davis. His green blouse was stained. A black hat was pushed back on his head.

"I'm Andy Farrell."

Davis read "horse liniment" on the bottle label and politely declined. Farrell quickly reclaimed the bottle.

"You are not one of us!"

"One of what?"

"A Fenian brother."

"Uh, no. My strength is spent." Davis had a story prepared. "I was wounded during the war and took a bullet in the lung. I tire quickly."

"Ah, my sympathy." Farrell lifted his hat to let the lake breeze flow through long brown hair.

"I was never wounded. That's why I'm here. Well, not to get shot but to see action."

"Where will you find that?" Davis feigned ignorance.

"Why, across the river when we take Canada."

Another new party marched from the depot and whooped as they met long-lost friends.

"Where you from?" Farrell called.

"Cincinnati by way of Cleveland," a man answered.

"Where you going?"

"California," several men replied and roared with laughter.

Davis was mystified, and his face showed it.

Farrell chortled and began to explain. "The authorities aren't quite sure what to make of us, so we've been told to say we're on our way to the gold fields of California, even though our trains are moving in the opposite direction."

"Are they all Union veterans?" Davis noted the prevalence of blue uniforms.

"Mostly." Farrell had the bottle back in his hand. "But a few Southern boys are with us. Good fighters, you know."

"Oh, I'm well aware," Davis agreed. "And all foot soldiers… infantry? Is there artillery or cavalry?"

"Damn. Empty!" Farrell tossed the bottle into a vacant lot. "What was you asking? Oh, guns and horse soldiers? Yeah, well, I seen a few cannon up the street, and Southern cavalry is on the way—the remnants of Jeb Stewart's division or so I hear. But they better hurry or they'll miss the show."

"Farrell!"

Another green blouse appeared close by. "We're going to eat."

"Not without me," he shouted back. "You sure you don't want a drink, mister?"

"No, the doctors say I must abstain." Davis faked a tired smile. "And I'm feeling in need of rest."

"Well, you take care not to excite yourself. Buffalo is safe, but don't cross the river until we have Canada under control."

• • •

Al McGregor

Niagara-on-the-Lake, Canada West
May 31, 1866

"Bloody foolish! What did you expect to accomplish in Buffalo?" The piercing eyes of John Breckinridge showed growing anger.

Sam Davis played with the straw hat to avoid the glare.

"I wanted to see if it was serious."

"You could have been arrested!" Breckinridge stormed. "I've warned you time and again. You could be recognized. Your former commander Henry Wirz was hanged. Andersonville is still a sore point in the North."

"But I wasn't recognized." Davis sounded petulant. "And I'm not in the army anymore. I make my own decisions. I appreciate your concern but I wanted to see for myself."

"My God, man," Breckinridge thundered. "Don't you learn? Didn't that woman who showed up asking questions about her prisoner son have any effect? She seemed to know you were part of the Andersonville camp administration. Do you want another spell in a Yankee prison?"

"I couldn't help her," Davis muttered. "Besides we didn't ask for nationality at Andersonville. The only Canadian I saw was a fellow called Chickamauga, and he was right crazy and maybe wasn't even from here. One fellow that was hung was supposed to Canadian, but the prisoners organized the trial and the hanging. I wasn't involved. Besides, the force in Buffalo is the threat now."

"So what did you see?" an exasperated Breckinridge finally asked.

"Lots of men." Sam Davis gave him a shy smile. "Tough, hard-looking, and drunk, and more in the same condition arriving on every train."

"And the Americans are doing nothing?" Breckinridge asked.

"No and maybe there's nothing to do until the invasion begins. I know I wouldn't want to be a Canadian farmer in the next few days. A few men can strip a farm clean. A few thousand will raise all kinds of hell."

"And the Canadians? What was happening in Fort Erie? Where are their troops?"

"No sign of them," Davis told him, "and business as usual in the town. The Fenians have their eyes on the railroad. Grab the rolling stock at Fort Erie and move the men right up the line."

"And take the canal," Breckinridge said, slipping into military planning. "Seize or destroy the Welland Canal, disrupt the shipping traffic on the Great Lakes and slow any British troop movements. Let's just hope the major cities, Toronto and Hamilton, are better targets than tiny Niagara-on-the-Lake."

"That's what I thought, too—" Davis began.

"Get our people together." Breckinridge was past listening. "We have to watch out for each other."

"Perhaps I should collect Anna—I mean, Miss Mason," Davis suggested. "She and a companion went to the Clifton House at Niagara Falls yesterday. I can bring them back."

"Yes, yes, good idea. But don't go alone." Breckinridge thought for a moment.

"Take Early. He's bored. In the meantime, I'll send another warning to Denison. I hope someone is listening."

XIX

Ottawa, Canada West
May 31, 1866

T he sharp knock and call from a messenger interrupted
Forsey's concentration. He had remained in the office as
other workers departed for the day. On the desk was a list of cabinet ministers who might give him a recommendation and ensure
his survival in the ranks of the employed. He slipped the list into
his pocket before he responded.

"Come!" He tried to sound officious.

"Two more telegrams."

The messenger was hardly more than a boy, but a boy with
connections or he would not have the job.

"Wait outside."

He doubted there would be a reply, but a youngster must
learn patience.

The first envelope warned of three thousand Fenian troops
at Buffalo. Denison was persistent, but it was the type of persis-
tence that made enemies. His very public warnings of the sorry
state of the militia over the past few years had angered both the
military and the politicians.

Forsey opened the second, later telegram, again from
Denison.

"Small boats crossing Niagara River, main force assembled on American shore. Telegraph line from Fort Erie cut."

He read it a second time, trying to decide what to do.

The sound of laughter and singing erupted as the door burst open.

"Burning the midnight oil? Come have a dram." John Macdonald steadied himself in the doorway, and in the shadows was the outline of a woman.

"Mr. Macdonald, you should see these telegrams."

Macdonald snapped his head back, as if the motion would clear the fog, and then grasped the messages.

"Take my new friend, Josephine, to my office," he whispered loudly. "Tell her I've important business but will return directly."

Macdonald was scratching out a note when he returned.

"No time to waste." The speech was less slurred than it had been only moments before.

"We'll call out the militia, every last man. Send a messenger to the governor general and call for Bernard. We'll need him too."

Hewitt Bernard arrived an hour later to find the office in a frenzy. He took one look at Macdonald and the woman before dragging Forsey to the hall.

"You fool! Look what you've done! He's in no condition to make decisions."

"But he is," Forsey countered. "He sobers quickly."

"Look at these orders." Bernard held a list in his hand. "He's called out the regulars and virtually every militia volunteer in the Western District. Units like the Komoka Rifles, the Seaforth Volunteers, and militia units from other tiny villages. Komoka must have all of ten men, and they probably share a rifle. It's silly! But worse, it will end Macdonald's career. His colleagues tolerated the drinking as long as it didn't harm the government, but this is sheer nonsense. If this comes to nothing, Macdonald is done," he said, poking his finger at Forsey, "and you will be too."

Fort Erie, Canada West
June 1, 1866

The sounds of a shunting engine echoed across the rail yard. A trainman stepped from between the cars and waved to his engineer, and the locomotive backed down the track to connect to the last cars for the morning train.

"Some strange men around the yard gate this morning." The conductor shouted to be heard as he climbed into the locomotive.

"Ah, not you too." The engineer tapped the steam gauge and watched the needle bounce. "I've heard enough. Everyone at the boarding house last night was talking about an army poised to attack. Nonsense! And besides, what would they want with a local freight train on the Buffalo and Lake Huron?"

"Those men weren't the usual local gawkers."

"Damn!" The engineer tapped the gauge a second time. "The wood is green. We're slow to build up pressure."

"What else is new?" The conductor settled into his seat. "Green wood, a poorly maintained track, and a rickety bridge before we reach the main line. The railway executives are saving money."

"We only have five cars, so the old wooden bridge will shake, but we'll get across." The engineer hung from the cab and signalled to the brakeman on the caboose, but as he swung back, a metal twang echoed off the locomotive.

"What was that?" The conductor sprang across the cab to peer back down the track. At the same moment, the glass in the window shattered.

"Someone is shooting at us!" he yelled. "Get the hell out of here!"

The engineer released the brakes, and the engine began to crawl forward. "Pressure is still low. This will be a slow run. Take another look behind."

The conductor gingerly stuck his head out the window. "Jesus!" he yelled as another bullet struck the cab. "A hundred yards back there are a bunch of men with rifles."

The engine slowly gained speed, but a hail of bullets forced both men to their knees.

"We'll make speed once we're across the bridge!" the engineer yelled. "And be damned if I'm slowing till we reach Ridgeway. It's only five miles. We can telegraph a warning from there."

"Fenians," the conductor gasped from the floor. "The damn Irish."

• • •

Levitus Hurley swore as distance lengthened between his men and the train.

"Sergeant Reagan! Tell the men to save their ammunition and use it on the British later. That train will carry a warning up the line."

Reagan spoke quietly to the men around him, and the gunfire ended.

"Bring up the kerosene," Hurley ordered. "Soak the bridge and light her up. There will be no more trains to or from Fort Erie."

• • •

Niagara Peninsula, Canada West
June 1, 1866
"Dublin's calling," the rider said, reigning to a stop on the limestone ridge.

"County Cork," Wilson gave the countersign for the scouts.

He was nursing his animal to conserve energy in the unusually hot June air. By contrast, the other scout's horse was almost winded.

"I'm going back with a report for Colonel O'Neill."

Like the horse, the rider appeared to be on his last reserves. "No sign of resistance, but the Redcoats must be close."

"Tell O'Neill, I just left Ridgeway, that little village," Wilson said, pointing. "Troops are coming in by train. No horses, no supplies, no food, but the men appear young and eager. One unit is university cadets, the Queens Own Rifles…some men are dressed in dark-green uniforms; others are in scarlet. Pass on those colors. There may be some confusion with our men."

"I'll tell him," the scout said, pressing the spurs into the horse to produce a grunt and a startled jump. He left a dusty trail in the direction of the main unit where O'Neill's men were already building entrenchments.

Wilson slid from the saddle. A few minutes wouldn't make a difference and horses were hard to find. The British forces might be unprepared for invasion, but local farmers were. In the last few hours, horses and other livestock were driven west or hidden in woodlots and ravines. Any hope for large numbers of mounted cavalry was gone. The men would have to press forward on foot.

As Wilson remounted the horse, he heard a bugle. The British units in Ridgeway were on the move. He turned toward Hoffman's Tavern, as good a place as any to watch the road. He was shocked to find Erin standing by the door.

"What are you doing here?" he demanded, the feeling of dread mixing with the pleasure of seeing her. "Didn't you get my warning?"

"And where was I supposed to go? The Hoffmans have taken all but an old swayback team and left me to watch the building."

"You are going to be in the middle of it. The British will be here within the hour. The Irish are digging in up the road."

For the first time, she began to understand the danger.

"It's too late to leave," he told her. "Is there a cellar, a basement?"

She thought for only a moment. "The Hoffmans don't like to talk about it, but there's a secret room under the tavern. This place was known as a smuggler's nest."

"Let's go." He wrapped the horse's reins around a post and pushed her inside.

"Blankets, food, water," he ordered. "You may be there for a while."

He collected supplies, including several bottles from the well-stocked bar.

"Take these. I'll smash the rest. You don't need a bunch of drunken soldiers tramping about."

"You will stay, too?"

"No. But when the British are by, I'll circle back."

Suddenly she was beside him, pressing her body against his. "Thank you," she whispered, not knowing what else to say.

"Stay quiet," he warned. "Don't come up until it's over."

She pressed her lips against his.

"We should have tried that before," she told him.

A smile was the last she saw as he pushed her below and closed the trap door.

A movement outside caught his attention. The first Redcoat was inching along the dusty road. Owen hurled a chair toward the bar as he dashed from the room, untied the horse, and was aboard in one swift movement. The Redcoat raised his gun, but Wilson was too far away.

• • •

Al McGregor

Lundy's Lane, Canada West
June 1, 1866

The carriage was borrowed from the owner of a local hotel. Southerners were frequent guests, so despite the growing tension, the manager made the vehicle available. Sam Davis worked the team hard to cover the miles and listened to a steady stream of oaths as the carriage rocked over bumps and potholes.

The former Confederate general, Jubal Early, sat beside him. Despite the heat, Early wore a full gray suit and a white-linen duster. He clutched a white slouch hat with a black plume in his hand so he could easily salute any woman who caught his eye.

"Something's doing," Davis offered as the carriage met a line of wagons and carriages moving in the opposite direction. Several of the wagons were piled with household goods and trunks.

"Don't like a retreat," Early told him. "Brings back unpleasant memories. Oh say, ain't she a dandy." The hat rose and fell as a young woman on horseback cantered by.

The drive took four hours. Time enough for Davis to hear of Old Jube's struggle to save the Confederacy, the bid to join General Kirby Smith in Texas and fight on when Lee surrendered, and his disappointment with the conditions in the exile community in Mexico. He heard the general's view on Confederate policies and the high command; and every few minutes, he found himself responding to questions.

"You sweet on this girl? Why else would we be traipsing across country to collect her?"

"I've known Anna—Miss Mason," Davis corrected himself, "for several years. The Yankees grabbed me in February '65 when I was carrying a message between Toronto and Richmond. It was her letters that kept my spirits up when I was in prison. I owe her."

"Young fellow could end up repaying that debt for years and years," Early warned. "Don't get tied down. Marriage changes a man. Look at old Dick Ewell. Hell of a general till he lost a leg.

The new wife comes along and nurses him, but he's no good as a soldier. Wife began to run his life. Now me, I do like the ladies, so me and Miss Julie get along fine without vows and have four children to prove it. Man doesn't need the approval of a parson."

Davis nodded politely. Jubal Early's views on life and marriage weren't about to change. His living arrangements had been the subject of hours of hushed conversations in the officer corps, but his military achievements saved him from serious censure.

"There! This is it," Early said, leaning forward. "The rest house is up the hill. The field will be across the way."

"General," Davis said, knowing that Early preferred the title, "I'm not sure we have time. The Clifton House is still a couple of miles off, and with this commotion, Anna—Miss Mason—will be worried. We should push on."

"God Almighty, she's already got you living under petticoat rules. I'll set you free. We'll stop and inspect this site. I've heard about the War of 1812 and the Battle of Lundy's Lane all my life, and I am not about to pass it by."

"General, we'll find ourselves in another battle if we don't hurry."

"This won't take long. Pull up below the hill and rest the horses. There's an observation tower. Climb up for a bird's-eye view. I want to be at ground level."

Minutes later, the slouch hat and plume bobbed among the gravestones at the top of the hill.

"It's so close to the falls. You can see the mist rising, a pretty spot."

Davis fidgeted and pulled out his watch.

"It's almost eleven. Miss Mason will be worried."

"Let her wait," Early snapped and continued his inspection.

"Good ground. The artillery would be placed here. Of course, the guns weren't up to today's standards but they were capable of cutting a swath. The battle was at night, you know. Men saw by the flash of the guns. It was a nasty little fight with about seventeen hundred casualties."

Early walked slowly along the crest of the hill.

"The American army was wearing gray. Did you know that?"

Davis made a show of looking at his watch.

"Did you know that?"

"No, sir, I did not." Davis returned the watch to his pocket.

"The cadets at West Point wear gray to honor those men," Early continued, "Gray, not blue."

"General, we should be going," Davis tried again.

"I never liked to fight in a cemetery."

Early bent to examine the markings on a gravestone. "But sometimes it had to be done. History is a funny thing, isn't it? And a lot of it is forgotten. We have to make sure the country remembers what we did. The Yankees don't own history. We're got to tell the stories and teach the truth, or the South will be as forgotten as Lundy's Lane."

Early grew more intense as he studied the ground and rested on a gravestone.

"General Winfield Scott was here—'Old fuss and feathers.' He got his baptism of fire in the Niagara campaign; took a bullet and made his career. He died this week. Did you know?"

Davis had no choice. "Yes, General. I do read the papers."

"I never cared for the man," Early continued. "His type convinced me to give up on the army before the war, too much red tape and rules. But just because I didn't like him doesn't mean I didn't respect him. Just like I respected most of the fellows I fought. Phil Sheridan was a ruthless bugger but he could fight. These Fenians tried to recruit him, but it didn't work. Maybe Grant sent him to Texas to keep him away from all this."

Davis watched as the general rose from his perch and took a series of deep breaths. "We should go to pick up the young lady now." Early's mood had changed. "My nose is sensitive. I smell gunpowder. There's fighting, and not that far away."

• • •

Ottawa, Canada West
June 1, 1866

"And the Americans, what are they saying?" The tension was wearing on the chief government clerk. The events of the previous hours had taken a toll. Convinced the invasion was a false alarm, Hewitt Bernard left the office at midnight only to be summoned back upon confirmation of the Fenian landing. His mood darkened more when he learned that the junior clerk was working with the governor general, and he had to wait to hear Forsey describe the events.

"All of official Washington is distracted by the funeral for their General Scott. The Americans have come to love the pomp and circumstance of a state funeral. The British consular officers are being told that no one is available and won't be until the mourning period is complete."

"I can't believe it," Bernard exploded. "Their northern neighbor is being invaded by troops from their soil, and the Americans are doing nothing."

"The governor general is angry," Forsey spoke with an air of authority. "He believes the Americans are waiting to see what happens and will make their choice based on the winner, and uh…" He paused, pretending to reread a line from the proclamation that would be issued within the hour.

"And what?" Bernard asked, trying to be patient.

"Well," Forsey said and then silently counted to five before he continued. "The matter of who is in charge. President Johnson has fired up the radical Republicans to the point where they are threatening to impeach him…that's remove him from office."

"I know what impeach is," Bernard growled.

"Against that sort of background, the politicians are careful of what they do and say. And with millions of Irish votes at stake, nothing will happen until they see how the invasion goes!"

"I can't believe it," Bernard repeated in disgust. "The Americans may think we need a taste of what they went through with the Confederate raids. But this is different. The Confederates used twenty men at Saint Albans. The Fenians have thousands."

"And Monck has to be careful," Forsey continued. "He knows the British don't want to be dragged into a major war. In fact, his proclamation doesn't mention the Americans. It says, *"The soil of Canada has been invaded, not in the practise of legitimate warfare but by a lawless piratical band in defiance of all moral right and in utter disregard of all of the obligations civilization enforces on mankind."*

"See nothing there to excite anyone but a Fenian," Forsey commented.

"Fine words," Bernard agreed but added, "and all we have to do is wave it under the nose of the Irish, and they'll see the error of their ways. A fat chance!"

"What of the cabinet?" Forsey asked. "It met today?" Bernard had attended the meeting while Forsey worked with the governor general.

"Nothing to do but rubber-stamp what Macdonald started," Bernard explained. "Each minister wants extra help for his home region, so they were bickering over where to send the militia. MacDougall was riled. A unit was missed when the orders went out. Denison's cavalry—what's it called? The Governor General's Guard—well, it wasn't activated."

"It was on the list," Forsey stammered. "I'm sure I saw it."

"Perhaps someone removed it; maybe Macdonald. He wouldn't want the gallant commander bathed in glory. At any rate, McDougall railed on about it, and the orders were sent. Denison may be late but he should get there."

"Any other word from Niagara?" Forsey asked.

"All kinds of rumors," Bernard scoffed. "The Welland Canal blocked, and people fleeing the region, but nothing confirmed. I'm not really concerned. The Fenians will turn and run at the sight of the British and probably won't fire a shot."

XX

Ridgeway, Canada West
June 1, 1866

"Colonel O'Neill, your honor, sir." Another courier snapped off a salute. Dust and sweat stained his green blouse. "Dispatches from Buffalo."

John O'Neill fit the image of a fighting colonel. He stood five foot ten before adding the campaign Stetson and stood rigidly erect. For a moment, he ignored the messenger; he was more intent on a smattering of gunfire a few hundred yards down the road.

The British had stumbled into his first set of pickets. The men were to draw back slowly to the main entrenchments, a line of trees and barricades that spread in a half circle on both sides of the road, and with seven hundred rifles poised to fire. The men were quiet, guns loaded, and waiting only for the command.

"I'll take them." O'Neill extended a hand while holding the spyglass to his eyes with the other.

"Nothing in writing," the courier said. "I'm to make a varbelle report—I'm to tell you about it, sir."

O'Neill glanced about. No one else was close.

"Go ahead," he ordered.

"Sir, there's trouble crossing the river. The tug captains are slow-moving buggers and demanding extra money. The only men getting over are on rowboats, so only a few at a time. The main body will be delayed until we get tugs to pull the canal boats."

"And what am I am to do?" O'Neill snapped. "Ask the British to wait? For Christ's sake!"

"I don't know, sir. They didn't say. And oh, the gunship called the *Michigan*, sir, is sitting offshore. But she's not doing anything. She's just floating out there."

"Hah!" O'Neill laughed. "And there she will stay. Andy Johnson is an old friend of mine, and he won't move against us. You know who Andy Johnson is, don't you, Private?"

The courier was dumbfounded. "I knew a Johnson that was a blacksmith, sir, but I don't think his name was Andy."

The colonel fought the urge to laugh. "Don't worry your head about it. Go back and tell them not to worry about the *Michigan*. Tell them to hurry the men across. The British are coming in force. This group down the road is an advance party."

"Yes, sir." The courier turned to go.

"Wait!" O'Neill looked through the spyglass again. "I can see men in kilts, a highland regiment, perhaps two regiments."

He turned back to the courier. "Tell them I am making a stand near the village of Ridgeway. If I have to retreat, I'll regroup at Fort Erie."

"I understand, sir!" The messenger tipped his hat and hurried off.

"Hurley!" O'Neill shouted and motioned to the officer leaning on the edge of the fortification. The captain spit a wad of tobacco juice and sauntered forward.

"Take ten men, move off on the right, and annoy them. When we hear your fire, we'll hit them hard."

"Yes, sir. I'll send the men," Hurley replied. "I'll collect extra ammunition and follow directly."

O'Neill swore softly and stuck his head in Hurley's face. "I was warned about you and the idea of leading from the rear. Go with them."

"Make damn sure he goes," Owen Wilson said, stepping from behind the barricade. He had recognized Hurley only seconds before.

"I don't need orders and suggestions," O'Neill snarled.

"Oh, but you do when dealing with that one. He has a reputation of shooting men in the back and looting bodies. Tell him about Gettysburg, Hurley."

The recognition slowly dawned. Hurley's face contorted with rage. "He's a lying bastard, a deserter. I tracked him into Canada during the war. He and his friends robbed the Union blind."

O'Neill's temper flared. "Fer Christ's sake! I won't have a court martial in the middle of a fight. We'll settle this later. Hurley, see to the men."

"You!" O'Neill pointed at Wilson. "I saw you ride in a few minutes ago. Collect your horse and go around the right side. You can be Hurley's advance scout."

"The man's a murderer—" Wilson began.

"Later!" O'Neill barked. He pointed. "The first of the men are going now. I want you with them."

Wilson swore, but another look at the colonel's face sent him to the horse.

Within minutes, he was with the skirmish line working through the undergrowth.

The whistle of a bullet reached him before the sound of the gun, but he twisted in time to see Hurley aim a second time. He slipped down the side of the horse as the shot whistled by above. A third threw splinters as it glanced off a tree.

Almost by instinct, he felt the revolver in his hand, straightened in the saddle, and wheeled to face Hurley. "Bastard!" he screamed, spurring the horse forward.

He didn't remember pulling the trigger but felt a surge of sweet revenge as the top of Hurley's head exploded.

"Bastard!" He yelled again, urging the horse to stomp on Hurley's jerking body.

"He's killed the captain!" a young soldier shouted, raising his rifle.

Wilson jerked the reins to send the horse into a spin but he felt the sharp sting of a bullet. The pain reinforced his belief that his days with the Fenians were over.

A hundred yards away, a British officer spotted a man on a horse and shouted the warning, "Fenian cavalry!"

The bugler didn't wait for an order. The signal to form square sounded, and the young militiamen dutifully formed in the road to repulse cavalry. They only had time to see a lone horseman fighting to stay on his mount before the square was punctured by a Fenian volley, and men began to sink to the ground.

"Bugler! Sound regroup!" The officer's voice was ragged with frantic breathing.

The bugle notes quavered over the din of the gunfire.

"No, dammit! That's the wrong call! Sound regroup! Not retreat! Regroup!"

But the damage was done.

The British force scattered toward the apparent safety of Ridgeway.

Fenian snipers followed to speed them on their way.

• • •

Hoffman's Tavern, Canada West
June 1, 1866
Erin heard glass smashing and hurried footsteps above her. Minutes later, she heard boots as someone walked through broken glass.

"Buggers tried to destroy the bar, but we're lucky. There's some left." The voice was young; the speaker could be no more than a boy.

"Get your sorry ass out and up the road."

The second voice was older and had an English accent.

"Yes, Sergeant Major." The response was followed by hurried footsteps.

Erin waited, straining for a clue as to what was happening above. A pair of heavy boots moved behind the bar. She could hear doors creak open and knew that the fresh supplies of whiskey had been found. The silence lasted for all of five minutes before the boots made their way back across the room.

She waited another ten minutes before raising the trapdoor just high enough to see that no one was in the room. She waited another five minutes before she emerged.

Smashed bottles littered the bar, and the heavy cabinet where the Hoffmans stored a small collection of expensive whiskey was empty. The glass easily could be swept aside, but the owners would demand an explanation when they returned.

"You shouldn't be here, Miss."

She had been so intent on the wreckage that she hadn't heard the man approach. He stood in the doorway, carried a small black bag, and wore a white apron over his shirt and trousers.

"But since you are here, you can help. I'm Dr. Abbott and I want this room cleaned. Sweep out the glass and pull the tables together. We'll need them for the wounded."

The girl was Irish, he guessed. Red hair tied behind her head and what he assumed was used clothing covered her slim and delicate body. She would be little help in holding a man down but she was all he had.

"Get to it!" He pointed to the broom near the door. "Clean the room! American doctors think soldiers have a better chance of survival when the area is clean. They should be right. They've had lots of experience."

He saw confusion on her face as he reached for an undamaged bottle and pulled the cork. The look turned to amazement when he poured the contents over the top of a table. "Whiskey cleans as well or better than water. The Americans learned that, too, in their war. When you finish sweeping, I want every undamaged bottle lined up on that bar."

He poured another bottle over a tabletop. "What's your name?" he asked.

"Erin Brady."

"Hear that?" he asked as a series of gunshots echoed in the distance.

"I'd have to be deaf not to!"

"When the injured men begin to arrive, keep your mouth shut," he ordered.

"They're fighting the Irish and won't take kindly to that fine Irish lilt."

She bit her lip and began to sweep.

• • •

Later, she pieced together the events of the following hours. The first wounded soldier had been clad in a green wool uniform.

"Fenian?"

Her question was answered with a scowl.

"That's your last question," the doctor told her, cutting the sleeve to reveal spreading blood.

"But no, he's one of ours. Many of the Queens Own Rifles are fitted in green. But it doesn't matter. We'll treat all who come."

Later she remembered British troops marching up the road, the steady chorus of gunfire, and then the stream of wounded men. And it seemed only minutes later, and the British were back—boys, really—only a few in ordered ranks. The majority was disorganized rabble, moving toward the town of Ridgeway.

What she suspected were Fenians arrived next. A few wore green, but most were clad in blue. A few looked inside and quickly moved on.

A Fenian officer finally told them of the skirmish. The British had been routed, but had put up more of a fight than expected. The invaders would regroup at Fort Erie, and any man capable of walking must follow. The remainder would be left to the tender mercy of the British. The doctor and his assistant were free to carry on their work.

It was midafternoon before she was able to leave the makeshift hospital.

The yard was littered with knapsacks, discarded rifles, parts of uniforms, and near the door, a severed arm wrapped in bloody rags. She blotted out the worst of the operations, the screams and moans, but the pile of human debris was something she would never forget.

She had wandered to what was left of the rail fence when she saw him, face down, a stream of red pooling on the ground. Before she saw the face, she knew it was Owen.

"Doctor!"

Her voice broke the silence that fell as the armies separated.

"Here's another one. Come quickly!"

Together, they carried him to the tavern, where the doctor removed the bullet.

"It's not deep," Abbott told her. "But he's weak from loss of blood. If there's no infection, he'll recover. He needs rest. And judging from his clothing, he's not British."

"No," she lied. "I've seen him before. He's a farmer from Port Colborne."

"Well, he can be moved to a British hospital instead of the jail where the Fenian wounded will definitely go. The other British columns should be here soon, along with someone to relieve me. Let them sort it out."

She waited until the doctor collapsed on the Hoffmans' bed before she moved.

She found the horses that the owners had hidden, hitched the animals to a rickety manure wagon, laid blankets on the dirty floorboards, and roused the groggy Owen Wilson.

The roads to the river would be full of armed men, so she pointed the horses away from the Niagara and onto the road leading inland.

• • •

Fort Erie, Canada West
June 2, 1866

Mike Flynn swore as he tripped over a section of broken stone wall. Wilson had been right. The fortifications had been abandoned years earlier, and only a few blocks of stone remained.

The Fenian units clustered by the Niagara River, waiting to make good on O'Neill's threat to turn the ruins of the fort and nearby town into a slaughter pen for the British army, but also waiting for the Irish reinforcements expected from Buffalo within the hour.

"The British are a bundle of nerves," a scout was explaining to O'Neill as Flynn approached. "I drove an old cow up the road, and they shot it. They didn't see me. But the cow is in bovine heaven."

O'Neill was in no mood for humor. "What sort of force is out there?"

The demand brought a hesitant answer. "Well, near as I can tell, militia; but there are a few regulars, and one of the boys overheard them talking about the cavalry. One fellow says trains have been bringing in troops from the West since early this afternoon. I can't give you numbers, but there must be lots of them."

"We'll fight here," O'Neill announced. "We may face thousands, but the seven hundred of us will make them pay for every square inch of ground."

"Excuse me, Colonel." Flynn edged into the glow of the campfire. "I'm Mike Flynn, messenger from our Fenian head center in Buffalo."

"Don't talk to me about Buffalo." O'Neill grabbed Flynn by the collar. "Where are the reinforcements? Where was the help when my men were dying in the streets? We retreated from Ridgeway, and had to fight in Fort Erie. Men were watching from the other side of the river, and not a one lent a hand."

"I don't know about that," Flynn confessed, feeling his jacket tighten at the neck as O'Neill lifted him off his feet. "I was at the headquarters arranging for supplies. I didn't see any fighting."

"Supplies for what?" O'Neill demanded. "Supplies for men who haven't arrived or supplies for the dead men lying on that limestone ridge and around Fort Erie?"

"I'm doing what I'm told," Flynn panted. The pressure was cutting into his throat.

"So what are you being told?" O'Neill released his grip so fast that Flynn teetered for balance.

"Another five hundred men are loaded to cross the river, a couple of canal boats full of reinforcements."

The colonel considered for only a moment. "Too bloody late and too few! Go back and stop them."

"But you wanted men." Flynn was confused. "And more will follow."

"It's too bloody late!" O'Neill repeated. "My men are demoralized. Soldiers are tearing planks from the wharfs and using the lumber to paddle across the river. Many will drown. And I already have scores of dead and wounded."

Flynn offered the theories from headquarters. "Perhaps you should withdraw and regroup on the American side. In a couple of hours the canal boats can be over to pick up the boys."

"Two hours!" O'Neill exploded again. "Our pickets from these country roads can't be recalled in two hours. We'd have to abandon them." He scowled at Flynn. "There may be only twenty or thirty, but at least I know they fight."

"Two hours is what they said," Flynn repeated. "They said, 'Tell him if he's coming back to do so with haste.' Something is going on with the *Michigan*. The Yankees have armed a pair of tugboats that are sitting out on the lake beside her, so my superiors think it best you move under cover of night."

"The Americans will not move against us," O'Neill proclaimed. "I have personal assurances from high-placed friends in Washington."

"Acting awfully strange for friends." Flynn was slowly finding the courage to confront the military commander. "Anyone trying to cross the river is being arrested. That's why more men haven't crossed."

"Ah, shit." O'Neill kicked at the fire, sending a spray of sparks high in the air.

"All right," he gave in. "The ferry dock in two hours. We'll take everyone we can gather. And you!" He glared at Flynn. "Tell them I want a meeting as soon as I'm back."

"Yes, sir!" Flynn moved into the shadows so fast that he stumbled into a scout standing nearby.

"Gilhooly!" O'Neill shouted. "Show this gentleman to the river. He's likely to get lost on his own."

"Gladly."

Flynn felt a rough push from Gilhooly.

"You're a scout?" Flynn asked.

"I am."

"Have you seen Wilson?" Flynn asked.

"I know who you mean," Gilhooly replied as he navigated the ruins. "But I haven't seen him since this morning. But don't worry. He's a Canadian. He'll know his way around. I never understood why he joined us anyway. He certainly didn't care about the cause."

"Yeah, he was drifting," Flynn agreed. "Not like the rest of us. He wasn't ready to lay down his life for Irish freedom." Flynn felt his confidence grow as he heard the lapping of the water and knew safety was a rowboat ride away.

"Still, if you see Wilson," he told Gilhooly, "warn him to come away. With the invasion, he's guilty of treason against the British crown. People are hung for that! I'd look for him myself, but as you heard, I have my orders."

XXI

Goderich, Canada West
June 2, 1866

"Put more muscle in it. Both cannon have to be in place on the cliff. And today, not sometime next week."

The sweating gun crews pushed and strained, and as evidence of the urgency, the captain stepped forward to join the effort.

"That's it, another foot."

The crew pushed forward again and finally collapsed as the guns settled in place.

"Next time, sir, perhaps we could use the horses," a corporal grunted. "I'll catch my breath and go back for the ammunition wagon."

"Good, good!" The captain turned away, quickly lifting a spyglass to scan Lake Huron. A summer mist and fog cut the visibility to only a few hundred yards.

"Captain Barnes, I don't like the looks of this," a private said, pointing up the road to the north. "There's an awful lot of dust from a normally quiet road. Is there any danger the Fenians have landed and flanked us?"

"What? Where?" Barnes swung his glass to where the private pointed. He fought to steady his arms so the men would not realize that he was shaking. Militia units from across the region were on alert after news of the invasion on the Niagara. The tension rose with warnings that a Fenian fleet was off Goderich preparing to open a second front. Through the dust, Barnes was able to glimpse the leading riders and exhaled with relief.

"Not to worry. I recognize the commander. It's the Bruce Regiment out of Kincardine. Our first reinforcements will be here in a matter of minutes."

It was an anxious half hour before the first of the new men reached the cliff top.

"I need twenty men—ten on each side of the guns," Barnes ordered. "If there's an attack, their job will be to protect my gunners."

"And who the hell do you think you are?" the commander of the Bruce volunteers demanded as he ran his eyes across the site. "I'm Captain Bill Caters and I have seniority. My men have been drilling for over a year, unlike this ragtag group. The so-called artillery only began training in March. I rank you."

"Can your men load, aim, and fire these cannon?" Barnes forgot the threat lurking in the mist offshore and turned to the adversary in front of him. The answer was a cold glare. A full minute passed as the citizen soldiers looked on.

"All right," Barnes relented, "but we do need help to protect these guns."

Caters maintained a stony silence.

"All right...sir," Barnes delivered the key word.

"Glad we agree," Caters said, smiling. "Company A to the left, B to the right," he called and watched the men take up positions.

"Follow me," he told Barnes and strolled to a quiet section of the cliff ledge, away from the guns. "Better tell me what's happening."

"Every now and then, the mist thins." Barnes pointed to the lake. "My best lookouts are sure they have seen masts in the fog. We've been warned about a force from Chicago. With a landing here, their army could force their way into the interior of the province."

"Won't it be a surprise when we open up with grapeshot." Caters smiled, thinking of the chaos that the British artillery would cause.

"We don't have grape or shrapnel." The gunner lowered his voice. "All we have are a few balls of round shot. And the guns are old, maybe from the war of '12. The pieces were moved here during the revolution of '37. The locals use them to fire a salute on the queen's birthday."

"But they work?"

"We hope so. I didn't want to waste ammunition so I've ordered a test fire with powder only and—"

Both men froze as a sharp blast interrupted the conversation, and the cannons vanished in a cloud of smoke.

"Accidental fire!" a sergeant screamed, his voice mixing with a louder scream of pain.

A rifleman writhed on the ground behind a smoking cannon, bright scarlet already streaming from his leg.

"Recoil," the sergeant announced, before he bent over the soldier.

The two officers trotted to the scene.

"Damn fool was standing right behind."

"I suppose he had never seen a cannon fire," Caters surmised, the shock already fading.

"Not to worry. Call for Dr. Secord. God knows he's seen his share of blood, what with service with the Confederates in the American war. But let's not waste time. The gun obviously fires. Reload and prepare for action."

"Ships!" A sharp-eyed volunteer pointed to the lake. "I saw two masts."

Barnes quickly ordered the gunners back into position and trained his spyglass on the mist. The screams of the wounded soldier faded as he was carried to the rear.

"I can see the outline of the boat!" Barnes shouted. "Looks like a big one. Load!"

The mist broke momentarily to reveal a ship on course for the harbor mouth.

"Elevate!" Barnes screamed at the crew. He peered through the gunsight as a ship knifed through the outer bands of the fog. In a few seconds, he would have the shot.

"Stop! Wait!" A ragged civilian was running toward them. "She's ours. That's the *Betty Lee*, a fishing boat. She's no Fenian warship."

• • •

"Report!" Captain Caters stood in the doorway of the shack.

A table was surrounded with oil lamps to improve the light for the surgeon, and Caters could see the bloody rags on the floor.

"Enjoy playing soldier, Bill?" The insolent tone of the question shocked the captain.

"I'll have you up on charges, Secord."

"Ah, stuff it." Dr. Solomon Secord shook his head. "I've dealt with officious officers before and I'm not afraid. Besides, this little war appears over. No invasion. No glory for a militia commander."

"The Irish may still come," Caters snapped. "My instructions are to hold this position."

"That's good." Secord smiled. "Goderich is a lovely spot to spend the summer."

"What of the boy?" Caters pointed to the injuried figure on the table. "When can he return to duty?"

"Never," Secord answered quietly. "I was able to save the leg. He'll live but he'll never walk properly again."

"Oh, no." The grim diagnosis transformed Caters. "I know his family."

"Be glad there weren't more hurt."

"Yes, yes," Caters agreed. "And, perhaps I can arrange some form of recognition. A medal, perhaps; maybe a medal for all the volunteers, something struck on the orders of the queen. I can make the recommendation."

"I'm sure that will speed his recovery." Secord shrugged. "I've seen this so many times before. A boy has one day as a soldier. The rest of his life will be spent as a cripple."

$$\bullet \ \bullet \ \bullet$$

The Niagara River, Canada West
June 3, 1866

Both Lake Erie and the Niagara River were calm. Only a few ripples washed against the tugboat and the two scows she pulled.

"Can't you make more speed?" Colonel O'Neill demanded.

The tugboat captain spit before he answered. "No, sir. She's a small tug. She's pulling the weight of seven hundred men and fighting a strong current that flows toward the falls."

"I didn't ask for a lecture on navigation. I need to get to Buffalo fast. We may be able to reload with fresh troops and recapture Fort Erie before the British entrench."

"Doing my best," the captain protested. "I don't have the power that the *Michigan* and those armed tugboats muster. Look at the way they can move through the water. And look, sir, they're coming alongside."

"Finally." O'Neill broke into a smile. "My Washington friends had promised help."

The *Michigan* slowed, but a surge of water from her paddle-wheels lifted the tug and scows. From the wheelhouse, O'Neill saw that the cannons on the gunboat were manned.

"Prepare to be boarded." The order came from the gunboat. "Stop your engines!"

"A damned fool order." The tugboat captain sprang to the wheelhouse door and yelled, "If I stop my engine and can't restart it, we could go over the Niagara Falls. I'll slow but I won't stop."

"Then slow and prepare to be boarded. We have orders to inspect the vessels."

"Inspect? What the hell for?" O'Neill had joined the captain in the doorway.

"For weapons," the officer on the *Michigan* called back. "And evidence that any on board violated American neutrality laws by unlawful excursions into British territory."

· · ·

Ottawa, Canada West
June 5, 1866

"So the *Michigan* comes alongside when they're halfway across the Niagara River and captures the lot of them, all neatly confined on barges."

Paul Forsey adjusted the heating duct to hear the conversation from the adjoining office. Silently, he thanked the designers of the new parliament buildings for the flaws in engineering that allowed him to eavesdrop.

"But we don't know if the captain of the *Michigan* moved on his own initiative or if there was an order from Washington."

The cabinet minister William MacDougall was trying to explain a very confusing situation. "General Grant was in the area, along with General Meade, but the president didn't issue his official order to restrain the Fenians until after the weekend. At any rate, the bulk of the raiders are in American custody."

"And what about the prisoners we took?" Georges Cartier asked, the high-pitched voice carrying easily through the ductwork.

"We have about a hundred," McDougall told him, "and there are a few more to round up. Denison captured a handful around Fort Erie, mostly stragglers and men lost or drunk. Their main force is still encamped near Buffalo."

"No, no!" Cartier harshly corrected him. "I am sure the main force is along the Saint Lawrence. The Irish are gathering in Saint Albans, so that miserable little town is afflicting us again. First, there was the raid during the American war and now this. My people in Montreal say the Irish army is gathering on the border, and even if it's not true, it is the way we must tell it. Better that everyone feels threatened in both provinces. Fear will benefit our work and bring new unity for the Confederation movement."

Forsey smiled to himself. Cartier was showing the qualities that had made him a powerhouse in Quebec.

"Where is Henri Le Caron?" MacDougall asked. "He infiltrated O'Neill's inner circle but sent no warning."

Forsey scratched out the name "Le Caron" as he listened. He knew someone was relaying messages from inside the Fenian organization.

"How can you trust paid spies?" Cartier was asking. "Choose men with pride, a deep sense of nation, not those who spy for money. I learned that during the rebellion. Trust those with the strongest convictions, not those who are most hungry."

Forsey scratched furiously to get every word.

Cartier rarely spoke of his involvement in the revolution in Lower Canada in 1837, the charges laid against him, or his escape to the United States. The minister's modern-day French opponents claimed that he was a less of a patriot than popular legend suggested.

"We'll take any information we get," MacDougall said. "McMicken's men are hungry and warned us in the past. We know that only a few insurgents will cause no end of trouble, so we have to root out the hidden supporters. Put them all on trial along with those captured on the Niagara. Hang them and be through with it."

"Review your history," Cartier cautioned. "Look at the hangings in Canada West after the '37 revolt. What was accomplished? Put the raiders in prison. Or better yet, banish them. But don't create martyrs."

Forsey could sense MacDougall's anger and could image his scowling face.

"Don't go soft, Georges! No weak-kneed crying over legal rights. I admit the timing is dreadful. We meet for the first time in the new parliament buildings, and instead of enjoying the surroundings, we have to deal with this."

"You misunderstand," Cartier interrupted. "I just want to be sure everything is done properly."

"And it will be!" MacDougall grew calmer. "Besides, we've another issue with our militia. Seven are dead on the Niagara, and several of the wounded won't survive. Denison says the troops had no food, no shelter, and their commander had led troops on parade but had no battle experience. On top of that, many soldiers had never exercised with live ammunition. When this comes out, there will be hell to pay!"

"Order an inquiry," Cartier suggested. "Those things take time. Delay until the shock wears off."

"We're considering that," MacDougall agreed.

"Macdonald might not like it," Cartier interjected. "Remember, he's had control of the militia portfolio. An inquiry could reflect badly on him."

And on Georges Cartier, Forsey thought. Cartier had held similar responsibilities in Canada East.

And Macdonald has enough trouble," Cartier warned.

"No one cares about the woman on the night of the invasion, but he was drunk. Imagine the uproar, a minister too far gone to perform his duties."

"The clerk says he sobered quickly." MacDougall's observation froze Forsey's pen.

"And who listens to a junior clerk?" Cartier asked. "Hewitt Bernard thought Macdonald was too far gone and stepped in to cover mistakes."

"Bernard will stay quiet," MacDougall replied. "We'll have to hope the young clerk keeps his mouth shut."

Forsey felt the pen slipping through his clammy fingers.

"If not, he could be transferred to the Selkirk Settlement. A few years in the back country or the prairies would do him good…if the little bugger didn't quit first."

Forsey imagined himself in a drafty, log hut counting beaver pelts.

"Let's wait," Cartier urged. "See if it blows over."

"You may be right. Besides, there's other work to do," MacDougall agreed. "All of Canada West is on edge, and we're already receiving claims for compensation. Look at this one."

Forsey could hear the papers rustling in the office before MacDougall resumed.

"A Niagara tavern owner claims the Irish maid, obviously a Fenian sympathizer, destroyed the liquor supply, stole a team of horses, and made off with a manure wagon."

"Why would anyone take a manure wagon?" Cartier scoffed. "As to the liquor…she drank it! It's the sort of thing we'll have to deal with eventually, but for now, keep the attention on those who died. Turn them into heroes. Deal with what went wrong later when the passions have cooled."

• • •

Saint Albans, Vermont
June 5, 1866
American troops met the train in Saint Albans, and the latest Fenian arrivals were herded to where several hundred compatriots already waited.

"This here is Saint Albans?" a young soldier asked a mounted officer.

"Yeah, you came to the right place."

The soldier cast his eyes along what appeared to be a prosperous main street. A few figures in green were making their way toward the depot, but the town appeared tranquil.

"I heard the Confederates burned this town during the war, but it looks fine."

"Nah, the rebels robbed the banks, but the fires burned out."

"So, what are you doing here?" the Fenian asked.

"Making sure you don't burn anything on either side of the border." He raised his hand and pointed across the railway yard to where a Union captain stood.

"Men of the Fenian brotherhood!" the captain yelled, appealing for quiet. "Under orders of the United States government, you are to return to your homes. The government will provide the train fare. The attempt to cross the Canadian border at Pigeon Hill was a complete failure and General Sweeney has been arrested by the US Army. Go home. This adventure is over!"

XXII

Toronto, Canada West
June 6, 1866

The church bells began to toll, joining muffled drums and a slow dirge from a military band. Yet another funeral procession was on the way.

Toronto entered deep mourning when the steamer carrying the dead and wounded from the battle on the Ridgeway appeared in the lake mist off the Yonge Street wharf.

Donald Smith took the unusual step of closing his shop for a day, a reluctant decision, but one forced upon him by other store owners. It would be a proper sign of respect, they argued, and Smith was nothing if not proper.

Today, however, the store reopened. Business was business, and Smith was determined to wring out every last sale. Rolls of black crepe were displayed in the front window, a sign of mourning and a reminder that the cloth was available for sale. He would summon his employees to the sidewalk at the proper moment so that little time was lost.

Sillery Fraser worked from a desk at the rear of the store. For her, the recent processions rekindled memories of Richmond. The same mournful music, the same sad parade of officers and men; but in the days of the Confederacy, the processions had come daily—sometimes several times a day—for months and then for years. In the morning mail, she saw the familiar handwriting of her friend in South Carolina. It would be news of her daughter, who was now approaching seven, and based on the earlier letters, becoming a proper young lady. She corrected herself as she tore at the envelope. Shasta would be a proper young *black* lady. Her teacher at the African school described her as bright and intelligent. Someday soon, she would join her mother. But not until Sillery was more secure.

The bells from a nearby church began to toll as the funeral cortege drew closer. She heard Smith call for the staff to assemble. She should read the message later but decided to sample the news immediately. The single-page letter was only ten days old.

Donald Smith planned to be the last to leave the store. He would stand in the doorway in case anyone tried to slip inside and pilfer stock. His appearance with the shop girls lined in front of him would also convey the image of a prosperous Toronto merchant.

The hearse was a few hundred feet away when he realized someone was missing. After a quick survey of the staff, he stomped back into the store.

"Mrs. Fraser?"

She sat at the desk with tears coursing down her face.

"Oh, for heaven's sake." He roughly forced her to her feet. "Get a grip, woman! We all feel bad for the young men of the Queen's Own, but let's not have a female outburst. Come on. Straighten up and out on the street with the rest of the girls."

He pushed her as he would a window manikin until she joined the other staff.

"Now buck up," he whispered fiercely. "This will be over soon."

The band marching in slow time led the procession, followed by the hearse and ranks of young soldiers.

"Another of the wounded died last night." The hardware-store owner slipped onto the step and whispered to Smith. "Who knows how long this might go on? Only a few minutes ago, a cousin told me of an invasion at Windsor. I don't know what to believe anymore."

Smith gave him a glance that suggested silence was appropriate.

Mrs. Fraser, he saw, almost collapsed as the coffin passed. Only the strong arms of a fellow worker kept her from falling.

The sound of the church bells, the drums, and the measured beat of the passing troops mixed with the sobs of those lining the street. The procession was a half-mile long with troops, family, civic dignitaries, police, and firemen all paying homage to the latest victim of the Irish menace.

Smith decided he had seen enough when representatives of local clubs began to appear. He could dispatch the mail as the final units passed the store.

The letter was face up on the stack. The handwriting was poor but legible, and the envelope addressed to a *Miss* Sillery Fraser. He read the lines slowly. The woman had lied. She was unmarried and had a child. The letter explained how the girl had stepped into the street in front of a runaway horse. Death had come a few hours later. "She's in a better place," the letter writer concluded. "There ain't much future for a black child in these times."

He heard Sillery sob as the staff members brought her back into the store.

"Mrs. Fraser, I will see you!"

He had once thought her pretty, well mannered, a woman who could climb in society.

"You lied!" He waved the letter in the air. "You claim to be a widow. The letter is addressed to "Miss."

She lifted her head to stare and try to comprehend.

"You had a child. A black child! Are you a victim of rape?"

A gasp came from the other staff, but there was no response from the woman.

"Did you lie freely with a black man, outside of marriage, and outside of race?"

The tears ran down her face as she braced against the desk for support.

"Are you a harlot?" he demanded.

She was silent for only a moment.

"No!" she screamed, her grief mixed with anger. "I am a free woman of color!"

Smith stared in shock, and for the first time understood the ivory hue of her skin.

"You are dismissed!" he hissed. "Go now. Your final payment will be sent to your lodging. Get out of my sight."

• • •

Brantford, Canada West
June 1866

"I have a team," Erin Brady said, bartering with the owner of a livery stable, "but a single horse and a small buggy would be better. Maybe we could trade?"

She had left Wilson resting at a campsite near the Grand River. He was too weak from loss of blood for heavy work. The team of sway-backed horses taken from the Hoffman Tavern wore down quickly, and needed rest, and the axle in the old wagon had bounced over its final rock and collapsed.

"What kind of horses?" the stable owner asked. "Heavy horses might fetch a good price. The army is buying up anything it can lay hands on. But don't think a woman can deal with the Redcoats. Better to deal with me. And see that?" He pointed to a small buggy with a fraying leather cover. "Take that and the little mare out back. Treat her right, and she'll carry you for many miles."

Erin knew that he would have the best of the deal but she couldn't wait. The sooner they were on the road, the better.

"Which way you going?" the livery stable owner asked.

"West." If she could reach Chatham, Amos Baker could guide them to the safety of Michigan.

"Troubled country," he warned. "Great Western has been running extra trains for the last few days and all packed with troops. The Irish have their eyes on Windsor. Hell, you may drive right into a battle."

He pulled a long blade of grass from the haystack near the door and picked at his teeth.

"Course, there's also trouble in the East. The prisoners in our jail were all sent to Toronto yesterday. No chance of escape, because our soldiers lined the street from the jail to the depot. The prisoners didn't look like much. Good strong rope will do away with the lot."

He thought he saw the woman shudder.

"Feeling all right?"

He wasn't about proposition a sick woman.

"A chill," she told him. "The nights are cool."

"Woman on her own needs a roof over her head. I could let you stay here for a couple of days." There was a long pause. "Let's say, for the right kind of payment."

"This woman prefers cash money."

The answer surprised and encouraged him. "Might have that, too." His voice quivered with anticipation.

"When I bring the horses later today." She forced a smile. "Have that buggy greased."

She returned several hours later leading the team, expertly examined the buggy and the harness, and carefully inspected the feet of the mare.

"Guess we've got a deal. Now let's go inside and consider the other matter."

"Good idea." He had washed and doused himself with cologne.

"And don't you smell nice." She smiled as they approached the tiny room that served as office and living quarters. "But I'll need to see cash first."

Her hand lightly skipped across his crotch.

"Yeah, sure!" He stepped stiffly to a small desk, opened a drawer, considered for a moment, and withdrew a handful of coins. "That should get us started."

She glanced quickly at the cash.

"It certainly should." She began to loosen the neckline of her dress. "Come closer. You'll want to see this."

She felt his hot breath and squirmed to loosen the fabric while he fumbled with his belt. The trousers slipped to the floor around his boots.

In one gentle movement, she pressed against him and then raised her knee to smash hard against his groin.

"Son of a bitch!" he groaned, staggering. He tripped on his trousers and fell heavily, losing consciousness as his head slammed sharply against the rough, wood floor. He didn't hear her move to the drawer, open the small metal case, whistle, or empty the contents into a feedbag.

● ● ●

"I have a bit of money," she told Owen two nights later, as she explained the decision to take a room in a country inn. In the morning, she planned to trade the horse and buggy for another wagon and team.

"Best we continue north," she suggested.

Erin sat cross-legged on the end of the bed, a newspaper spread in front of her. An item on the robbery of a Brantford horse dealer told of an innocent man attacked and beaten by a red-haired Irish woman, who then stole a horse and buggy.

"The papers say the whole province is on the lookout for Fenian sympathizers," she told him. "But perhaps no one will notice a couple looking for their first home."

"So we're a couple now?" Owen laughed. "Well, why not give it try!"

He crossed the room to stretch on the bed beside her.

"For a while," she told him. "I have enough money to buy land. You can work to pay for half. Let's see how it works."

"Why wouldn't it work?" he asked.

"Because people change," she told him.

The last rays of the sun found a break in the clouds and streamed into the room to bathe her in the soft golden light.

"We both know that. We've seen what can happen. We have to take what we can now. The future is too uncertain."

XXIII

Ottawa, Canada West
June 1866

The legislators were barely in place when an opposition member sprang to his feet.

"Mr. Speaker. It is an honor to rise for the first time in our new parliamentary chamber. My congratulations to all involved in the construction. But Mr. Speaker, we live in dangerous times. Can the attorney general Canada West tell us how many raiders are in custody?"

John A. Macdonald made a show of slowly rising to his feet.

"Mr. Speaker, I too wish to congratulate the contractors. As to the question...No, I won't."

The legislature erupted in a chorus of boos and cheers.

Macdonald leaned toward D'Arcy McGee and winked. "New house, same old rabble!"

"Mr. Speaker," the opposition member tried again. "Will the house be asked to endorse a motion to suspend the right of habeas corpus? And if so, how can the attorney general defend an attack on fundamental rights? Will our people face prison without knowing the charge against them?"

Again, Macdonald made a show of rising slowly.

"Mr. Speaker, the honorable member will be asked to approve the suspension within the hour. We are under attack. Our brave men shed blood on the Ridgeway in Canada West and repulsed the invader at Pigeon Hill in Canada East, but an enemy lurks inside and outside our borders. This government is in good company revoking habeas corpus. The British suspended the writ last year to pursue Irish rebels. The late President Lincoln took the same action during the American war. Why, even Jeff Davis did it."

Macdonald's supporters thumped their desks.

"Mr. Speaker!" Another opposition member was on his feet. "We are all aware of the member from Kingston and his political tricks. Is he inflating the risk to pump new life into the Confederation scheme? Has he now found a way to frighten the population to support his notorious plans?"

Macdonald sat quietly as the house erupted. He waited a full minute before he responded.

"Confederation will go forward. Nova Scotia and New Brunswick have accepted the principles of union. The representatives from the Maritimes will join us in London, come fall. As to frightening the population...I will not dignify the question with an answer."

• • •

Ottawa, Canada West
June 1866
Lieutenant Geoffrey Ralston fought to keep a straight face as he watched the squad drilling on the grounds of the parliament buildings. Only the matching blue tunics and pillbox hats offered any hint of a cohesive unit. The Civil Service Rifles were drawn from the ranks of government clerks. No one had bothered to match the men by height or build, and the ranks had all the uniformity of the neighboring Gatineau Hills. The short, tall, fat, thin, and bespectacled were in training to defend their country and to impress their political masters. The ranks seethed with whispers of invading armies and the coming decision on who would stay with the federal

public service and who might be demoted to the lesser provincial governments.

"Dismissed," the senior deputy minister croaked. He cleared his throat and added, "It's coming nicely. Everyone was in step this morning."

Ralston made his way across the lawn. The grounds were littered with construction debris as workers applied the finishing touches to the exterior. He crept up behind a trooper.

"Forsey," he hissed.

The rifle shot out of the clerk's grip to bounce on the ground.

"Christ!" Forsey spun to face the red uniform and froze before recognizing his friend.

"Ralston, you took me by surprise." He retrieved the rifle but almost nicked another trainee with the bayonet.

"Be careful with that," Ralston cautioned. "One of the Fenian raiders dropped a gun. It went off and killed a companion."

"No worry there. We have no ammunition. We haven't reached live fire drill."

He saw the telling smirk on Ralston's face.

"But probably next week. We've only been drilling for a few days."

"Ah…Ottawa will be protected." Ralston smiled. "The infidel hordes will be hard-pressed to seize this capital."

The clerk gingerly removed the bayonet from the gun and fumbled to return it to the sheath.

"Here, hold this," he said, thrusting the rifle at Ralston. He then used both hands, one to hold the sheath and the other to insert the bayonet.

"What brings you to Ottawa?" His eyes darted about to ensure that other clerks were returning to their offices.

"Had a dispatch for Monck," Ralston answered. "Can you get away for an hour? We should catch up."

"No. Picket duty. Join me. I'm posted to the rear of the center block to watch the river. It's not onerous duty but it is important."

They walked unhurried to the outlook above the Ottawa River as Forsey loosened the tight buttons on his uniform. "Monck comes down each morning by boat." He pointed in the direction of the governor general's new residence.

"A full crew of oarsmen, British sailors, row him from the residence at Rideau Gate. It looks very regal, and the sailors are well trained in case anyone tries to do him harm."

"It's a waste of manpower," Ralston told him. "And he may not have that crew for long. We'll need every sailor if new gunboats are fitted out for the Great Lakes."

"I'm sure Monck will give them up. He's that sort." Forsey tried to sound nonchalant. "I've been working with him more lately. Besides, when the Civil Service Rifles are fully drilled, we can protect the capital."

"That will be a relief to the empire." The sarcasm was lost on the clerk.

"Have you heard of the plot to blow up the parliament buildings?" Forsey asked. "The constables were searching for dynamite down in the bowels of the place. Just imagine. Millions of dollars spent on these buildings and up they go in a puff of smoke. I suppose if they found any explosives, it would be hushed up and kept from all but a few of us."

He turned to scan the river to the north. "We don't know how they might come. A lot of Irish settlers have moved into the Ottawa Valley. An assault down the river would be an unpleasant surprise. We'd know if they were coming from Montreal or up the Rideau Canal, or raiders could already be here hiding among the Irish in the city. You never know."

"So the capital is on the verge of panic," Ralston surmised.

"Well, it is a symbolic target and the seat of government, at least for now."

"And what does 'for now' mean?" Ralston asked. "The new parliament buildings are barely christened."

"The buildings are magnificent; great, imposing structures." Forsey turned away to study a rowboat emerging from the mouth of the Gatineau River and exhaled with relief when two men dropped fishing lines.

"The building will be fine, if the heat and gas works are ever completed, but the rest of Ottawa is a mess. Sawmills and wood shavings, no sewers, open drains, and the water supply is questionable. We buy water in barrels and pails and don't know where the suppliers find it. In fact, I don't want to know."

Despite their solitude, he dropped his voice and leaned closer to Ralston.

"The governor general fears the capital may have to be moved. He doesn't think the proper sort will spend the political season here. He and his family aren't happy about the new residence. The building is certainly not as grand as what they're used to."

Forsey lifted the rifle to his shoulder, swung the weapon slowly around the grounds, but saw only a few workers struggling with a load of supplies.

"All of the government employees are renting accommodations. Building lots are for sale, at good locations, but no one wants to risk the money if the government is going to move."

"You can't be serious." Ralston was shocked. "After all the time and money spent on construction and in a good strong location that even the Civil Service Rifles could defend."

"I'm just telling you what I hear," Forsey explained patiently. "Not everyone has the access to information that I do."

"But what does that say about the new Confederation? Have those plans gone bust?"

"No, but they are seriously delayed."

An approaching steamboat from Montreal caught the clerk's eye. "Do you think the military has extra spyglasses? I could use a set."

"The proper requisition would produce the equipment," Ralston assured him.

Forsey trained his eyes on the steamer. Women milled about on deck, preparing to disembark, but who knew what might be lurking behind the cabin doors?

"The Fenians won't give up," Ralston agreed. "Their organization is wracked by internal dissent, but more raids are possible."

"We live in uncertain times," Forsey said. "Volunteers on one of our ships almost fired on an American vessel on Lake Erie. Some one thought the Irish had seized the boat. One accidental shot and we could have been at war with the Americans."

"And that's why trained people need to take over. Actual British crews will replace the volunteers on the lakes. The first men are already en route to Windsor, and later, gunboats should police the lakes and the Saint Lawrence."

The steamer reached the dock, and the women stepped off with no sign of raiders.

"Well, that's a relief." Forsey began to relax. "But we'll continue to train. The citizen militia saved the colonies in 1812—stood up to the Yankees and gave them what for."

"General Brock and the British regulars were there, too," Ralston reminded him.

"Oh, they helped, I suppose," Forsey grudgingly admitted. "But we may think too much of British legends. We need our own symbols and our own stories. The children of the future will learn how the citizen militia turned out to repulse the Irish armies. This won't be forgotten. Macdonald and Cartier believe it will draw the colonies together."

"Well, some good has come from it then. The new Canadian history will probably overlook a lack of supplies, poorly trained militia, and inept officers."

Forsey didn't seem to hear and turned his attention back to the river.

"I have other news," Ralston continued. "I'm resigning my commission. Francine and I will be married. Her family need

English blood if their business is to grow outside of Quebec. I'm the chosen vessel."

"Congratulations, I guess. I always liked her." Forsey blushed as he thought of her lithe figure. "But I didn't think you were serious about leaving the army."

"I want to be with Francine. And I have no desire to see the empire, to trudge across India or Afghanistan. I like what I have here."

"Yes, that's really good news." Forsey wasn't sure he understood or cared. Women were pleasant company but shouldn't stand in the way of a career. Instead, he asked, "Did she say whether she has been receiving my packages?"

"She did," Ralston replied. "She says she's filled a second trunk. What is that about?"

"Oh, old files; keepsakes, I suppose. Look, I'll keep my ears open in case there are any positions in the Canadian militia. An army veteran like you could help with training. You never know what I might hear."

• • •

Halifax, Nova Scotia
June 1866

"So the fat's in the fire!"

Joseph Howe watched as the printer at the *Chronicle* arranged type for the morning paper. The telegraphic dispatches on the invasion and repulse at the Ridgeway would be the major story.

"What you print will go into history," Howe sighed. "Blood has been spilled. Macdonald will use this to his advantage. He will say it shows how we need a strong defense and united colonies? The sacrifices must not be in vain! You watch the way he plays it."

"Not much two men in Halifax can do about it, then," the printer murmured.

"Don't count us out," Howe spat.

"The earlier scare at Campobello convinced New Brunswick to support Tilley and the union. Dr. Tupper used the same tactic to win the support of those cowardly devils at the Nova Scotia legislature. But what's happened since? If an election were held today, Tupper would be beaten. We have thousands of names on the anti-confederation petitions. Great Britain can't ignore us. Macdonald and the Upper Canadians think we are beaten. It's not so!"

"So off to London, are you?" the printer asked. Typesetting was easier when there was less pacing and shouting.

"Very soon," Howe told him. "I have friends in the imperial circle who will listen. The Canadians are delaying. They blame the unrest, but there is more. The brilliant minds of Ottawa have no final agreement. There is too much unfinished business. Newfoundland dropped out, fearing the loss of local control. Prince Edward Island couldn't get the financial package it demanded and walked away. The foreign office may be on Macdonald's side with his grand Confederation scheme, but we'll see if they feel that way after I've had a go at them."

XXIV

Jones Falls, Canada West
August 1866

"About ten minutes, Mr. Macdonald," a canal worker called. The water was rising to lift the steamboat for the next stage of the voyage up the Rideau Canal. Macdonald had jumped from the vessel as the locking process began and spent the time happily conversing with the lockmaster and his wife.

"Old friends?" D'Arcy McGee asked as Macdonald returned.

"I like to chat as I'm passing through. It never hurts to meet a voter."

"And what could you offer today?" McGee watched as the crew hauled the ropes to keep the boat snug to the limestone wall.

"Reassurance," Macdonald said softly. "The sight of British soldiers has disturbed the quiet of the Rideau lakes. The lock-master's wife had heard of a plot to blow up the canal and now knows it was nothing but another wild rumor."

On the edge of the lock, a worker began to crank the gates open. The captain ordered a blast of the whistle, and the vessel moved toward open water. McGee and Macdonald stood by the railing.

"So here, too." McGee sighed. "Miles from anywhere, but the fright continues. We have to collar the leaders. Ordinary Irish want nothing to do with this. The men captured on the Niagara were led astray. I would swear to it."

"I once helped put down a revolution," Macdonald reminisced. "All the young men joined the Kingston militia in '37, but I kept getting the sword caught between my legs."

McGee shared the laughter, but Macdonald grew serious as other memories returned. "Nicolas Von Schoultz was the leader of that misguided American adventure. He, too, expected the local population would rise to revolution. But I doubt our present-day felons have his courage. He was prepared to shoulder the responsibility and he hung for it."

"I'm more worried about the ordinary folk," McGee explained. "Fenianism is another black mark against the Irish. We're cursed by poor choices and bad luck. Look there." He pointed to a stump visible below the water. "An Irish workman probably cut the tree. Thousands of them worked here and hundreds died. Accidents, overwork, overindulgence...malaria and the other diseases all took a toll."

"They accepted the work," Macdonald reminded him, "and those that survived live well in Ottawa and Kingston."

"But we should offer more for the immigrants," McGee suggested. "After an Atlantic crossing, the plague ships, leaky vessels, quarantine, heart break, and then back-breaking labor. After all of that, we should offer something more."

"More immigrants will be coming," Macdonald predicted. "The Hudson Bay lands will need settlers; but please, no expensive promises to help new arrivals. Let them make their own way. Don't invent a new role for government."

"If we encourage them, we should protect them and help them. What can they farm in this area?" McGee pointed to the shoreline. "Rocks?"

"Men make a good living supplying wood for the steamers," Macdonald answered. "But you are right. The land in this area is poor and not the fertile soil found around Toronto or along the Saint Lawrence."

"Quebec is interested in opening new lands," McGee told him. "And encouraging their French speaking people to return from the United States. The province wants more settlement in the eastern townships and north of the Saint Lawrence, well to the north. The French may not join the rush to the west and instead settle more of their own province."

"Another issue for Cartier," Macdonald decided. "And he already has a full plate. A small but very vocal group opposes Confederation. Cartier is attacked as a '*Vendu*'...a sellout to the English, but he is wily. He will survive."

• • •

Bruce County, Canada West
September 1866

An early pioneer tried to claim the land but gave up. Erin Brady could see where the effort began, the twenty-five acres cleared and a rough cabin built. The remainder of the property was covered in virgin bush, a potential bonanza if the trees could be turned into lumber.

The land had been registered to Owen Cash, a play on the bargain driven with the lawyer. Hard cash was at a premium, and the price dropped when the lawyer saw that Erin's money would cover the cost of the property plus a handsome stipend for legal services. Owen's name change was a matter of safety in case anyone searched for the Fenian scout. She had learned he had already changed his name several times. First to circumvent British neutrality laws when he joined the American army and later to avoid American justice when he deserted and re-enlisted under a new name.

In the distance, she heard the crash of another falling tree. A mill owner in Kincardine would send a winter crew to load and move the logs over frozen roads. With the extra money, workers could be hired to clear the stumps and prepare virgin ground for seed. It was better than she dared hope.

The journey to the backcountry had been slow and cautious. Even tiny villages were on edge. Any stranger with an Irish accent was viewed with suspicion, and she tucked her red hair under a wide sunbonnet and kept her mouth firmly closed. As Owen regained strength he played a larger role.

The fear of invasion grew like summer weeds. Local militiamen drilled in dusty streets by day and by night slept with guns. Each week, the newspapers carried a new alarm or a description of the desperate characters in the provincial jails waiting for Her Majesty's justice.

But Erin had her own struggle, produced by Owen's private demons. Many nights she crept from the bed unable to sleep with his thrashing, mumbling, and groans. On other nights, they came together with a wild passion that made her forget everything, even the smell of cheap whiskey on his breath or the bottles hidden in the barn. Gradually he had shared the secrets of his past life, the time with the American army and with the Fenians.

Her own secret was buried near the wild rosebush, a jar with a sack of coins. The land was in his name because they both agreed it was a man's world. But she had convinced him to sign a document giving her rights to half of the property. It was buried with her money.

She heard the jangle of the harness. The horses would be tended before he came to the cabin. She dropped another piece of bread into the stew and sampled the dinner. By design, it was greasy and thick with lumps of fatty meat—greasy enough, she hoped, to soak up the alcohol. His drinking habits, she feared, might be the one major obstacle to their happiness together.

"Erin," he slurred.

"Dinner's almost ready." She watched him sway into the room.

"Dinner can wait!"

He ran rough, cold hands under her dress.

"A man needs more than food, and this man is going to get it."

• • •

Ottawa, Canada West
November 1866

Engineers continued to struggle with the Parliament Hill heating system as the fall chill took hold. More coal and wood would add to the expense of heating the offices, but Paul Forsey wasn't paying for the fuel and dropped two fresh logs into the fireplace. A man couldn't be expected to work in the cold, he thought, as he removed his jacket to settle at Hewitt Bernard's desk.

The chief clerk wouldn't need the office for the next few months, and Forsey was taking full advantage. Bernard had chosen to take another clerk to England for the London Conference on Confederation, leaving Forsey to face the bitter Ottawa winter. He suspected that the decision was a form of punishment. Relations with Bernard had not improved since the Fenian invasion, and when the *Globe* reported that Macdonald was drunk during the crisis, Bernard made it clear that he held Forsey responsible.

Macdonald said nothing publicly. The government relied instead on D'Arcy McGee, who stepped forward to praise John A. But McGee also quietly raised questions about the state of the militia, and Forsey suspected that the minister, too, was being punished. After the near disaster on the Niagara, the cabinet decided a senior minister must be available to handle emergencies in the capital. Macdonald had decided that McGee would stay and so miss the opening round of the London Conference.

Forsey was to prepare monthly reports for the delegation in the British capital. He smiled as he thought of the potential reaction to his latest report. George Denison's inquiry into the skirmish with the Fenians at Fort Erie had produced a damning indictment of the officer in charge, while another dispatch told of the conviction notices for the first of the prisoners. Provincial judges wasted no time. Seven were condemned to hang.

"Forsey." McGee had entered the room unnoticed. "Forget the work for a few hours. I have Buckley, John A.'s driver, on call. I need company." McGee was aging rapidly, walked with a distinct limp, and needed a walking stick.

"I really should stay and finish the dispatches. I'm picking up the slack for Bernard and the others. It's a lot of work." He waited to see if McGee would acknowledge his dedication.

"Oh, I'm sure," the little man answered. "But the senior minister is ordering you away."

Forsey needed no more urging.

• • •

"So, Mr. Buckley, you've been driving for John A. for many years."

McGee quickly turned the ride into a three-way conversation. He sat with the clerk in the rear of the carriage but talked cheerfully with the driver on the high front seat. The weak November sunshine was only slowly warming the air.

"Yes, sir." The driver's accent matched McGee's. "In Toronto, then Quebec City, and now in Ottawa."

"Well, tell us some secrets." McGee winked at Forsey. "Have you driven his lady friends? How many times have you seen him...tight?"

"Aw, Mr. McGee," the driver replied. "I shouldn't be saying a word but I hear a lot of talk about the woman in Kingston. She's called Eliza and helps on his campaigns, and seems close to him, but whether she's more than a friend, I wouldn't know—except publicly, it wouldn't be right to have a tavern keeper consorting with a cabinet minister. And as to tight, well, he is always fine company—like you, sir."

"Hah! Good answer." McGee chuckled. "But I've taken the temperance vow. Not a drink in months. The doctors say alcohol could kill me."

"Every man picks his poison," Buckley shot back. "Learn a lesson from John A. He takes the abstinence pledge at election time, but when the campaign is over, he allows the temperance membership to lapse."

"Hah." McGee laughed easily. "A fine day for a ride, but don't stop in Hull. Take us into the hills."

"Right you are." Buckley smiled and pointed the carriage toward the Gatineau.

Forsey lifted a blanket from beneath the front seat.

"Mr. Macdonald also minds the cold!" Buckley glanced back to see the civil servant wrapping the blanket over his body, "Like you, he wants the extra comfort."

"On the other hand," McGee told them, "I prefer the sunshine and the fall air."

The minister waved to the people walking along Wellington Street, tipping his hat, and offering greetings.

Forsey dropped into a sleep, filled with images of Ralston's Francine. He was reaching to undo her dress when the room began to shake.

"Wake up, you'll miss the view." McGee's voice drifted into his consciousness.

"Quite a sight, isn't it?"

The object of McGee's affection was not the dream woman but the parliament buildings in the distance. The new complex dominated the horizon.

"I sent Buckley away. Told him to take a walk and return in an hour. You've been fast asleep."

Forsey tried to clear his head as McGee spoke.

"Ottawa looks more charming from a distance. The mills and the river make it appear a rich and prosperous place where great deeds will be done."

Forsey forced the memory of Francine swaying across the tavern from his mind to concentrate instead on McGee. Only the eye and mind of a poet would see beyond the logs and sawdust of the city of Ottawa.

"Commerce will make the country grow," McGee said. "And government must be part of it and not removed from reality of the ordinary folk. A government can become too absorbed in its own world and satisfy only friends. The problem spreads to the public servants. Too many are chosen for their connections or ambition, rather than ability. And that becomes more dangerous as the numbers grow. The Americans have thousands of government employees, and I suppose we will follow. The trends trickle across the border."

"I suppose," was the best Forsey could muster, as Francine was still dancing in the corner of his mind.

"I didn't care for the attitude in the states," McGee continued, "a land of opportunity for many, but not all. Of course, my home country offered opportunity only for the very few."

"But you did try to change Ireland years ago." Forsey was finally moving back into the present and he was eager to hear of McGee's past.

"Oh, the young Ireland movement." McGee smiled sheepishly. "This old man was once a revolutionist, but I remind people that we all change. Don't berate a man in his forties or fifties for the ideals he held at twenty-one. I do have ideas on how to improve the conditions in Ireland and I intend to share them with the British. But Canada is home now, so we'll concentrate on the new nation. We need to encourage immigration and bring people to settle the western lands."

"And the right kind of people," Forsey interjected. "We don't need troublemakers."

"Careful, lad," McGee cautioned. "I was a troublemaker, and many think I still am."

"I meant Fenians," Forsey told him.

"We only have to worry about the leaders," McGee assured him. "Take the head off the viper before it can strike. Even our driver, Buckley, appears to have been bitten, but I doubt he is dangerous."

Forsey's eyes widened as McGee continued. "He's taken in by rhetoric. Like most of them. The rank and file follow the leaders blindly, so if we eliminate the leaders, the movement will wither. I have the names. When the time is right…I'll expose them."

"And the Fenian prisoners. Executions will send another warning."

"Hanging?" McGee snorted. "No…don't create martyrs. That's what their leaders want. Let's create work for John A.'s constituents in Kingston. Lock the offenders in the penitentiary."

"But the sentences have been imposed. The executions are next month."

"Our colonies are blessed with ample supplies of creative lawyers, and lawyers can find grounds for appeal—especially with the anger over the conduct of the trials."

"What anger?" Forsey demanded. "Not among people I know."

"In the Catholic community," McGee told him. "An Irish priest, no doubt another misguided soul, but a priest, is convicted and sentenced to hang. An Episcopalian minister captured in the same circumstances faces the same charge and is acquitted. That doesn't sit well with an Irish Catholic or a French Catholic or any Catholic. They see a double standard in judging Catholics and Protestants."

"Perhaps the priest was guilty," Forsey argued.

"Read the evidence. Both were equally involved," McGee responded. "The case was essentially the same against both men. But the jury for the priest was primarily Protestant—or perhaps included members of the Orange Lodge. The Orange Order has caused as much damage as the Fenians."

"But the Orange Lodge doesn't seem dangerous, and in Toronto, the membership includes the major men of society."

"But that's a problem, too," McGee explained. "The old Anglican, Loyalist set, descendants of the family compact, wants to control the country and do it their way. Orange leaders want to be silent puppet masters. But it does the country no good and creates more bad feelings. The Catholic religion should be protected. The Protestant religions should be protected. But leave it at that. When we're all working to protect our own interests, we lose sight of the future. And that's what is so exciting about Confederation, a common future."

"And you want to play a major role?"

"I want to be a minister in the first cabinet of the new nation and have worked hard to deserve it." McGee turned from the river to face the clerk. "But if I can't be in the cabinet, perhaps I would be better off finding a secure government position. Can you imagine me as a lighthouse keeper or postmaster?"

Forsey laughed aloud, and McGee broke into a wide smile. "However, I'll tell you confidentially. I have another idea. As a writer by training, I'd like to write the story of the new country."

Forsey felt a knot develop in his stomach. "What kind of story?"

McGee warmed to the new subject. "The inside history of how a nation is formed. I was there. I saw it. People know my name and hopefully trust me. The others that were inside won't do it. George Brown might, but he's trained to write short items like editorials. My book should be like the country: big, sweeping, and majestic."

McGee laughed again. "And don't think I'm an egotist. The story should be told."

Forsey thought of Francine and of the packages faithfully stored in the trunks in the tavern attic.

McGee was an accomplished writer, with volumes of work to his credit. Which book would people buy? The work of an unknown civil servant or one from the pen of D'Arcy McGee?

"So you've been keeping notes and all?"

"All in here," McGee said, tapping his head. "The London Conference is the final chapter. I want to be there, both for the conclusion and the new beginning."

• • •

Fort Jefferson, Dry Tortugas
December 1866

The guard rattled his key against the bars, and the two prisoners rose in unison to face the penal postmaster.

"Sam Mudd," the guard drawled, shoving an envelope through the bars. "But nothing for George St. Leger Grenfell."

"Bastard," Grenfell growled and returned to his bunk.

Mudd studied the envelope, savoring the pleasure of a new message.

The cell mates had spent over a year in Fort Jefferson, an aging relic off the coast of Florida. They survived disease, the stifling summer heat and humidity, and guards who took special pleasure in making their lives miserable.

"Our esteemed prison administration is probably holding my mail. There should have been an answer by now." Grenfell stretched on top of the bunk. "My friends often send newspapers, but I haven't seen one in weeks. And I wrote a letter to the British consul suggesting a trade—myself in exchange for the Fenian prisoners in Canada. The Americans claim to be worried about those poor Irish lads. It would be an ideal trade, but

Stanton might block it. The secretary of war wants me to rot in this cell."

Mudd listened, still clutching the unopened envelope.

"But Stanton won't win." Grenfell slammed his foot to the floor. The bugs scattered. "I do have a chance of escape."

"To where?" Mudd asked.

"Cuba, the Caribbean, South America," Grenfell replied. "Anywhere but the United States, and when I go, people will never hear from me again. I offered my story to the American magazines, and not one was interested. When I am free, they will have questions. But the tables will be turned, and I won't talk."

"Aren't you setting up for disappointment? Look at the obstacles to escape. First, the cellblock, the main courtyard, the sharks in the moat outside the wall, and the expanse of the Gulf of Mexico. Escape would require outside help."

"And I may have it!" Grenfell spoke with conviction. "When the time comes, my friends will come through. I may be an old man in my middle sixties, but I have my health. Who knows where the future might take me?"

"The only place I want to go is home," Mudd told him. He ran the envelope under his nose but could detect none of her scent. Gently, he worked the envelope open.

For a few minutes, there was silence save for the crickets singing in the tropical night.

"She thinks there's a chance." His voice choked. "She's making progress in Washington. It won't happen immediately, but I may be released."

"Can you trust anyone in Washington?" Grenfell asked.

"No, but I trust Frankie. My wife has good sense and is reaching the right people. She knows what to say and what not to say. You see, I did know Booth. I met him during the war, but after the assassination when he came to me as a patient, I acted as a doctor."

"Leave the prior meetings as well-kept secrets." Grenfell intoned. "Reread your letter, savor the moment. As for the past, may it not haunt us. And as for the future, may we both know freedom."

XXV

Journal of Paul Forsey
January 1867

*T*he British colonies live on luck. Two years ago, we feared American
invasion. In the past few months, we appear to have weathered a
Fenian storm. The legends will grow, but a keen observer will realize it
was more good luck than good management.

Our political leaders appear on the verge of cobbling the Confederation
agreement in place but not without opposition. Still, if their luck holds, a
new nation will be born in the coming year.

While we have been obsessed by the big picture, smaller events have
been obscured. For example, that rogue, George St. Leger Grenfell, has
reemerged. The latest demand from his Florida prison cell offered a unique
exchange: the old Confederate for the Irish prisoners held in our jails. The
offer was quickly rejected—one of the easiest decisions Macdonald and
company have made.

The way ahead has no doubt more controversies, more issues the ministers would rather keep private. The surprise will come later when my
book exposes their opportunism. In the meantime, I watch, collect information, and wait for my opportunity.

Hamilton, Canada West
January 1867

The train was late, but the day was mild for January, and George Brown welcomed the chance to pace the station platform and enjoy the sunshine.

"It is. It's George Brown! Good day to you."

"I'm Bert Collins, Reform party agent. We share a proud political allegiance."

Brown smiled. He would use his political instincts for a few more months.

"Of course, Bert. Hello."

"I worked on your campaign in '63," Collins reminded him, "before I moved to Hamilton. I don't like to intrude, but I have to ask. Is it true? You won't run again for parliament?"

"Oh, it's true." Brown smiled. "As I've told my wife, I'll be a free man."

"But why?" Brown's leadership had brought Collins from the Tories to the Reform party.

"The coalition was necessary to pass the Confederation proposals, and that work is nearly done. As to the rest of the government operation, I found myself in the minority. The old crowd stick together. The attempt to patch up a trade agreement with the Americans was botched. The Tories wouldn't listen to my advice. I stayed as a member for a full year after resigning from the cabinet. But now it's time to go."

Collins stuck his hands in his overcoat. Brown didn't seem to mind the cool breeze and reveled in the fresh air. Other passengers stayed close to the depot to escape the wind, but Brown stood hatless at the very edge of the platform.

"You will give up politics?" Collins was mystified.

"I will continue to support Reform," Brown answered. "But a new leader is needed. Mackenzie of Lambton county would be my choice."

"The stone mason?" Collins was surprised.

"A stone mason and solid," Brown replied. "A good man for the job."

Collins was disappointed. Alexander Mackenzie was quiet and reserved. Brown was an outspoken fighter. "And what will you do?"

"I'll speak through the *Globe*," Brown said, laughing, "and spend more time with my wife. For recreation, I have a plan to build a model farm at Brantford."

"But what of Bothwell?" Brown was once called the 'Laird of Bothwell' because of the land he owned near the oil fields of Lambton and Kent counties.

"Selling it," Brown announced and leaned close to Collins. "A warning. Don't speculate in oil. I had a stake but over the past few months I've come to see the petroleum game is almost played out. I've been liquidating my investments."

The train whistle sounded again and was much closer.

"Well, thank you for the advice," Collins answered.

"We Reformers have to stick together. The Tories do." Brown's voice rose as the train neared. "The coalition days are numbered and we'll be back to the old party system. I won't be the leader but I know how to beat Macdonald and his cronies. For a start..."

The arrival of the locomotive drowned out the rest of his words.

· · ·

London, England
January 1867
"Good morning."

A beaming John A. Macdonald sauntered through the lobby of the Westminster Palace Hotel. He carried a stack of papers under one arm. The other arm was in a sling.

"Assemble in the conference room," he called to the Nova Scotia delegates. "D'Arcy McGee just arrived. I'd like to speak with him privately, so let's say fifteen minutes."

"He's in a happy mood, and he has good luck" Charles Tupper whispered to his secretary. "The man has a brush with death. A candle sets off a fire in his room, and he escapes with only a bad burn on the arm."

"Make it a half hour," Tupper called back.

"And," he continued quietly again. "People said he was drunk and fell asleep, but those closest to him say he's stopped drinking."

Across the room, Macdonald smiled and laughed as he dropped the papers and pumped McGee's hand.

"Maybe there's a woman?" Tupper suggested. "He's acting like a young pup. You don't suppose there's something going on with Bernard's sister. They have been seen together. She's an intelligent and forceful woman, but my heavens, she must be half his age."

"Ah, McGee, good to see you," Macdonald said, smiling. "I'm sorry you had to delay for so long before the crossing, but we did need a senior minister at home…just in case."

"I've been anxious to come," McGee admitted. "But where are we? Progress, failure, or stalemate?"

"Progress, very important progress. I'll make this very brief before the other delegations join us. The agreement is intact with only a few very minor changes to the Quebec accord."

"So, almost there," McGee was relieved. "But I hear old Joseph Howe is fighting hard against us."

"Oh, but he's isolated," Macdonald explained. "The official delegations, including Nova Scotia, are for union. The British listen to us and not Howe."

"The schools question?" McGee asked. "The protection of the religious schools?"

"Protection for the minorities in both Canada East and West, and I believe enough guarantees to satisfy you and Mr. Galt. The British North America Act will soon be introduced in the House of Commons and the House of Lords. I'm told not to expect opposition. In truth, I'm not sure they care. Most of the lords are more concerned with legislation on local taxes and foxhounds."

"You've done it, then! Congratulations!"

"A very productive period," Macdonald said, beaming, "very productive."

XXVI

Toronto, Canada West
January 1867

The chill came from more than damp winter air. It began when John Breckinridge saw the morning paper. John Surratt, the Lincoln conspirator, had been arrested in Egypt. His forced return to Washington would reopen freshly healed wounds.

The chill deepened when the maid announced a mysterious woman caller and the name Sarah Slater.

With one glance, he knew the woman was an imposter. He had met Slater only once but could instantly recall the stunning Southern beauty. No man would forget the golden hair and the deep-blue eyes.

"Well?"

He waited on the woman in front of him. She was another striking Southern beauty but of the type the South wished to ignore.

"I'm Sillery Fraser," the woman announced. "I worked with Sarah Slater."

Breckinridge found the poise to point to a chair. The woman carried herself well and could easily pass for white.

"I need help," she began.

Smith, the storekeeper who had employed her, had kept his word and sent her last pay but he also told fellow merchants of her secret. Each request for new employment at white-owned shops was met with polite refusal. She had found no work in the small, black community, and the supply of money that once seemed inexhaustible was almost gone. Worse yet she was consumed by grief over the death of her daughter but kept the pain hidden from those around her. Her few friends would never know her anguish.

"I need to make a fresh start, far away from Canada or the United States. I need a passage to Europe and enough funds to get on my feet."

"Miss Fraser," Breckinridge said, forcing a laugh, "you are badly misinformed. The Confederacy is finished. There's no money left. I can do nothing."

The black eyes bored into him as her face tightened. "Read the papers. John Surratt is to stand trial in the Lincoln murder?"

"I'm well aware," he said, feeling the chill again. "But it's none of my business. I'll read the accounts of the trial along with everyone else."

"And Mr. Davis remains in prison?" she asked.

"Yes, but what does that have to do with anything? The Yankees don't have enough evidence to ensure a conviction if they bring him to trial. He'll eventually be released."

"Imagine what would happen if Surratt was convicted. He'd try to save himself. He let his own mother hang. Do you think he would go to the gallows for Jefferson Davis?"

Her speech was rehearsed, planned just as she and Sarah Slater had planned their conversations each time they crossed the Union lines.

"Miss Fraser! Our meeting is at an end!" He rose to escort her out.

"And what if there was another witness who could link Surratt and Booth and Richmond to the assassination?"

Breckinridge had opened the door but as quickly, closed it.

"It would be a lie!"

"Would it?" she asked.

"What if someone could tell of messages that Jacob Thompson and George Sanders sent to Richmond and the replies that came back?"

"Blackmail!" He fought to keep his posture rigid and the urge to sink back into a chair. "I could have you arrested."

"But you won't." Fraser smiled and tried to keep a light and sweet tone in her voice as Sarah Slater had. "Surratt will try to save himself and you hope there are no other witnesses. I'm proof there is."

"And what would you say?" Breckinridge demanded.

The war department had been in shambles when he took control in February 1865. He had tried to learn as much as possible but could have missed something. Davis, Benjamin, or other government staff might have had secret correspondence.

"I could tell them of the attempt to spread yellow fever in the Yankee army, Dr. Blackburn's plan."

Breckinridge relaxed slightly. The yellow fever plot was in the newspapers.

"Or of the plans to burn New York and Chicago."

"All in the papers," he told her.

"That Lincoln was to be kidnapped and taken to Richmond."

"Again, in the newspapers."

"That rebels were waiting in Virginia to carry him to Richmond, and that a special train would carry him partway on an order from the highest levels of the Confederacy?"

The dread returned. Only a few people knew the details of what was planned for Lincoln.

"And that Booth used the Confederate line to make his way from Washington after the assassination, and that he was expected. I know all of those people."

She saw the color draining from his face and knew her suspicions were correct. The file she had found outlined part of what had been planned, but she suspected there was more. It only stood to reason that Booth would make contact with the members of the old rebel underground.

"And you would know that *most* of the papers and files were destroyed before Richmond was abandoned, but could those in charge of the destruction have missed something?"

It was her final card. She had saved and protected the file that Mcgruder had inadvertently lost during the evacuation of the Confederate capital. Now it offered the hope for another fresh start.

"And wouldn't it be awful for Jefferson Davis and his cabinet officers if someone was to appear in court to testify? To relate a story that John Surratt knows only parts of? And what if she had documents to back up her story?"

"Lies. All lies."

Breckinridge began to fear that the woman presented more problems than either he or she knew.

"Help me get to Europe and I will disappear! I'm not as stupid as Surratt. Once I disappear I won't be found again. I need ten thousand dollars and passage to Europe immediately."

The only sound came from the ominous ticking of the wall clock.

"Suppose—just suppose—I believe any of this. I don't have that kind of money."

"There was money to send Surratt to Europe."

Again, it was a guess, but she saw she was correct. "Find more. I'll be back in seven days."

• • •

Ottawa, Canada West
February 1867
"Married? Married? 'Randy Jack' is *married?*"

Forsey regretted the words as soon as they left his mouth.

"He is John A., or better yet, *Mr.* Macdonald to the likes of you," Edgar Meredith, the new ranking clerk, corrected him sharply.

"And never let Mr. Bernard hear you speak that way. His sister is now John A.'s wife. A quick tongue could be cause for dismissal."

"I'm sorry," Forsey told him. "It won't happen again." And, he thought, certainly not in front of you. Edgar Meredith had climbed to rank alongside Bernard in the civil service hierarchy. Either man could make or break a career.

"But what a surprise," Forsey tried to explain. "Agnes—er, Mrs. Macdonald—was at many functions in Quebec City a few years ago. And now this. They meet again on a London street and a few weeks later are married. She's so much younger... there must be twenty years between them and—"

"I don't see how any of that concerns you," Meredith interrupted. "The man's personal life is not your business."

"I'm surprised there was time for romance, what with the meetings on the Quebec proposals and the negotiations on the final terms."

"Well, there obviously was time for both," Meredith told him. "But our concern must be the shape of the new government. And all seems to be in hand in London."

"Oh, that is good news."

"I'm sure they will be delighted to know you approve," Meredith told him coldly. "I didn't invite you to seek your opinion. I was instructed to ask for the latest intelligence on the Americans and the Irish. For some reason, Governor General Monck believes you keep watch. I note it is not part of your job duties, but since he asked, I will prepare a report."

"Yes, sir." Forsey was surprised by the request.

"If all is in hand, the delegation will stay in England for a few weeks and tie up other matters," Meredith explained. "If, on the other hand, there is urgent reason for a quick return..."

"I'm not an expert," Forsey said, opting for modesty. "But I try to keep up with the journals and the papers from the states and I do see the confidential McMicken reports."

"A very superficial approach," Meredith observed. "But go on, I'm not about to question a request from the governor general."

Forsey silently gathered his thoughts before he began. "Well, sir, the Fenian movement appears spent. We hear of internal squabbling and a lack of funds. A major attack would seem unlikely in the next few months. There's also a desperate nature to their talk, as if they were trying to convince their own people to hold on. Their operatives claimed to have set the fire at the Westminster Palace Hotel, where Mr. Macdonald was burned, but he says he fell asleep and left a candle burning."

"Yes, I see," Meredith mused. "I'll send that along."

"And there's less worry about the Americans. Their war is over, but they continue to fight among themselves, a struggle for power."

"I'm not interested in theories," Meredith sniffed. "Tell me what you know."

Forsey hesitated a moment, trying desperately to collect his thoughts and separate fact from opinion.

"The Union party suffered a setback in the fall elections. President Johnson lost the support of Irish voters, but there's more. The attempt to reconstruct the South is failing. New secret societies are being formed to oppose the government, and groups of hooded men—"

"Hooded men?" Meredith interjected.

"White men who don't want to be recognized are terrorizing the Negro. Klu Klux...it's called...the Ku Klux Klan. The members are almost certainly former rebels. Several blacks have been lynched, and Memphis and New Orleans have had bloody white-on-black riots."

"Sounds typical of a mob," Meredith pronounced. "People love secret societies, and especially the Americans."

Forsey nodded and pressed on.

"Their army has been demobilized to a fraction of what it was, and the navy has begun to sell surplus ships. So, the military threat has diminished, but the Americans believe annexation of our territory is still an option. Settlers are slipping into the Hudson Bay lands. These squatters apparently believe the prairie lands will someday become United States territory."

"I don't really care about eventually. I care about now," Meredith interrupted. "The cabinet will deal with the West after a new government is formed. Now, I gather you think the next few months will be peaceful."

"Er, well." Forsey took a deep breath. "I think you will find the Americans are distracted by other problems. We will be considered a very minor issue."

"Good!" Meredith grunted. "Let's hope it stays that way."

• • •

Toronto, Canada West
February 1867
James Mason brushed flakes of snow from his topcoat before passing it to the maid.

"Hang it near a fire," he ordered. "Nothing worse than wet clothing."

"Yes, sir," she answered. Her accent produced memories of his time as a Southern diplomat in London. She bowed politely before leaving the room."

"Where did you find her?" he asked as John Breckinridge appeared in a doorway and beckoned him to follow. "She's English?"

"Trained in London," Breckinridge replied. "And worked for one of the old Toronto families. Denison recommended her."

"Denison?"

Mason struggled to connect a face to the name. Members of the small Southern community were easy to remember, but the Canadians who drifted about were a different matter.

"Militia officer," Breckinridge prompted, "well connected in the city, the fellow writing the book on cavalry tactics."

"Ah, yes," Mason responded. "I'm afraid I couldn't help him on that."

"Early has agreed to a critique," Breckinridge said, smiling. "Denison may be doing us a favor. Old Jube will be occupied."

Mason nodded wearily. "We need privacy."

Breckinridge led him to a book-lined study and closed the door. "I'm glad you are available. I can't discuss this with the others. Men like your new son-in-law, Sam Davis, or Bennett Young are well intentioned, but I didn't want to involve them, and Jubal doesn't do well on delicate issues."

"Oh, I agree," Mason replied. "And I wish we didn't have to deal with her, but what can we do?"

"She said she'd come back and agreed to be patient."

"How patient?" Mason asked absently, glancing over the book collection.

"Five hundred dollars patient."

Mason removed a leather-bound volume from the shelf.

"The books came with the house," Breckinridge explained. "I can't afford a fine collection."

"Oh, understood." Mason replaced the book. "We're all tight on funds. If we agree to meet her demands, we'll need cash. But we'll deal with that later. What have you learned?"

"Everything she told us seems true," Breckinridge began. "She worked with Slater and Colonel Mcgruder, but both of them have vanished. She created hard feelings with a local storekeeper here in Toronto, so hasn't worked in months. But she lives and travels mostly between Montreal and Chatham, one of the smaller cities."

Mason turned away from the shelf to give the Kentuckian his full attention.

"We have connections there. Chatham is generally sympathetic to the Africans and mixed races, but she didn't get along. She has a haughty attitude at times. An uppity side."

"And in Virginia?" Mason asked. "Is she remembered?"

"Oh, very few people would forget her or Slater, but most who worked the Richmond–Montreal line felt it best to disappear, and the few that are left don't discuss the war."

"What about Richmond?" Mason asked.

"Anything could have happened with the confusion in the evacuation. Secretary Benjamin and I ordered the destruction of many files. Unfortunately, Mcgruder was assigned to carry out the order. This woman left the city with Mcgruder and Slater, but then we don't know anything else until she surfaced in Canada."

"And the files?" Mason prodded.

"A few may have survived," Breckinridge confessed. "We did our best. John Taylor Wood recalls destroying papers. I've had a recent letter from Wood, by the way. He's doing well and working with one of the old Confederate suppliers in Halifax. He may be able to advance some cash. The papers he destroyed were burned, and the ashes scattered. The Yankees claimed to find documents when Richmond fell. But if there was anything incriminating, they would have used them by now. President Davis did manage to carry off letters, which are safe in a bank vault in Montreal. The Yankees used their influence to see them, and again, if there was anything serious, we would have heard."

Mason thought again of his diplomatic experience.

"In England and in France, in all of our European dealings, we were very careful about what we put on paper."

"As we were in Richmond," Breckinridge told him. "But it is possible that someone wrote something. There was so much confusion at the end. Davis and Benjamin took a harder attitude in the final months and talked of fighting on at all costs. But the

Lincoln business, I don't know. And quite honestly, I don't want to know, and I doubt that you do either."

Mason grasped at a straw. "Could she be bluffing?"

"She could be." Breckinridge shrugged. "But there's another problem: this Surratt business. Booth kept a diary."

Mason slumped against the bookcase as Breckinridge continued.

"Secretary of War Stanton has it. Booth wrote about his travels and hints that he hatched the kidnap plot in Montreal. But apparently nothing truly damaging."

"So nothing to worry us?" Mason asked hopefully.

"Not that we are aware of…But part of the diary is missing."

"Missing?" Mason asked.

"A section was removed, and it's the period around the assassination."

"Why? I don't understand," Mason stammered.

"I have no answers," Breckinridge told him. "Booth may have removed them, perhaps for toilet paper while hiding in the swamp. Booth also had a bevy of women. Maybe it was a record of sexual conquests. No one knows, but a lot of people want to find out."

"And you say it was from the period of the assassination," Mason repeated.

"That's what my informant believes. Secretary of War Stanton had the diary, so perhaps it contained sensitive material on Washington interests. He might have removed something. Goods were flowing through the lines. A few Northern men became rich in the cotton trade. Maybe Booth helped them. And what about President Johnson? Booth left his card at Johnson's hotel and all—"

"I can't believe that," Mason interjected. "His involvement would be preposterous."

"Ben Butler doesn't think so," Breckinridge retorted. "He's Senator Butler now and wants a new investigation of the assassination."

"What will that accomplish?" Mason asked.

"We both know Washington," Breckinridge reminded him. "Butler may be trying to enhance his image or settle old scores. He may be looking for a Southern connection to justify a harder line on reconstruction. But there might be something more. We never understood why Booth turned to assassination."

"What a mess." Mason shook his head.

"I agree completely," Breckinridge explained. "I've been thinking about nothing else. It's why we have to deal with the Fraser woman. The last thing we need is to add fuel to this fire."

"So we negotiate," Mason said. "You are right. We have no real choice."

"I'll try to deal with her," Breckinridge told him. "Although I wish there was someone else to turn to."

"And if she doesn't deliver the documents or has made copies?" Mason asked.

"Leave that to me! But let's get her out of the country. Is there any money in our London accounts?"

"I doubt it," Mason told him. "We were running short of funds before the war ended, and since then more has been drained away. Still, in a true emergency..."

• • •

Toronto, Canada West
February 1867

Jubal Early tapped the thin ice and smiled as it shattered. The sun was finally winning the annual battle with the winter cold. Across the brown grass, frost was melting from the glass on the hot house at Heydon Villa. George Denison's staff would soon prepare the seeds to hurry the season forward. Spring would come much faster in Virginia, but Early wouldn't be there to see it.

A special clerk was working at the White House to process thousands of Confederate parole applications, but the former general refused to seek a pardon. The simple act of filling out a form would indicate he had done something wrong and was asking forgiveness. Jubal Early was not about to give old foes any measure of satisfaction. The only mistake he saw was losing the war.

Denison beckoned from the door. The Canadian colonel wore a simple civilian suit, probably one of many in his closets. Early wore the same gray suit each day. The buttons, cut from his old rebel uniform and polished daily, reflected the sun.

"Good afternoon, General," Denison said, smiling. A butler hovered nearby to take the great coat.

"Very nice house, Colonel." Early gazed around the entrance hall. The furnishings compared well with pre-war Virginia mansions.

"We've been blessed," Denison told him. "Over the years, the family made the right business decisions."

"Hah! Yes!" Early smiled. "The good lord helps those who help themselves. Or in our line of work, God is on the side of the largest army."

"A quote from Napoleon, isn't it?" Denison asked.

"I believe so," Early answered reluctantly. He would have preferred to take the credit.

"Brandy," Denison called as they approached the roaring fire and another servant appeared.

"Writing a book, are you?" Early settled into a plush armchair.

"I was told you were direct," Denison said with a laugh. "I'm working on several projects, including a history of the cavalry."

"Well, good luck." The tone was dismissive. "That will take years of study."

"I'll do it gradually. I'll start with tactics and drill. We need new training material for our militia."

"I'm not sure about book learning," Early said, trying to be gentle. "Many of our men couldn't read and learned best by doing."

"I don't mean for the ordinary soldier," Denison explained. "I mean material for officers."

"Like at West Point?" Early asked.

"Precisely," Denison replied. "We're going to build an officer corp. We can't always rely on the British. Training is a first step. I would appreciate your thoughts. I discussed the subject with General Hood and General Pickett when they were in Canada."

"Ain't they a sad pair?" Early interjected. "Sam Hood is a cripple. He takes too much laudanum. And Pickett is hurting from the failed charge at Gettysburg. At least Pickett has Miss Sally to console him. Sam is mooning over a lost love. And to put it politely, both men have a blemish on their military records. Say, why don't you write to General Lee and get his opinion?"

"My letter has already gone," Denison told him.

"There are others that handled cavalry. Forrest is still above ground. Stewart and Morgan could have taught you more."

"I spoke with Morgan's men here in Toronto," Denison told him. "But most were junior officers."

"A lot of them were scouts or spies or partisans," Early explained. "I never did care for guerrilla operations. If you write about that, you might as well be writing a dirty French novel."

"No, no. You misunderstand," Denison told him. "I want to write about the cavalry as an element of an army."

"Oh, the massed charge? Lancers riding stirrup to stirrup, banners flying, swords whirling?" Early left the statement hanging before he continued, "That's over. You won't see that anymore. War has changed."

Early lifted his glass, took a deep swallow, and washed the brandy around in his mouth. "Cavalry is effective for scouting. That was Stewart's forte when he rode around the Northern armies. Morgan's raids had a nuisance value, but his real strength came with dismounted cavalry. His men could fight on horseback or on the ground. With today's rifles and artillery, the grand mounted attack can be blown to bits in seconds. It makes for high drama...like the British at Balaclava and the Light Brigade, and look what happened to them."

"But surely there is a role for the mounted attack," Denison argued.

"For shock value, perhaps, or an attack on an undefended position, but not against artillery or men who are entrenched. Hell, a horse charge on the trenches at Petersburg would have been suicide. No! Actually, with the power of the new guns, it would be murder. War has changed. The navy has ironclads. The land forces are next. Will it be armored wagons, armored trains? Maybe it will be infantry in trenches firing across a no-man's-land—like at Petersburg? But, of course, Mr. Denison, that's only my view. General Lee may have a different perspective."

"I've extended an invitation for him to visit us."

"I'm not so sure he'll want to travel," Early replied. "He's in poor health, but probably a written reply would help your project."

"Have you thought of staying here?" Denison asked, abruptly changing the subject. "Of staying in Canada? We could use your knowledge as we build our army."

"Stay in your new Confederacy?" Early laughed.

"Why not?"

"For a start, the weather. God Almighty, Canada has a miserable climate."

"It's not all that different from Virginia," Denison told him. "Seriously, you could stay."

"And become a Canadian general? I'd say something and spark a war inside of a week. No, wouldn't work. And in all honesty...I'm not sure your new Confederacy will work. It looks like the old Washington game of consolidating power at the top. And..." He took a breath before charging forward. "If you want another reason, I suspect you will soon become American."

"That won't happen!"

"It doesn't come with force," Early explained. "Or even annexation. I read American news in your newspapers. I buy American products. They don't have to conquer you. They take you by stealth. You become American by osmosis."

"Not so." Denison's voice rose. "We are different. And we're going to create a great Anglo-Saxon nationality in the North."

"Anglo-Saxon? Doesn't that mean English-speaking and white?" Early was warming for a good argument. "What about the French? What do they say to that?"

"We'll deal with them." Denison was growing angry. "We'll keep them in their place."

"I've heard that before," Early told him. "We said the same thing about the African. And now they want to run the country."

He tipped the glass to drain the brandy and rose to leave. "I won't stay for dinner but I will read your manuscript. And good luck with your new Confederacy."

XXVII

Ottawa, Canada West
March 1867

It was another moving day for Paul Forsey, and for an instant, he regretted hiring Buckley and the wagon to haul his meager household goods, the single armchair, a small desk, and three heavy trunks stuffed with books. He had never read the books and never would, but classic literature was an imposing sight on a bookshelf. Today, however, books added only weight and expense.

Hewitt Bernard's note, an eviction notice, had been terse to the point of arrogant. John A. and his new wife would need additional room at the Quadrilateral. Forsey must vacate. Bernard would stay, and Brydges, the railway executive, would easily find richer accommodation.

"All loaded up, my friend?" Buckley glanced around the room. His eyes came to rest on a small carpetbag. "This last bag and we're away?"

"No." Forsey realized the response was too sharp. "I'll carry that, just a few files I need to review."

He planned to separate the papers. A few could be destroyed, but most would be sent to Quebec City for safe storage. He had learned a great deal from Macdonald and Brydges. Bernard was content to retreat to his room and his Bible, but the other two enlivened the evenings with conversation ranging from railway construction to campaign finance. The secrets shared before a warm fire and with a full glass would have shocked their opponents and still might.

"We can go, then?" Buckley asked. "I charge more if we go beyond dusk."

"We'll go. I can't afford any more."

A year earlier, he had overheard George Brown telling of the speculations in the oil fields of Lambton County, and the clerk had quietly invested in a property adjacent to Brown's holdings. The once-quiet hamlet of Bothwell had exploded into a boomtown, and it should be only a matter of time before his investment would pay off. Until then, he must live frugally.

"We'll be finished well before dark."

His new home was a single room, small but very inexpensive. Fellow public servants had conquered fears that the capital would be moved and were buying local property, but the returns from the sale of a house would be much less than the profits he expected from petroleum. Oil was safer than a bank. For more evidence, he need look no further than Kingston, where the bank for which Macdonald was a director and legal counsel was in trouble. Macdonald's plate would be full when he returned to the capital. There was a new wife to support, a bank teetering, and the new government demanding his attention.

"I'll wait at the wagon," Buckley announced.

Forsey glanced around the room. For a moment, he considered sweeping and collecting the dust. But only for a moment. Bernard—or even, Macdonald—could pay for cleaning.

Minutes later, he climbed to the wagon seat. Buckley remained on the ground and carefully inspected the horse's feet.

"Like to check the shoes before the darkness sets in," he announced as he stepped up to the seat and gently urged the horse forward. The animal plodded into the late-day traffic.

"Be glad when John A. returns. Business is a slow without a regular customer."

"The delegation should be back soon," Forsey assured him. "The transatlantic cable has been restored. Confederation can take place on July 1. Any questions for the home office can be answered almost immediately by wire. No need for them to stay."

"Ah, good news." Buckley smiled. "And John A.'s work is paying off?"

"All coming together very nicely," the clerk announced knowingly. "We know the names for the provinces. The people who wanted to call Canada West 'Toronto' will be disappointed. The new name will be Ontario. Quebec will still be Quebec. And the country as a whole will be known as the Dominion of Canada. I suspect that is a sop for the Americans. Yankees don't like royalty, and the Kingdom of Canada, right next door, might be too much for them to swallow."

"Whoa!" Buckley called and stopped the horse. He jumped down and shook the front wheel. "Thought I saw a wobble." He slipped to his knees to inspect the running gear. It was several minutes before he returned to the seat. "Can't see anything. Light is fading fast."

"Perhaps if we moved a little faster..." Buckley was obviously delaying and ready to demand extra payment for additional time. "I, too, would like to finish. I don't care for some of the characters I see on the streets at night."

"Then perhaps you need extra protection." Buckley kept the horse in a slow walk. "I know a fellow who could get you a small handgun. People order them through American magazines, but this would be a better price."

"And if I ordered a gun, could we be move a little faster? And if I ordered a gun, would you demand extra payment?"

"We can come to an accommodation." Buckley smiled and flicked the reins to urge the horse into a trot.

"I hear things. A man must be careful. People are floating dangerous ideas. You never know who might be about on those

dark nights when the parliament sits late and a clerk or a politician has to brave the streets."

• • •

Quebec City, Canada East
April 1867

"I'll see this bag is taken to the cabin, Mrs. Fraser. Your man will
bring the rest?" the steamship porter asked.

"Yes, sir. I's gonna take them," Amos Baker said before she
could reply. His dialect came easily, along with the large grin.
"Don't you worry none, mister. Miss Fraser has been kind to
old Amos. She given me my 'mancipation papers. I be free."

The porter didn't care. "Passage for one," he reminded her.

"Oh yes." Sillery's smile came easily. "My servant will be
staying here or returning to Virginia or whatever they do."
She appeared unconcerned. "We have no control of them
anymore."

Sillery was anxious to reach the safety of the cabin. The
crowds swarming the docks to watch the first departure of the
season frightened her. She took one last, hasty glance across the
sea of faces, fearing someone was looking for her.

Breckinridge had delayed and played for time, but finally
provided the ticket and half of the money. The other half was
to be paid in Europe. And Breckinridge had demanded proof
of what she knew. Her answer was a list of the men who oper-
ated the Confederate line between Washington and Richmond
and their instructions for the Lincoln kidnap. She promised the
actual file when she received full payment.

Amos Baker had convinced her of the danger. Baker had
been one of the black men waiting for business when her train
arrived in Chatham, a city considered a Black Mecca. Despite her
dismissal from the Toronto shop, she had given Canada another
chance, but in her heart, she feared failure. And as Baker toured
her around the town, the fear grew. The black population was

dropping. Even successful shops were feeling the squeeze. Baker guided her to a boarding house, where he shared his time and knowledge.

"You could pass," he told her, "but I know, and eventually others will catch on. It's not all that different in British territory. Even a little black makes life hard. Although sometimes I think it's easier here because there are fewer of us."

"How did you know about me?" she asked him.

"Smell." He began to laugh. "White folks talk about the way we smell. We don't smell any different than they do."

She grew to trust him. When John Surratt was arrested, and as her plan took shape, she confided more of her secrets. The confidence was returned a few weeks later when Baker appeared suddenly at her side. "People are asking questions. You need someone to keep you safe."

"Scuse me, sir."

She heard him now, as he made his way toward the cabin.

"I's got to get through to Miz Frasieere's cabin and get off this here boat. Ol' Amos has a fear of water. "Scuse me again, sir."

A muffled curse was the only answer.

"Miz Frasieere?" he drawled. "You all in there?"

She bit her tongue to control the laughter as he lurched inside. The trunk hit the floor with a loud crunch.

"Now look what you've done," she said loudly and slammed the door.

"Amos," she said, laughing, "you are incredible."

"All part of the entertainment. You want help putting stuff away?"

"No, I'll have lots of time at sea, but we don't have much. You said the money was enough, but I want to thank you. I doubt I would have made it without you."

"I wouldn't worry too much right now. That fellow that was following you had a little accident and didn't see you change your ticket, so you'll be safe on the water. Just be real careful on the other side."

"Amos, why do you keep warning me? Do you know something you don't want to tell?"

"Not much to say, except I did some work for the Confederates. There's a little fellow from Kentucky I consider a friend, but I know he's done real rough things, and so have other rebels. One fellow that crossed them went over the Niagara Falls. End of story. You have to be careful."

"I will, Amos," she said quietly. She cupped her hands gently on his cheeks and gave him a soft, lingering kiss.

"Now what you do that fo?" The dialect covered his embarrassment.

"Ol' Amos will step off this ship looking like he got a piece of lumber in his pants."

"We might have, Amos," she told him.

"Yes, we might have." He pulled the cabin door open. "And I will regret that we didn't. I'll wait for your letter, and I'll arrange to see Breckinridge."

"Scuse me, sir." He trotted toward the stairway as another passenger emerged from a stateroom. "Ol' Amos don't like a boat. He wants to be on dry land."

XXVIII

Niagara-on-the-Lake, Canada West
May 1867

T he strains of "Dixie" had barely faded when the townspeople began to chant, "Davis! Davis! Speech! Speech!"

The reaction brought new life to a thin and haggard figure.

"I'll just give them a few words, and we can speak in peace."

John Breckinridge and James Mason rose and followed as the Confederate president stepped onto the veranda. The glow from flaming torches illuminated Davis but left the two companions in the shadow.

The cheers grew until he raised his hands.

"My friends," Jefferson Davis said, his voice a croak. "I hope that peace and prosperity forever will be the blessing of Canada." The voice gained strength. "For she has provided the asylum for many of my friends." He bowed politely to Breckinridge and Mason before taking a deep breath. "As she is now for me. I hope Canada will remain forever a part of the British Empire."

The crowd erupted in cheers. He stood looking at the upturned faces before waving again as the little band struck up another chorus of "Dixie."

"I think that will do!" Davis offered a rare smile as he returned to the gathering in the parlor.

"The people in the small towns in the South are the same. They don't ask for much, and when you do give them something, they appreciate it."

"The cities welcome you, too."

Davis turned to the speaker, trying hard to put a name to the face. "Ah, thank you, Mr. Denison." The militia officer had introduced himself on the steamer crossing Lake Ontario.

"I understand you organized the gathering in Toronto. I thank you for that welcome," Davis said.

"There were two or three thousand people to see you," Denison told him. "And it didn't take any work once word spread that Jeff Davis was coming."

"Perhaps someday I can return the compliment."

"Thank you, I—" Denison began to respond.

"But now I must ask you excuse us," Davis said, adopting a sterner tone. "I have private business to conduct."

Denison could barely conceal his disappointment as group left the room.

In the hall, a woman spoke quietly. "He doesn't look any better up close. Pale, thin, and I thought I saw a nervous twitch."

"At least he's bailed from prison," a companion told her. "If we spent two years confined in Fortress Monroe, we'd look bad, too, and returning to Richmond must have been hard. He and his wife, Varina, slipped away to visit their son's grave before he appeared before the court. And can you imagine those vile New Yorkers lining up on the platform to shout insults as the train came north."

"If you ask me, he should have stayed in Montreal until he regained his strength," the first woman suggested. "I don't understand why he came here so soon. With time, we could have arranged a proper greeting, something better than a wretched local band."

"But he did enjoy the reception," Denison said, offering an arm to each of the women. "Let's leave him in peace so he can get a good night's rest."

Mason waited until the voices faded before producing a box of cigars.

"Yes, thank you," Davis said, bending to accept a match and taking a deep puff. "So, we have a problem that demands my attention?"

Breckinridge sighed before he began. "We believe the issue is in hand but wanted you to know."

"I've been thinking since Mr. Mason outlined the situation in Montreal," Davis spoke quietly. "With all of our problems, we find ourselves considering the case of a misguided mulatto woman. But I concur, the best thing was to get her away. Still, you don't know what papers she has."

"No," Breckinridge answered. "We don't. We tried to follow her, hoping she would lead us to them, but she's clever. She slipped away. The ticket we provided was exchanged in Quebec City. She may have taken another ship or she may be somewhere in Canada. She was well informed of our operations and she was in Richmond the night of the evacuation. But we don't know about this file. I don't recall seeing anything, but…"

"But you wonder?" Davis finished the sentence. "You wonder if our people had a hand in the assassination. I can assure you there were no direct orders. Is that enough?"

He puffed on the cigar and watched the smoke rise toward the ceiling. Mason and Breckinridge stood in silence.

"As to indirect—a secret mission that went sour," Davis continued. "I suppose anything is possible."

For an instant, the old presidential steel showed in his eyes.

"Mr. Breckinridge will recall the confusion. I wanted to fight on. I issued a proclamation in Danville, where I said we were entering a new phase in the struggle. Our men could fall back into the hills and continue to fight and wage a guerrilla war. And I imagine there were men prepared to take the war to the North with torpedoes, explosives, or guns. We needed desperate men for desperate times. I have since come to discover," he said, looking directly at Breckinridge, "that my cabinet was not in agreement. There were those working for an early surrender, men who had the misguided belief that the North would be more compassionate if we simply gave up."

Breckinridge looked on in silence.

"Look at the South today." The president's voice rose in anger. "Federal occupation, a ruined landscape, people starving, gangs of armed men, the poor Negro wandering aimlessly in poverty and destitution, while shoddy Yankee businessmen make a fortune. Would my way have been any worse?"

Mason shifted uncomfortably. Breckinridge stood firm.

"So could something have been written to encourage desperate attacks?" Davis continued to stare at Breckinridge before he sneered, "Of course! Did I write it? No! Would you, as my secretary of war, have written it? Not when you were working to undermine my authority and arrange an early surrender." He glared at Breckinridge.

"Could the secretary of state have written something? It's doubtful! Judah Benjamin supported me to the very end, as every cabinet member was expected to do. But could someone in his department have written something? It's possible. And never forget that as hard as we tried, Northern sympathizers and spies wormed their way into our government. Perhaps they wrote something to cause trouble."

He jabbed a finger toward Breckinridge. "Did cabinet members see every file, every letter, or was something forged? It's possible!"

"Mr. Davis?" Breckinridge deliberately dropped the presidential title. "The Confederacy was in a shambles. Continuing the war would have accomplished nothing. General Lee could see that. We tried to keep the army intact so we could negotiate with a semblance of strength, but you did everything in your power to prevent the peace talks. I agree, the South is in a terrible plight and will be for years, but partisan attacks were not the answer.

Hell, we had seen what was already happening in the West. No one was safe."

"We can't refight the war," Mason interjected. "We should be dealing with the problem at hand. What do we do about the woman?"

"Silence her," Davis barked. "Pay her off or find another option!" He shrugged. "Have someone in London take care of it. Is Sanders in London? He enjoyed cloak-and-dagger drama. Have him look into it. Give him a free hand. He'll find a solution."

"But the man was unstable," Breckinridge snapped. "Why would you want him to handle something like this?"

"Because he'll find a way to do it. One way or another," Davis replied.

"Mr. President," Breckinridge appealed to what he hoped was a higher instinct. "One way or another? Are we talking about the same thing?"

"Of course." Davis smiled. "Have Sanders handle it."

"I don't like this," Breckinridge announced.

"I'll send a letter." Mason tried to defuse the tension. "And I had information today that may take the pressure off the court case. A new storm is about to burst. The lawyers preparing for the John Surratt trial have stumbled across a new document. The court martial recommended clemency for his mother, but President Johnson didn't see it. The document may have been hidden from him. Johnson has to deal with that, and so fewer people will be paying attention to your trial."

"I'm not worried about my trial," Davis told him. "I can defend myself as long as I have a fair jury. I do fear the Yankees may stack the jury with uninformed Africans. But if the jury is made up of true Virginia men, I will be acquitted."

Davis turned again to Breckinridge. "After all, I had served in the United States cabinet before the war but I was out of office when I was summoned to the presidency of the Confederacy. I violated no oath. It's the men who held positions of authority and turned their backs on the union that really upset the Yankees… people like a former vice president, a candidate who ran against their beloved Mr. Lincoln, and a man actually sitting as a senator when the war began. The Yankees consider that treason."

"Mr. Davis," Breckinridge spoke coldly, "I stayed in Washington and worked to prevent the war. I worked for compromise. It was only when I faced arrest that I went south."

"Oh, I remember." Davis smiled, but his tone was harsh. "We were so pleased when you came. People thought you might become president of the Confederacy. Was that in your thoughts, too?"

"Let's call it a night," Mason jumped in. "The president is tired."

He gently pushed Davis toward the door. "Perhaps tomorrow a touch of sightseeing here in the Niagara. It's delightful country. And the local fair is this week. We'll take that in."

Davis resisted.

"Silence her," he repeated. "No matter what you think of me, no matter what you have to do. Do it for the cause."

"Mr. Mason will write to London," Breckenridge told him quietly. "And when this affair is finished, my service to the Confederacy will end."

Jefferson Davis demanded the last word.

"It already has Mr. Breckinridge. I believe it ended some time ago."

XXIX

Ottawa, Canada West
June 1867

John A. Macdonald displayed a gentler, more serene demeanor, and those who knew him best wondered if it could last. Returning from England, setting up a new household, with a new wife, watching over the final details of the Confederation plans, and never once the excuse that he was "indisposed."

"A few loose ends to tie up," he said, as he welcomed Paul Forsey to the east block office. "Everything is in place. Take a seat; make yourself comfortable."

Macdonald was acting as he had in the evenings at the Quadrilateral, warm and friendly but sober. Other public servants told of the empty glasses surrounding a pitcher of cold water.

"I suppose you can guess why I asked to see you." Macdonald settled into the chair beside the desk. "The other clerks will be jealous. You've done a marvelous job, and Hewitt Bernard says you deserve a promotion. Meredith does, too. And those two gentlemen are hard to please."

Hard to read, too, Forsey thought. The senior clerks had been cold and had ignored him in the last few weeks. He had done everything in his power to win their approval. Only a few senior government positions were left unfilled. Senior positions paid well, and he needed money more than ever. His lucrative investment scheme had failed. The oil boom at Bothwell was dying, and the value of his property was falling fast.

"Are the new rooms comfortable?" Macdonald asked. It was the first time either he or Bernard had indicated any interest in Forsey's life after the time at the Quadrilateral.

"Oh, a little cramped, but one gets used to it."

With a new higher salary, he would be able to afford better.

"Thinking of buying a house?" Macdonald inquired.

"No," Forsey confessed. "Couldn't afford to buy."

"Just as well," Macdonald sighed. "A man gets burdened with property and mortgage payments. The banks have to protect their shareholders."

Forsey nodded in understanding. Banking would be a big issue on Macdonald's mind with the Kingston bank rumored near collapse. The salary that flowed to him as a bank director and legal counsel could be lost.

"Yes, banks must be careful," Macdonald mused. He was silent for a moment. "Well, look, let's not beat around the bush."

Forsey leaned back in the chair, crossing his legs. He wore new plaid pants, the style Macdonald favored.

"I've decided on the premiers," Macdonald said, and absently scratched at his hair. "Ontario was the toughest decision. I've offered the post to Sandfield MacDonald."

Forsey smiled and nodded. He didn't really care, but sending the Cornwall MacDonald into the political wilderness was typical of John A. The provinces were minor players, and the appointment would eliminate an opponent at the federal level.

"And he's agreed to accept and will take the post in Toronto."

Forsey enjoyed the confidence. It would be this way in the future, with Macdonald confiding in him. As for the Cornwall MacDonald, he wished him well. Toronto was growing as a business center, but a premier of the new province would have no more prestige than a mayor. He would deal with local issues—education, roads, and canals—and not the big projects at the federal level.

"So have you guessed what we want you to do?" Macdonald had his attention again.

In his mind, Forsey could hear the conversation: "Go and see Forsey. He has as much clout as Bernard or Meredith."

Macdonald smiled. "We want you to go with Sandfield."

Forsey froze.

"It's only the number three position in his office," Macdonald explained, "but the provincial work force will grow. The salary will be close to what you earn now, and you have demonstrated that you live frugally."

Forsey sat in shock.

"I wanted to speak to you because I hope we can keep in contact." Macdonald glanced to a file on his desk. "You did excellent work over the years with the Confederate raiders, the Fenians, and so on. You keep your ear to the ground."

Forsey tried to speak, but no words would come. Macdonald pushed on.

"It's the issues in the future that concern me. Sandfield MacDonald is not stupid. He'll look for ways to weasel subsidy money from federal coffers and claim he's defending the province. Quebec will try to make a special case, and that too is to be expected. I'd like to have had a stronger clause on federal and provincial powers. Oliver Mowat prepared the language, and I thought he was up to no good. It's why I offered him the post on the bench as soon the position opened, and I was damn glad he took it. I didn't want any more of his meddling. But that's in the past. I will need to know what the premiers are up to. What they're thinking, what they're planning. You can be my private set of ears in Ontario."

Macdonald looked again at the speechless Forsey.

"Oh, I know this new responsibility must be a shock, but you're the man for the job. The political coalition will soon end, and the parties will be back in vogue. We've got to be ready to fight the Reformers with the elections scheduled in the fall. Report anything you hear."

Forsey felt the hand lifting him from his chair and moving him toward an uncertain, financially strained, and no doubt boring future.

"Glad this went well!" Macdonald patted his back. "My next meeting will be harder. I have to tell McGee he didn't make the cabinet. There are too many factions to appease. Protestants, Catholics, Quebecers, the East Coast crowd, and I can't fit him in. Damn fool made it harder with the Fenian business. He's lost support in the Irish community. But if he can win re-election, I'll consider him another time."

He opened the door and followed Forsey into the hall.

"Don't move too quickly," he said, chuckling. "We'll have quite a show when Confederation is proclaimed on the first of July."

Forsey opened his mouth to speak, but Macdonald cut him off. "No, don't thank me. Just keep me informed."

• • •

Ottawa, Canada West
June 30, 1867
Gaslights flickered to life as the summer twilight began to fade, but the grounds around the parliament building would be well lit for parties and receptions. From the Russell House hotel, a home-away-from-home for many of the politicians, well-dressed men and woman were making the short walk to the grounds of Parliament Hill.

Paul Forsey carried only a small satchel and moved in the opposite direction. In a few short blocks, he would be in the darker sections of the capital. The poorer Irish and French would have to be content with a glimpse of the festivities.

He touched his pocket lightly and took comfort from the feel of the revolver. The gun was added protection in the seedier part of the capital, a world away from the buildings and the people he was leaving.

John A. had worked until nightfall and then climbed into Buckley's rig for the short drive to the Quadrilateral and Agnes. "Lady Agnes," Forsey thought to himself and "Sir John A."

The knighthood officially would be announced in the morning, but already word of the queen's decision was creating controversy. Georges Cartier had been given a lesser honor, and the rumor mill said that the French leader felt he deserved more. The little family of the new Canada was bickering before the ink was set on the birth announcement.

Forsey had made notes on it all before he had slipped the last papers into his case. He had sent a telegram to Quebec City asking Ralston and Francine to ship the trunks to his new address in Toronto. There would be ample time to start the book. With luck, he would be finished before McGee put pen to paper.

The blast of the first cannon startled the town.

Forsey turned in time to see the flash of a second celebratory blast and, in the brief illumination from the gun, the row of artillery pieces facing the Ottawa River. With the third shot, smoke from the powder began to rise above the parliamentary towers.

"What the hell?" a voice called as a tavern door opened and the clientele spilled into the street.

"Finnegans," said a man reeking of whiskey, who bumped hard against Forsey.

"Finnegans!" he shouted. "The Finnegans are attacking!"

Another cannon shot blasted into the twilight.

"Where is our bloody army? The Irish bastards will kill us!"

"Ah, you damn fool," Forsey said, pushing him out of the way. "It's not Fenians. It's a cannon salute for the new Dominion of Canada."

The glassy eyes tried to focus on the speaker.

"It's for the new country. It's for Confederation!" Forsey wanted to shake him.

The glassy eyes slipped toward Parliament Hill as yet another cannon joined the chorus.

"Confederation?" the man asked, and Forsey nodded.

"Confederates!" The little man lurched toward his companions. "It's the damn Confederates!" he shouted. "And the whole Yankee army will be right behind them!"

"Ah, you are daft. Come on, we'll watch the show." The crowd shoved the man along as it moved toward the hill.

• • •

Halifax, Nova Scotia
June 30, 1867

"Here's a good copy." Joseph Howe beamed over the latest edition of the *Morning Chronicle.*

The black-bordered paper was headlined, "Died, Last Night at Twelve O'clock the Free and Enlightened Province of Nova Scotia."

"That should stir things when it hits the street in the morning," Howe told the printer. "But add a bit more ink to the border. Make it black as black can be."

"That will take a few minutes," the printer said, glancing toward the clock. With Howe in the office, it promised to be another long night.

"Go ahead. We won't win this fight in a night. Sharpen the line where we say, "Her ungrateful sons betrayed her to the enemy."

"Again, it will take a few minutes." The printer grimaced.

"This is just the start," Howe explained. "The British let us down at the London Conference and pushed through Macdonald's scheme. But we've an election coming. The anti-confederate movement will sweep the province. Wait until the voters learn how Ottawa is spending their money."

"And then what?" the printer asked. "Fight it out at Province House?"

"No." Howe shrugged. "Our legislature can now deal only with local issues. The men we elect will carry the fight to Ottawa."

"But you won't have a majority there?"

"A dedicated minority can accomplish a great deal. The other provinces have reservations about the British North America act. We can win support from other dissidents. And if that fails, there's always secession."

"The Southern states tried that, and it didn't work out so well," the printer reminded him.

"Let's just wait and see."

XXX

Quebec City, Quebec
July 1, 1867

Geoffrey Ralston heard the shouts at the same time he felt Francine leave the bed.

"Get up." She lit the oil lamp. "Something is wrong. Something is happening. Can't you hear the noise?"

Ralston opened his eyes in time to see her naked body disappear under a dressing gown.

"Huh?" He rolled across the bed to reach for her.

"Get *up!*"

"Come back to bed. The army is to fire a special salute at dawn. The artillery units are getting ready to mark the Confederation. The whole day will be a festival. Come back to bed. Get some sleep, so we can enjoy it."

The dressing gown hung from her body as she looked frantically for the belt that would pull it together.

"I don't think so," she told him. "The voices are in French! The artillerymen speak English. It's something else."

"Don't be silly. It's—"

The pounding on the door below cut off his words, and she rushed from the room.

"Get *up!*" she shrieked a minute later, returning to gather her clothes. "It's a fire! The tavern is burning. The flames are coming from the attic! I was up there last night to gather Forsey's papers. Oh, God! Did I snuff the candle?"

Toronto, Ontario
July 1, 1867

The church bells were pealing. One after another, the sound swelled until the bells echoed across the city.

"Are you going out to join the celebrations?" she asked.

"No, Molly." D'Arcy McGee used his wife's pet name. "I have no official duties so I believe I will stay here."

"D'Arcy McGee should be playing a larger role," she told him, as she had repeatedly in the last two weeks. "You should be making a speech and sharing the glory."

"Spoken as a true wife." McGee smiled. "But it's not your decision or mine."

"Macdonald should have included you."

"He can't listen to the wives. He's doing what he thinks is best."

"By having you lie low in Toronto while he parades about the capital and by leaving you out of his cabinet?"

"We've been through it before, Molly. He had to find a way to represent all of the colonies...a way to represent all of the interests—the businessmen and the farmers, the Protestants and the Catholics—and his way didn't include me."

"So will you quit then?"

The question surprised him.

"Give it up," she suggested hopefully. "Return to writing; publish poetry; perhaps take a government position until you get on your feet financially. He owes you that much!"

"No." Again he spoke quietly. "I will run in the next election, and there might be a place in the next cabinet. I have something to prove."

"What's to prove?" she asked sharply. "You helped pull this new country together. The Irish at home in Montreal always support you. You have nothing to prove."

"Then I'll do it to prove something to myself. I'm ready to name the major Fenian supporters, the people behind the scenes, and those men will want me stopped. But I won't let them destroy all that we have accomplished. This will be hardest campaign yet. It will be dirty, and it will tough. But I will win."

"Then you've made up your mind?" she asked.

"I have. I can't quit. Not yet."

• • •

Montreal, Quebec
July 1, 1867

"Ah, Mr. Lovell…we finally meet." Jefferson Davis forced a smile. "I'm not sure where we would be if you had not offered the use of this home. I'm used to spartan surroundings, but Varina and the children deserve better. And quite frankly, this is more than I could afford."

"A pleasure," Lovell assured him. "But, I hoped we might discuss some business while you are in Montreal."

"Business?" Davis tried to sound surprised, but the attempt fell flat. He could guess what Lovell wanted.

"I am a publisher, and every publisher in North America and Europe would like to print the memoirs of Jefferson Davis. We're a small house, but we do good work, and we can grow. I've worked with other members of the Southern community and know anything you write will sell well."

"I'd be happy to consider it, Mr. Lovell," Davis told him. "And as you are aware, I need the money, but there's nothing written, and I'm not sure when there will be. I recently opened the vault that contains my papers, and one of the first things I found was a letter General Lee sent before his surrender."

"Wonderful," Lovell enthused. "The sort of history our readers are waiting for."

"They'll have to be patient...very patient," Davis said, puncturing the optimism. "I found it too painful. I'm not ready to confront the unpleasant memories."

"Perhaps a monograph, a few pages," Lowell suggested.

"No." Davis left no opportunity. "Too soon!"

"Should you change your mind—" Lowell began.

"I won't," Davis interjected. "Look elsewhere for new material—maybe the memoirs of local politicians."

"A very small market," Lowell explained. "Trying to survive on the Canadian market will bankrupt a publishing house, so we look for material with wider appeal. We survive on government printing contracts, but to win that business we need...well... special friends, people with the right connections. Politicians become upset if I publish a book by one of their opponents."

"I'm sure this new Confederacy will bring new work," Davis suggested.

"I'd like to think so," Lowell agreed. "But while it's a new government, they take care of old friends first. Again, if you should change your mind..."

"I'll remember," Davis assured him. "But don't hold your breath. The story can't be told properly. At least not yet."

• • •

Niagara-on-the-Lake, Ontario
July 1, 1867

The man was stretched under the tree, a hat partially covering his black face. Later, John Breckinridge would realize that he should have paid more attention. Blacks were still rare in the small, white, Canadian town.

The remnants of the Confederate community were in a party mood when he saw them off on the steamer for the trip across the lake. Toronto would mark the birth of the new nation with a grander celebration than the little village on the Niagara. He encouraged them to go, and watching them wave from the boat, he wished again that he could join them.

Only a few Southerners, like Breckinridge, still waited for the amnesty that would allow a safe return home. But with the American president facing impeachment, forgiveness for the former enemies of the republic was low on the political agenda.

Breckinridge reached the house, lingering for a moment to gaze at a sailboat on Lake Ontario before climbing the short rise of the carriageway. The maid had been sent off in advance of what he planned to be a very private meeting.

Minutes later, Breckinridge watched a figure approach.

The Negro walked with a calm assurance, glanced at the path leading toward the rear of the house, but turned instead to the main entrance. His clothes were clean and gave no hint that only minutes before he had been stretched out on summer grass.

"Would you be John Breckinridge?" he asked. There was no hint of any Southern drawl or Negro dialect; instead, there was the crisp tone of an educated Canadian. "If you are, you are expecting me."

Amos Baker had found a picture of the Confederate general taken during the war. The man in front of him had aged but was still handsome and carried an air of authority.

"I should offer you some refreshment," Breckinridge told Baker.

"Thank you, but that won't be necessary. I don't expect to be long."

"At least take a seat." Breckinridge motioned to a chair.

"I'd prefer to stand," Baker replied coldly. "This is business."

Breckinridge noted something in the man's appearance, something beyond skin color that reminded him of a former servant. Jim Ferguson had been at his side though the war, during the escape across the Southern states and the perilous sea voyage by small boat to Cuba. But in one of the cruel ironies of the new America, he had been denied his freedom. The Emancipation Proclamation excluded slaves in border states, such as Kentucky, until passage of the thirteenth amendment finally brought freedom. Breckinridge hoped that Ferguson would someday have the confidence to act as the man who stood in front of him.

"I've had a letter from Miss Sillery Fraser," Baker began. "She wanted me to explain that the deal is off."

Breckinridge felt a now-familiar chill.

"She wanted to say," Baker continued, "that she trusted you, and you kept your end of the bargain. It's what happened in England that changed her mind."

Breckinridge struggled to maintain his composure. "I don't understand."

"She went to the address you gave her, and George Sanders was there. She recognized him from Montreal. Sanders refused to give her the rest of the money and threatened her."

Breckinridge knew that his worst fears had been realized.

"And after a suspicious fire at her hotel that night," Baker continued, "she has decided to disappear. I know she is safe but I don't know where she's gone."

"And the file?" Breckinridge asked.

"She'll keep it. She's made arrangements to send the documents to the newspapers if anything happens to her. She believes they'll know what to do with them."

"Long-term blackmail," Breckinridge said, sighing.

"She thought you would think that," Baker told him. "And I'm to tell you that you are right."

Breckinridge was silent.

"I suspect there are many secrets, many things the leaders of the North or South would rather not talk about," Baker told him. "She's a woman of her word. I came to know her well. If she stays safe, so will the file. She'll take it to her grave. But if she feels threatened, she'll fight. She wouldn't tell me what she knew. She felt I would be safer if I didn't know."

Breckinridge could only watch as the African turned and left the house.

A moment later, he heard the footsteps behind him.

"You won't need me."

Tom Hines stepped quietly into the room.

"You heard it all?" Breckinridge asked.

"Yes, and you can trust him. I used him many times."

"But the woman?" Breckinridge asked.

"I don't know her, but do you have a choice?" Hines asked.

Breckinridge considered the question for a full minute.

"No," he said. "We've run out of choices."

• • •

Kincardine, Ontario
July 1, 1867

The day was perfect. A soft westerly breeze from the lake cooled the picnic ground, and those who wanted to escape the early summer sun found shelter beneath a line of trees.

It had taken three hours to reach the village, and with the discomfort of a pregnancy, Erin Brady doubted she would travel far in the coming months.

The lumber had been cleared from the farm, and the new crops showed promise. Money would not be a problem. Her chief concern was across the field, conversing with the men who had cleared the land. His back was turned deliberately toward her, but she saw the arm move and the neck slip back before he passed something to another acquaintance. She should be pleased, she thought. It was almost noon, and he was partly sober.

A choir joined the local dignitaries on a small, makeshift stage. She was too far away to hear the speeches but she sensed the ceremony was ending as the people closest to the platform stood, the men removed their hats, and the strains of "God Save the Queen" drifted over the park.

She waited as the crowd began to drift off, carefully avoiding Owen and the men around him.

The first sign of trouble came as an empty jug was smashed against a rock. In mere seconds, the little group became a wild melee of arms and fists. She started forward when Owen went down.

"Better call the doctor," someone called as she trotted across the field.

"Hell, call the undertaker," another ruffian groused as the men scattered.

She reached him at the same time as a middle-aged man appeared with a black bag clasped in his hand.

"Let me look at him," he said, bending to examine the prone figure. "I'm used to such things."

Blood flowed from Owen's forehead. His eyes were closed, and his breathing was ragged.

"Head wound," the man told her. "They bleed like hell and make it look worse than it is."

He opened his bag and removed a towel.

"Hold this against the cut," he said, lifting Owen to a sitting position. "The bleeding should stop shortly."

He looked for any other wounds. "Don't see anything else, and his breathing is easier. He looks familiar, somehow. Are you from the town?"

"No. We came in for the picnic," Erin said.

"Press down hard," the doctor ordered. "We want the bleeding to stop. What's his name?"

"Cash," she said. The lie now came naturally. "Owen Cash."

She saw Owen's eyes flash open with a bewildered, lost look.

"Holy shite." He started to revive.

"Mr. Cash, do you know where you are?" the man asked.

Owen's eyes flickered as he tried to focus on the question.

"Dr. Secord?" He said as the face became clearer.

"So we have met?" Secord threw an angry glance at the woman.

"Yes, a couple of times," Owen told him.

"How much have you had to drink?"

"Just a couple of good slugs." Owen shook his head, and blood began to roll down his face again.

"Hold it tight!" Secord shoved the towel back on the wound and pressed Erin's hand on top of it.

"Slugs or bottles?" he asked.

"I lost count," Owen admitted.

"Never mind," Secord snapped. "Sit while I patch the hole in your skull."

Secord nodded to Erin, who carefully lifted the bloody towel. The surgery took only seconds.

"Bring the wagon." He wiped bloody hands on the grass. "I'll help you load up."

Erin moved to go but stopped when she heard Owen speak.

"Don't you know me, Doctor? We met at Gettysburg."

Secord stiffened and stared at the patient.

"You helped my friend," Owen told him. "And Payne was helping you. The one they hung for the Lincoln murder."

"You're nuts," Secord told him.

"He died hard," Owen continued. "The executioner had to swing on his legs to kill him."

"Is he often this drunk?" Second asked, turning to Erin.

"It's getting worse," she admitted.

"Doctors can't cure this. He has to help himself."

"And we met in Charleston, too." Owen teetered forward, raising his head and shoulders. "You treated another friend, and he got better. But the war eventually took him, too."

The effort was too much. He fell back, unconscious.

"Go and get that wagon," Secord ordered. "He'll come around but he won't be walking home."

Owen revived and passed out again as he was moved.

"I'm betting it's booze and not the head wound," Secord told Erin. "He'll sleep it off."

"I can pay you, Doctor." She slipped five dollars in coins into his hand.

Secord quickly gave two of them back.

"Your husband?"

"No." She saw him glance at her stomach. "At least not yet. Maybe never. I don't know."

"He was in the American war?" Secord asked.

"Yes. He doesn't usually speak about it. I don't know what he was talking about."

"I do," Secord now admitted. "I was a Confederate surgeon. I had a patient named Payne at Gettysburg. We were short of staff and he helped out as a nurse. I didn't put him together with the Lincoln conspiracy until today. His mind was damaged by the war in ways we don't understand. Your man has problems, too, and they may get worse as he grows older."

Secord was silent for a moment, and Erin waited.

"If he was in the American army, he might qualify for a pension. There's a veterans' organization called the Grand Army of the Republic. He may want to contact them."

"I don't think he'll do that." Erin's voice was full of regret. "He has too many secrets, too many different names. It could come back on him."

"Well, it's not much comfort, but he's not alone," Secord said. "Many Canadians served under false names because of the neutrality act, and it may come back to haunt them, too. An alias makes it harder to prove a man actually served. Their fellow Canadians don't care. They saw a foreign war and don't understand that it changed this country, too."

Secord extended an arm to help her climb to the seat on the wagon. Even in pregnancy, she moved gracefully.

"So all he has is you?" Secord asked a moment later.

"All for now!" She smiled and touched her stomach.

"Well, take care of him, and take care of yourself. If I can help, you will find me around Kincardine."

"Erin Brady thanks you," she said, smiling. "But after the baby comes, we may move west. He's much better when it's just me and we are far away from other people."

Secord could only smile. The woman had more than her share of spunk.

"Good luck, Erin Brady!" he called as she drove off and received a wave in return.

EPILOGUE

Ottawa, Ontario
April 7, 1868

Macdonald tried to read, but his mind was far from the report on parliamentary spending.

The Quadrilateral was quiet. Agnes had been asleep when he returned from a late session in the commons. Only Bernard, now his brother-in-law, still shared the house near the parliament buildings, and he, too, was asleep.

Macdonald wasn't ready for bed; too many thoughts were running through his mind. Confederation had been approved with the fall election, but the new union was a tenuous affair, especially with the secessionist members elected in Nova Scotia. He had to find a way to appease Joseph Howe and his band of Anti's, the name given to the men who vehemently opposed the new union.

And trouble might be brewing on the prairies. Whispers of discontent blew on the western wind, with predictions of new Fenian raids, of unhappy Métis, the descendents of the original European and native communities, as well as greedy Americans settlers. Their complaints or open rebellion could endanger the attempt to bring the prairies and British Columbia into Confederation.

A glass of water sat on the desk, and for a moment, he considered something stronger. But if Agnes awoke she might notice the liquor on his breath. Instead, he sat back in the chair and thought.

Four years earlier, he had been attorney general of a fractious little province and now he was the prime minister of a new country. He smiled, remembering the early days, the coalition that brought the breakthrough, the storms of politics, and the shifting alliances.

George Brown had returned to the *Globe,* but Georges Etienne Cartier was still a powerhouse in Quebec, and perhaps in a few months he could bring the poet back to the cabinet. D'Arcy McGee had charmed the parliament only a few hours ago with a plea for unity and a simple message.

"I speak not as a representative of any race...or any province...but thoroughly and emphatically as a Canadian."

Macdonald smiled before turning the lamp lower and allowing the glow from the full moon to light the room. The silence would be welcome.

His reverie was interrupted by the sound of a galloping horse and a shout from the street.

"Sir John, Sir John!"

He recognized the voice of his driver, Buckley, and opened the window.

"McGee!" Buckley yelled. "Mr. McGee is dead!"

Macdonald froze.

"It can't be. He spoke in the House just a few hours ago."

"No, it's so." Buckley sobbed. "I saw him. He was shot outside at his boarding house on Sparks Street. Shot dead...Assassinated!"

• • •

Montreal, Quebec
April 13, 1868

The Highland Regiment snapped to attention, and the mournful skirl of the pipes carried over old Montreal. The lament sounded as the body was carried from the Notre Dame Cathedral to the hearse. Eight gray horses waited to carry D'Arcy McGee to the cemetery on the mountain.

Paul Forsey stood with the other spectators. There had been no room for a mere provincial clerk from Ontario inside the cathedral. Instead, the pews had been packed with the old friends. Macdonald, Cartier, and the other major politicians had aged in a matter of days. Their faces were ashen, the shock still evident. They were a mirror image of the faces of the ordinary people, the thousands who felt a need to attend, if only to stand and watch.

The news of the assassination had spread quickly. McGee's Ottawa landlady had heard a noise and opened her door to find him dead on the step. There were no witnesses.

Anyone with an Irish connection was suspect; the local constables had even questioned John A.'s driver. But before terror could truly seize the capital, another man, an apparent Fenian supporter, was arrested. Patrick Whelan was a mere tailor but as good a culprit as could be found.

"Ah, good. You are here." Forsey turned to face Sandfield Macdonald. The Ontario premier had been invited inside the cathedral but now stood among the crowd as the hearse began to draw away.

"Come, ride in my carriage. We won't be going to the burial ground. We have work to do."

"John A. is up to his old tricks." The premier had barely taken his seat when he began to speak. "He says the murder investigation will be a federal responsibility, which means he wants to take all the credit for hanging the assassin. But policing is a provincial jurisdiction. I need you to go back through the Confederation accord and find the relevant article. John A. thinks he can run the country, but he forgets that provinces have power, too."

McGee's death had seemed to change the political world, but suddenly Forsey realized that little had changed. The poet was gone, but the world of political intrigue was very much alive.

"We might want a legal opinion," he suggested quickly. "As I recall, Judge Oliver Mowat had a hand in drawing up the formula for the division of powers, and he's no fan of John A."

· · ·

Lexington, Kentucky
April 16, 1868

The distant whistle produced a stir in the waiting room, and a few people began to make their way toward the track.

Basil Duke slowly folded the newspaper, stood, and waited as the room cleared. Through the dusty window, he could see the headlamp of the approaching train. He took a deep breath before removing his overcoat and stepping to the open platform. At first, the full dress uniform of a Confederate general produced gasps and then a smattering of applause from a small crowd. Duke squared his shoulders and glanced down the rails. The train was a few minutes away.

"Good day, General."

Duke hadn't noticed the man slouching against the wall. He wore civilian clothes and would easily blend into any crowd.

"I guess I'm in uniform, too," Tom Hines said with a smile.

Duke returned the smile. "I'm not as rebellious as I appear. I actually sought permission from the Union army before the uniform came out of the closet. Rebel attire still frightens Yankees, but as a sign of respect, they have agreed to allow this."

"Time we started the healing process," Hines suggested. "I meet a lot of people through my work at the newspaper. They're ready to bury the past even though they will never forget it. And we're finally tying up the last of the loose ends. Our friends in Florida have made contract with Grenfell. He'll need patience but some dark night in the next few months, he'll be offered a boat ride from the Dry Tortugas."

"And that would do it." Duke smiled. "He's last man that we can help, the last survivor from our band of raiders."

Both men stepped back as a wagon and team of horses passed and stopped at the end of the platform.

"I was reading about the trouble in Canada," Duke said. "The assassination of a major political figure doesn't bode well for their future. I hope our refugees are safe."

"Mr. Breckinridge will watch out for them. The northern refuge was welcome, but most want to come home and probably will soon."

"I'm not surprised," Duke admitted. "People are more comfortable around their own."

Hines glanced at the slowing train. "It's hard to explain. The Canadians aren't all that different from us. The trouble now is with the Irish, and that's not really their fight. Of course, we weren't their fight either, but we took advantage of their territory. They'll weather this latest storm. Washington thinks the provinces will eventually link with the Union. But that's not going to happen. The Canadians are quite content on their own…if for no other reason than they're not American."

"They'll need better fences," Duke said, laughing. "Good fences and good borders make good neighbors."

The sound of the locomotive bell signaled the train's arrival.

"Let's hope this is the last…sad…homecoming." Duke's words were almost lost in the hiss and clatter from the rails. The door to the baggage car was open, and both men could see a coffin positioned by the door."

Duke spoke quietly, his voice breaking under the emotional strain.

"Almost four years since General Morgan fell. Richmond gave him full military honors at Hollywood Cemetery, but we felt it was best to bring him back to the blue grass. And tomorrow, we'll have the final interment here in Lexington. He was there at the start, and we are here to finish the story."

The train came to a full stop, and only the hiss of the steam broke the silence.

Duke was transfixed and didn't notice as Hines made a small gesture with his hand.

A troop of six men dressed in gray stepped around the corner of the station. They marched in formation to the train, gently lifted the coffin to their shoulders, and carried it to the waiting wagon.

"We'll all be there for the service tomorrow," Hines said quietly. "And we wanted the family to know it was the men from Morgan's command who carried him home."

AFTERWORD

History has more to say about the real people of the novel.

Canadians can study the long political career of John A. Macdonald and will find more of Howe, Tupper, Tilley, MacDougall, Cartier, Brown, and the prominent figures of the era. George Denison continued to play a role with the Canadian military and later wrote *Soldiering in Canada* as well as a study of cavalry.

The rebels John Headley, Breck Castleman, and Basil Duke exchanged swords for pens in the postwar years and wrote of the exploits of Morgan's Cavalry. Jefferson Davis and Jubal Early wrote multiple pages on the war and became champions of the Lost Cause. Bennett Young played a prominent role in the Confederate Veteran movement.

And Tom Hines served for many years as a judge in Kentucky.

The trial of John Surratt ended with a hung jury, and in later life, Surratt seldom spoke about his association with John Wilkes Booth. Sarah Slater vanished in the aftermath of the Civil War, so perhaps she did meet with Judah Benjamin, who became a respected British lawyer.

And George St. Leger Grenfell did escape from Fort Jefferson, but the attempt was made during a violent storm. Searchers found no trace of him or his boat but an item from folk history tells of a mysterious English gentleman who passed through the Tampa area around the time of the escape.

I leave it to the reader to imagine the future for the fictional characters. Owen, Erin, Paul Forsey, Mike Flynn and company helped me navigate through and around the actual events that have served as the backdrop for both novels.

My thanks to the family and friends who have encouraged me through this writing adventure. Deborah Phibbs at Quantum Communications deserves special credit for the cover design as does Chris Partridge who created the map art.

The website at www.almcgregor.com has more background and I would be pleased to answer any questions.

Al McGregor
August 2014